RELENTLESS STORM

Claire Lorrimer

Chivers Press • Thorndike Press
Bath, England   Thorndike, Maine USA

This Large Print edition is published by Chivers Press, England, and by Thorndike Press, USA.

Published in 2000 in the U.K. by arrangement with the author.

Published in 2000 in the U.S. by arrangement with Claire Lorrimer.

U.K. Hardcover ISBN 0–7540–4068–2 (Chivers Large Print)
U.K. Softcover ISBN 0–7540–4069–0 (Camden Large Print)
U.S. Softcover ISBN 0–7862–2457–6 (General Series Edition)

The text of this Large Print edition is unabridged.
Other aspects of the book may vary from the original edition.

Set in 16 pt. New Times Roman.

Printed in Great Britain on acid-free paper.

British Library Cataloguing in Publication Data available

Library of Congress Cataloging-in-Publication Data

Lorrimer, Claire.
    Relentless storm / Claire Lorrimer.
        p.   cm.
    ISBN 0–7862–2457–6 (lg. print : sc : alk. paper)
    1. Abbeys—France—Alps, French—Fiction. 2. Family—
France—Alps, French—Fiction. 3. Alps, French (France)—
Fiction. 4. Large type books. I. Title.
PR6062.O77 R4 2000
823'.914—dc21
                                       99–089825

CHAPTER ONE

It was the Great Dane, Tristan, who gave the first warning of the events which were subsequently to change the whole of Alex's life. He quivered, lifted his massive head and gave a deep rumbling growl. His mate, Isolde, instantly alerted, pricked up her ears and barked. At that moment Alex, too, heard the hammering of the heavy iron knocker against the front door.

Alex glanced at her watch. It was half past five. Gilbert, the old butler, had not yet carried out his evening ritual of drawing the curtains. Through the tall casement windows Alex could see nothing. Darkness had fallen early tonight because of the snow storm that was sweeping the mountainside where the Abbaye St. Christophe stood, huge, grey, imposing, hewn from the same rock as the mountain itself.

Tristan and Isolde were both standing now, their brindled hackles bristling with nervous anticipation. Alex hushed them as she listened to Gilbert's shuffling footsteps crossing the flagstone floor of the hall as he went to open the great front door.

The Baron and Baroness Leyresse were away at their apartment in Paris; their young daughter, Eloise, was at school in Switzerland. Alex was alone in the abbey except for the servants and the two huge dogs. No one ever visited except by appointment. The abbey, situated as it was, was not a place where people stopped en route to some other destination, hoping to find the Baron or Baroness at home.

Tristan and Isolde were now standing side by side at the door, furiously barking as their keen ears detected the sound of voices. Beyond the *petit salon* in which she stood, Alex, too, could hear voices—the soft low tones of Gilbert and those less easily distinguishable of another man.

When she was at the abbey the Baroness was very strict with the servants. She insisted that the old standards be maintained regardless of the changing times. Had she been here now she would not have permitted Alex to go and find out what was happening, but would make her wait until the old butler came and announced their visitor. Fortunately for the Baroness, most of the servants were elderly and well enough paid not to resent the continuance of out-dated formalities.

As she thought of the Baroness, Alex's mouth curved in a mischievous little smile as she took advantage of her employer's absence to break one of the rules. With the dogs, now securely held by their chain collars, flanking her sides, she opened the door of the *petit salon* and walked into the hall.

'*Qu'est que c'est*, Gilbert?' she asked the old

man, her French almost flawless after six months at the abbey.

In front of her stood a young man not much older than herself. His dark brown hair and shoulders were covered with snowflakes, which were melting rapidly into a pool on the stone floor beneath him. He was in ski clothes but without an anorak, and it was small wonder, she thought, that he was shivering so violently he could barely stand upright.

In halting French he began to explain the reason for his presence, but Alex cut him short as she told Gilbert:

'A large cognac for *Monsieur*, quickly, Gilbert. And send Jules for some warm clothing from the Baron's room.'

She turned back to the young man, and with a smile said in English:

'There's a big fire in the study. Come and get warm whilst you tell me what has happened.'

The young man stared speechlessly at Alex. She was wearing a long wool dress of deep forget-me-not blue. It matched her eyes, which were too large for her pale, thin face surrounded as it was by a cloud of soft, shining fair hair. Flanked on either side by the Great Danes, the girl seemed totally unreal to him— an angelic apparition suddenly turning the nightmare of the last few hours into a miraculous dream.

The fire she had promised him was, indeed,

a big one. Huge pine logs burned in the massive stone grate. Colder than he had ever been before, the young man hurried towards the warmth.

'Here, put these underneath you,' Alex said practically as she handed him a bundle of newspapers. She smiled at him, the smile somehow dispelling his first ethereal impression of her so that now she seemed no different from any pretty English girl back home.

He stood with his back to the fire, his ski-boots, clothes and hair dripping onto the newspapers covering the crimson Bokhara rug.

'Can you tell me what happened?' Alex asked. 'Did you get lost?'

He took a deep breath. Until now, his teeth had been chattering too violently to speak.

'In a way, yes. But it's much worse than that. I was skiing back to Valory with my Norwegian friend, Knut Olsen. The snow-storm overtook us when we were only a third of the way down. Knut thought he knew a short cut and we were stupid enough to leave the *piste*. We ran into a pine forest and then . . .' His voice suddenly broke. 'Then Knut, who was leading the way, hit a tree. His ski broke and also, I think, his leg. It was horrible. I'm not much of a skier and I hadn't a hope of finding the way down by myself. Knut passed out and there was nothing I could do but wait until he regained consciousness. When Knut came round, he told me to take off my skis and leave them and walk downhill. If I just kept going downwards, he said, I'd be bound to reach the valley sooner or later and then I could get help.'

The sense of urgency suddenly returned to him. 'I must telephone at once. Is there a rescue team? I must get help to him. I left him my anorak but he'll freeze to death if he is left there for long. Besides, he's in great pain.'

Alex heard the rising note of hysteria in the young man's voice, and was grateful that Gilbert chose this moment to come in with the brandy and an old shooting pullover and jacket belonging to the Baron.

'Drink this!' she said curtly, handing him a generous measure of cognac. 'Then put on these clothes. I'll telephone the Rescue Service for you. My French is probably better than yours,' she added, and was pleased to see the visitor's taut white face relax into a brief smile. 'Before I phone, can you give me any idea where your friend is? It could be difficult finding him in the dark in this storm.'

She spoke lightly to conceal her steadily growing apprehension. The mountain had a reputation for claiming lives. In good weather it was no different from any other ski slope—a glorious sunny south-facing run down from the summit, the skiing not too difficult and the trails, or *pistes*, well marked and identified by posts stating directions and degrees of difficulty. But in bad weather, it was different.

5

The vicious storms seemed to gather unseen and break with startling suddenness over the jagged peaks, sweeping downhill into the valley and taking their toll of skiers and climbers who were inexperienced or unprepared. The chances of finding the Norwegian in this weather and in the dark seemed pretty grim.

'I can't describe the place,' the young man was saying. 'But I'm sure I can find it. I expect it sounds silly but I remembered the old story of Hansel and Gretel and I cut grooves in the pine trees as I came down. I think I could find my way back with a lantern or torch.'

Alex nodded, and went out to the hall to telephone. It crossed her mind that the wires could be down—they frequently were in such weather. But fortunately it was only a matter of minutes before she was speaking to the Mountain Rescue Centre.

When she returned to her guest, he looked much better. The cognac had brought some warmth back into his body, and his face had regained its natural colour. His hair was drying rapidly in the heat of the fire, and she noticed with amusement that it was beginning to curl in small tendrils round his neck and forehead, making him look a great deal younger. 'Everything's fine,' she reassured him. 'The men will be here in about fifteen minutes. They'll come up in the snow cat, pick you up and go on by foot. Meanwhile, would you like something to eat? You'll need to keep up your strength.'

'I don't think I could eat anything,' he replied. 'Thanks anyway—for everything. You've been marvellous.'

'We haven't introduced ourselves,' Alex reminded him, as much to keep his mind off his injured friend as to maintain the social niceties. 'I'm Alex—Alexandra Amery. I'm a kind of cross between an *au pair* and a governess, employed by the Baron and Baroness Leyresse who own the abbey. My home is in Surrey and I'm twenty-two years old. How about you?'

The young man held out his hand and shook hers formally.

'I'm more than pleased to know you, Alex. I was getting quite desperate when I saw the lights of this place glimmering through the trees. I thought I was imagining them—the snow kept covering my goggles and I wasn't sure at first. Then when I saw the Château— the Abbaye I mean, I thanked God, although to tell you the truth, I'm not very religious as a rule.' He gave a self-conscious smile. 'My name is Rory Howes, by the way. I'm from Hertfordshire. Knut, my friend, was at university with me. We've both been studying art and were on a trip we planned years ago. We intended to hitch our way across Europe to Italy and spend three months there seeing art galleries and museums and ruins—everything we could. Then Knut, who's a marvellous skier, suggested we stop in France for a couple of weeks of winter sport in the Alps. I'd not done much skiing and it seemed a wonderful idea. We booked in at a youth hostel and today was our third day's skiing ...'

He broke off suddenly and then said:

'I keep hearing the sound of his scream and the crack of bone ... it was horrible, truly horrible.'

Instinctively Alex put her hand on his arm.

'Don't think about it,' she said. 'Tell me more about yourself. You haven't said how old you are.'

'Twenty-three,' Rory replied. 'Knut's a year older than I.'

He stared around him as if only now aware of his surroundings.

'This place is fantastic,' he said. 'You called the building an abbey. It's pretty vast, isn't it?'

'It was a monastery at one time,' Alex explained. 'Some of the rooms are huge—too big really to live in. I spend most of my time in here when I'm alone. It's actually the Baron's study. I like the octagonal shape. Long ago it used to be the abbot's private oratory. It's a sort of anteroom to the main salon where the Baroness entertains.'

'Who did you say the owners are?' Rory asked, fascinated.

'The Baron and Baroness Leyresse. He's a French nobleman of ancient lineage. I believe

8

he can trace his family back to Agincourt. It's quite interesting, as a matter of fact. The family lost their estates in the French Revolution and the abbey was burned. The Leyresses went to live in England and for a while they had no money, only the patronage of aristocratic friends. Then the Baron's father married an American heiress and they returned to France and bought back a great deal of the land which had once belonged to the family. The abbey had been vacated by the monks during the First World War, when it was turned into a barracks. When the Baron's father bought the land he also bought the ruined abbey and spent a small fortune restoring it. The present Baron—he's now sixty—was born and raised here and he, in turn, also married money. His wife, the Baroness, is South American. She is twenty-five years younger than he, very rich, very beautiful, very cosmopolitan. A great deal of her money has been spent in modernising the abbey, so that it now has every conceivable comfort. But the Baroness spends most of her time in Paris.'

'And how do you come into this fantastic set-up?' Rory asked curiously.

'The Baroness wanted someone English here so that her daughter—the only child—would learn the language. I'm a companion to Eloise during the holidays. In the term time when she's away, I live here and look after

Tristan and Isolde.' She patted the huge dogs on their heads and their tails thumped the floor, the noise deadened by the thickness of the rug. 'The Baroness adores them. I sometimes think that she is fonder of them than of her own child, although I can't say I blame her. Eloise is a spoilt, precocious, egotistical little girl of twelve. Fortunately, I haven't had much to do with her.'

Alex's account was cut short by the arrival of the six-man rescue team. They stopped only long enough to collect Rory before they were off into the night again. Within minutes they were swallowed up by the darkness and Alex quickly closed the heavy door against the driving snow.

The huge house seemed suddenly deserted. Alex went back into the *petit salon*. Despite its name—the *petit* in comparison with the vastness of the other reception rooms—even this favourite retreat in which she spent most of her evenings had become permeated with a strange feeling of emptiness.

As if in sympathy with her mood, Tristan came across the room. As Alex sat down on her heels before the glowing fire, he lay down beside her and rested his heavy head on her lap. The huge dog had become very attached to her, far more so than Isolde, who was placid in temperament and friendly with anyone who cared to pay her attention. It was Tristan who padded after Alex when she left the room, who

10

insisted on accompanying her when she went skiing, who settled his large body at the foot of her bed as if placing himself on guard at night.

Alex sighed. The Baroness was obsessively jealous of the attentions of her dogs—as, indeed, of any living being. Although she admitted to being glad that Tristan no longer fretted when she was absent, the admission was grudgingly given when she was at home. Tristan was expected to follow *her* rather than Alex—an order he was becoming less and less willing to obey.

Until recently Alex had tried to shut her eyes to the selfishness of the woman who employed her. Inez Leyresse, many years ago, had been at a Swiss finishing school with Alex's mother and the two girls had sworn a lifetime friendship. When Alex's mother married a small-town solicitor and Inez a French Baron, it was inevitable the two lost touch, although they continued to exchange letters at Christmas. Her mother knew very little of the woman Inez had become when she had written asking her if she could find a place for Alex at the abbey. She had believed Alex would be received by a charming, beautiful and vivacious woman, who brightened the lives of all around her, as had the youthful Inez at school.

Alex had not had the heart to write the truth in her letters home. Nor, until a short while ago, had she surfaced sufficiently from

11

her own self-centred orgy of unhappiness even to notice those around her to any marked degree. Each day had been another one she must somehow live through; somehow tolerate, despite the fact that life had ceased to have meaning or purpose since her fiancé, David, had died.

She had tried not to think about David. Purposefully, she had made her mind a vacuum, performing the few duties the Baroness gave her, arranging flowers, answering the Baroness's letters, taking the dogs for walks, driving down to Valory to make occasional purchases. In the evenings she read, studied French, wrote letters home. She continued to live but only because it would hurt too many people if she, like David, were to die.

Now, unaccountably, the presence of the young Englishman here in the *salon*, looking at her from deep-set dark brown eyes like David's, had sparked all the memories she had tried so desperately to forget. David—the man she had been going to marry—would have married by now but for the appalling suddenness of that car accident. Alex had also been in the car but only David had died, the steering wheel penetrating his chest and killing him instantly.

For two weeks she had been spared the truth whilst she lay concussed in a hospital in Birmingham, her mother and father at her bedside. When they told her about the

12

accident she wished she had been killed, too. She tried to die but she was too young and healthy. Inexorably her body began to recover its strength, and only her mind remained scarred.

'You must make a new life for yourself, darling,' her mother had said.

But how did one make a new life when the only person you had ever loved would never again take you in his arms, make love to you, dance with you, walk with you, laugh with you. She and David had known each other three years and had been lovers for the last year before his death. In a way, their intimacy made his death more difficult to accept, and yet she did not regret that she had given him all the loving of which she was capable for that last brief year of his life. She wished now that she had had a child by him, a part of him to cling to. Sometimes, in the hospital, she had dreamed that she was pregnant, or that she held David's child in her arms.

It was almost a year now since David's death. Somehow she had managed to exist, building a cocoon around herself in which feelings, emotions, hopes, desires, played no part. Within this vacuum she walked, talked, observed the fantastic beauty of the abbey, of the Baroness, of the mountains, with total detachment. Only the dog, Tristan, had recently managed to penetrate the world of non-involvement in which she had found it possible to survive. Despite everything, Tristan's intense devotion to her evoked a response she subconsciously resented, so that on occasions she pushed him away when he nuzzled his great head against her arm, telling him not to be a nuisance.

Instinctively Alex had known she needed a period of time—a period of peace and solitude and quiet in which her bruised heart and mind could recuperate. Her parents had wanted her to find a job where there were other young people, with plenty of fun and laughter and activity to help her forget David. But wisely Alex had known she could not endure a life she could not share with him. The Abbaye, far away from anything either of them had known, isolated halfway up a mountain, remote, almost unreal, had had exactly the therapeutic effect she needed to come to terms with her personal tragedy.

The dramatically sudden appearance of the young Englishman, Rory Howes, had served as a minor electric shock to her system. She was experiencing now, for the first time since the fatal car accident, a feeling of acute loneliness, feeling the solitude as something alien rather than welcome. She was conscious of an urgent desire for the rescue team to return quickly, bringing Rory Howes and his friend here to the abbey where she would make them welcome.

But when, an hour later, the dogs began once more to growl and then to bark furiously,

14

it was not on account of the injured skier and his friend, Rory. As Alex quietened the dogs and opened the door to go through to the hall, it was to see Inez Leyresse and her husband, complete with her personal maid and the Baron's valet, arriving home unexpectedly from Paris.

'Ah! So you have not yet retired, Alexandra!' the Baroness said. 'We are late arriving—the storm, *tu comprends*!'

As always, when Alex saw her employer after an absence, she was struck by the flamboyant beauty of the woman. Although now in her early forties, Inez Leyresse still had the slender figure and flawless skin of a girl. Encased in a vast calf-length, white ermine coat, above white kid boots, her flaming red hair piled high in an elaborate Paris coiffure, the Baroness looked like a Russian princess. With her white skin and red hair she could not have looked less South American. Only the narrow, near-black almond-shaped eyes gave a hint of Latin ancestry.

No wonder the Baron is so crazy about her! Alex thought as her gaze went to the grey-haired, thick-set little man fussing over her many suitcases that Gilbert and the valet were bringing in from the car. Despite his rather plebeian figure, the Baron's face was that of an aristocrat, with a large hooked nose and piercing green eyes beneath bushy silver brows. A military moustache topped a thin,

15

narrow-lipped mouth and carved jawline.

He gave Alex a warm smile. She knew that he liked her and suspected that the reason was not so much personal as because of his wife's approval. Inez did not find it easy to keep female staff. She took quick dislikes to women, especially if they were young and pretty or had strong wills of their own. Her social secretaries seldom remained in her employ for more than a few months and those that did stay longer, did so only because they were snobbish enough to enjoy working for a Baroness; or because, ill-tempered and critical though Inez could be, she paid well enough to make the subservience worthwhile.

Alex, living in her self-created vacuum, had been happy enough to comply with Inez's arrogant orders, oblivious to the cruel little derogatory remarks Inez made from time to time about her appearance or clothes. Alex neither knew nor cared that Inez thought her stupid, spineless and harmless. Of her true nature, Inez had not the faintest inkling, and her sympathy for Alex's bereavement had been merely superficial.

'She'll soon get over it!' she had written to Mrs Amery as if David's death was of no more importance than a bad cold.

But tonight Alex found herself seeing her employer with a new perception. She was aware not only of Inez's extraordinary beauty, but of her arrogance and the hint of cruelty in

16

the delicately curved and painted lips.

Inez led the way imperiously into the *petit salon*, flinging her white ermine coat across a mauve velvet chair. It slipped on the floor and was promptly used as a rug by Isolde. Inez did not even notice.

'Tell Gilbert to bring drinks in here,' she told Alex as she spread long, scarlet-tipped fingers to the warmth of the blazing logs. 'I suppose it is too much to hope that the fires have been lit in the *grand salon*.' She gave an irritable sigh. 'Oh, well, I should have telephoned, I suppose, but we only decided on the spur of the moment to come back for the weekend. There will be a dozen or so visitors tomorrow, Alex. Tell the servants. House guests, of course. I'll see the chef in the morning about meals. You can do the flowers in the bedrooms. Go in to Valory and buy what you need. I suppose nothing has happened whilst I've been away? Nothing ever does happen in this place! *Mon Dieu*, why do I come back here?'

'But this time there's been an event!' Alex said, the hint of excitement in her voice unusual enough to make Inez pay attention. 'There's been a skiing accident. Two young men lost their way in the storm and one, a Norwegian, has broken his leg. The other—an Englishman—found his way here to the abbey to get help. He has gone off now with the rescue team to try and find his friend. When the dogs began barking, I thought it might be them returning.'

Inez Leyresse raised her thin dark pencilled brows and shrugged her shoulders. Alex's news was disappointing.

'These stupid foreigners,' she commented, as if she, herself, were a native of France. 'They deserve to lose their lives. Isn't that so, Bernard?' she addressed her husband as he came into the salon, Gilbert close behind him with a tray of drinks.

When she had retold Alex's story, the Baron said pacifically:

'But the storms in these mountains come down very suddenly, *chérie*. If you are not used to them . . .'

'Nonsense!' Inez broke in brusquely. 'One should always be prepared for snow at this time of the year. People have no sense!'

She yawned as she bent to pat Tristan's head. She was already bored with the subject of the lost skiers.

'And how is my beautiful Tristan?' she asked the dog, her voice changing to the soft cajoling a woman might use with a lover, but which she certainly never used with the elderly Baron. 'I hope you have been taking care of my lovely boy, Alex?'

But Tristan had begun to growl and Isolde joined in at the sound of a renewed commotion in the front hall.

Alex felt her heartbeat quicken in nervous anticipation. She wondered if the young

Englishman and the rescue team had found the Norwegian.

Inez was watching Alex with an amused smile on her lips. She had never before seen the girl's face so animated.

'Well, aren't you going to find out who it is?' she asked. 'I can see you are greatly excited. Run along. I won't stop you. Your young Englishman must be more attractive than you led me to suppose!'

For the first time since her arrival at the abbey, Alex felt a moment of real dislike for Inez Leyresse. The Baroness was talking as if this whole situation were little more than a minor divertissement; as if young men's lives were of no importance. She seemed totally unaware, or uncaring, of the fact that the Norwegian could have frozen to death on the mountainside.

Alex turned quickly away from that beautiful, smiling face and hurried out of the *salon* into the hall.

CHAPTER TWO

Rory opened his eyes and closed them quickly. Someone had come into his room and pulled aside the curtains, allowing the brilliant sunshine to pour through the casement windows. His eyes were sore and stinging; his

19

head felt heavy and throbbed furiously.

A woman came over to his bedside, her shadow between him and the sunlight. He caught the fragrance of a strong but attractive scent.

'*Bonjour, Monsieur*! Welcome to St. Christophe!'

Rory wondered if he were still dreaming. The woman standing over him was tall and slender. She was wearing black slacks and black tunic with a huge gold cross on an antique chain hanging between small perfectly shaped breasts. The most beautiful red-gold hair framed a flawless face. Her tantalising, heady perfume wafted from her as she moved her supple body to put a cool hand on his forehead. She was smiling.

'I am the Baroness Leyresse,' she announced. 'You are a guest here in my home, the Abbaye St. Christophe. You collapsed last night when you came down from the mountain. Do you remember?'

Rory jerked himself into a sitting position, fully awake now as the fear and horror of the previous night returned to him.

'Knut!' he said. 'My friend. How is he? Is he here? Is he all right?'

Inez put her hand against his bare chest and gently pushed him down into the soft pillows.

'Your friend was taken to the hospital last night,' she said reassuringly. 'Alexandra—I think you met her earlier yesterday evening—

is telephoning the hopsital now for news of him. You have nothing to worry about, *mon ami*. Lie still and rest. Gilbert will bring you some breakfast in a minute.'

Rory felt himself relaxing. The memory of last night and his exhaustion had returned in full. He felt weak with the relief of knowing that Knut was being properly cared for.

'I can't thank you enough, *Madame*,' he said warmly.

It occurred to him that this might not be the correct way to address a French baroness but she instantly put him at ease.

'You are very welcome, *Monsieur*.'

'I don't know what I would have done if I hadn't found the abbey last night,' Rory told her truthfully. 'I was beginning to despair when I first glimpsed the lights. When we found Knut one of the guides told me he would have frozen to death if he'd lain there another hour. It was horrible . . . a nightmare.'

Inez Leyresse looked at the young Englishman with increasing interest. Not only was he extremely handsome but he had an air of good breeding which never failed to fascinate her. No one ever referred to her own background, but her father had been of very lowly peasant origin and had managed to climb the social ladder only because of his unfailing shrewdness and ability to make money. By the time he was twenty-two, he was a rich man and was able to marry into a far

21

higher social class than his own. When Inez was born, he was a millionaire and the little girl was brought up with the idea that eventually she must marry well and in so doing, realise his dearest ambitions. Fortunately, the child was beautiful and since she had been taught by the very best of tutors and trained in all the social niceties by an English governess, she had no difficulty whatsoever in attracting the many titled men her father made sure were invited to the house.

The question of marrying for love was not considered. Inez knew it and accepted the part she had to play. She rejected several younger and more personable men before she finally consented to marry the middle-aged Baron Leyresse—an aristocrat whose family tree went back for centuries. The Baron's lack of money was unimportant. Her father settled an enormous dowry on her and promised her she would never lack for anything she needed.

Inez had been imbued with the snobbery of class distinction too young for her ever to see in other people their true value. Her friends were those who were her equals or above her in the social scale—never those beneath her unless some ulterior motive called on her to play the *patronne*. She had fallen mildly in love on a number of occasions, but only indulged her passion when she was sure her reputation would remain intact. Her lovers all had titles of a kind, and the affairs were of minor importance to her and carried on with the utmost discretion. She dared not risk the Baron's discovery because, like so many elderly men married to young wives, he was obsessively jealous and still as adoring and doting as he had been in the days when he had courted her. She bore him no love but she was secretly afraid of him. Underneath the easy-going, indulgent exterior, she knew him to be a violent and passionate man.

Nevertheless, the marriage had been a success, each partner getting what they wanted from it. Only now, as the years seemed suddenly to have slipped by and Inez was approaching middle age, did she begin for the first time to feel the pangs of dissatisfaction, of something missing, of youth lost in the search for position and pleasure. She was still beautiful but more and more time was spent now in beauty salons, warding off the tell-tale signs of age that were frighteningly apparent beneath the scrutiny of her magnifying make-up mirror. Tiny wrinkles were appearing beneath her eyes and at the corners of her mouth; her skin was losing that tight, firm elasticity that made her complexion so flawless. For the first time in her life she had to have her glorious red hair tinted to hide the hint of grey—only a hint as yet but there all the same. She was restless, increasingly so; bored as well as frustrated.

23

She had come to look at the sleeping guest from no more than idle curiosity. Her first glimpse of Rory had somehow shocked her. With his dark curling hair and bronzed skin, she saw in him a marked resemblance to Michaelangelo's famous sculpture of David, his throat thick and strong and his jawline clear-cut and boyish. His shoulders and arms, bare above the white embroidered sheet, shone with youth and health. She had found herself longing to touch him; longing for him to open his eyes; to see the look of recognition and admiration all men gave her when they first saw her.

Inez had drawn the curtains deliberately to waken him. And she was not disappointed. The look she had hoped to see was there in his eyes. It was there again now as she said softly:

'I'm very glad you found us. It is always satisfying to realise you have helped to save a life. You are by no means the first lost person we have rescued, you know. In the old days, when this place was still a monastery and the monks lived here, there were provisions permanently on hand for wanderers on the mountain who sought refuge.'

'I'm fascinated already by the little I've seen of your fantastic home,' Rory said truthfully. 'It's like a dream world. May I see more of it before I go? I'd like to thank Alex, too. She was very kind to me last night.'

Inez felt a tiny stab of irritation. She wished

24

now that she had taken the trouble to receive the rescue team when they had returned last night. Instead, she had pleaded fatigue from her journey and had allowed Alex to take charge. The Norwegian had been in urgent need of hospitalisation so there had been no question of his remaining at the abbey. But there had been nothing more wrong with Rory than total exhaustion and, as Alex had suggested, it would have seemed churlish not to offer him hospitality for the night.

With Gilbert's help, Alex had taken the half-conscious Rory to one of the guest rooms—former monks' cells that had been cleverly converted into small suites of rooms for visitors. Inez herself had not set eyes on him until a few moments ago.

'It will be my pleasure to show you my home', she said with a warm smile that made her look a great deal younger. 'But first you must have something to eat and you must rest. Later, when you are feeling stronger, we will make plans. You must tell me all about yourself.'

Rory smiled back at her.

'You're very kind. I'm afraid I've caused a lot of trouble.'

The door opened and Alex came in carrying a silver breakfast tray.

Rory noticed the swift frown that creased Inez Leyresse's white forehead.

'You should not be doing the servants'

25

work,' she reproved the girl in a sharp voice Rory found vaguely disquieting. At the same time he was intrigued to see the quick colour that rushed to the girl's cheeks.

'I was coming here anyway with news of Rory's friend so I took the tray from Gilbert,' she told the Baroness aplogetically. She placed the tray on the bedside table and smiled at Rory.

'I'm glad to see you're better. Your friend is better, too. I phoned the hospital and they have set his leg. When I spoke, he was sleeping comfortably. I'm afraid his fingers were frostbitten but not too seriously.'

'Thank God for that!' Rory said fervently. 'Knut, like myself, is an artist. If he lost a finger and couldn't paint . . .'

'An artist?' Inez broke in. 'You are a painter? That is most interesting.' She picked up one of Rory's hands and held it between her own. 'Yes, indeed, you have artistic fingers!' she said admiringly.

It was Alex's turn to feel irritated. As far as she could see, Rory's hands were no different from any other man's—well cared for but with no visible signs that he was a painter. She suspected that Inez was being purposefully charming to their visitor. Without understanding why, Alex resented it. Rory was attractive, she thought, as she poured coffee from the engraved silver pot and held out the delicate Sèvres china cup to him, but far too young to interest a mature woman like Inez.

Rory, in turn, was noticing Alex anew. Last night she had been a ministering angel in blue so that he had retained a picture in his mind of a young Madonna. But today Alex was wearing faded jeans and a boyish-looking checked shirt with a sleeveless red sweater over it. Her long fair hair was tied back in a pony tail and she looked to Rory like any other girl at home— only prettier. With her suntanned skin and large clear blue eyes, she was in complete contrast to the exotic and glamorous Baroness.

He grinned up at Alex and said:

'Thanks a lot for everything you did for me last night. It was all a bit of a nightmare. I was afraid I'd never find Knut.'

'Enough talking!' Inez commanded, a smile softening the sharpness of her tone. 'Now you must eat, my friend, and regain your strength. Then if you will come downstairs, I will be happy to show you around the Abbaye. As an artist you will have a special interest in my home.'

She stood up and touched Alex's arm.

'I'm sure you have much to do before my visitors arrive,' she said pointedly. 'We will leave our guest in peace to eat his breakfast.'

The imperiousness of her tone of voice amused Rory. Catching Alex's eye, he gave her a quick, nearly imperceptible wink. Alex felt a childish urge to laugh bubbling within her. Quickly she left the room, Inez following more slowly after her.

Rory emptied his coffee cup and began vigorously to eat the hot, fresh croissants. His artist's eye noted the delicate engraving on the silver tray, the fine bone china, the crested silverware. The Baron and Baroness Leyresse, he concluded, were obviously very wealthy.

His eyes roved round the room as he ate. The draperies were white lace, the carpet a deep green. The walls, covered in white silk, were hung with delicate Japanese prints. The whole effect was luxurious and charming. It was hard to imagine that this room had once been a monk's cell; equally hard to imagine that the snow-capped mountain he could see through the window was the same forbidding and treacherous mountain on which he had fought for his life, and Knut's, last night.

The brilliance of the sun hurt his eyes, sore this morning from the biting wind and the effort of seeing in the darkness. There had been moments when he had felt close to breaking point. Only Knut's helplessness had kept him going on and on, down through those dark dripping pine trees until he had found this sanctuary—the Abbaye St. Christophe! Even the name was romantic and unreal—as romantic as his glamorous hostess, Inez Leyresse. How he would love to paint her! That combination of white skin, red hair and extraordinary agate eyes was enough to fascinate any man, let alone an artist!

His thoughts turned to the English girl, Alex. In her own way, she was very attractive, too. There was a hint of sadness in her face that had a fascination of its own. He'd mischievously enjoyed making her laugh and her face had been utterly charming when she did so. Her position here in this great establishment was slightly incongruous. She belonged to England—the kind of girl he had known at his university, intelligent, likeable, fun to be with.

Rory finished the last of the croissants with relish and poured himself another cup of coffee. He felt very much better—even happy, although he tried to stifle the feeling out of sympathy for poor Knut lying in hospital with his broken leg. As soon as he could, he would go and visit him and they would have to rethink their itinerary. It might be weeks before they could go to Italy now. Then there was the need for cash.

They had each saved five hundred pounds for this trip, planning to stay in youth hostels wherever possible and save on transport by hitch-hiking from place to place. Now there would be hospital bills to pay and Knut's parents must be informed of the accident. Knut's family was not as well off as his own. His father, Sir John Howes, was a company director with a good salary besides his income from considerable inherited capital. Rory, himself, would be rich on his twenty-fifth birthday when he would come into money from a trust fund set up by his grandparents. But in the meantime his father believed it would be good for him to manage without money, so that he had the merest pittance of an allowance during his university years and had had the greatest difficulty saving enough for this trip. Rory could appreciate his father's motives. At least he had acquired a good understanding now of what it meant to be hard up.

He threw back the bedclothes and went over to the window. From where he stood he could see at one corner of the abbey a great church tower, the stonework covered with snow that was melting rapidly in the hot sun. Directly behind it was the thick pine forest through which he had fought his way last night. This morning, huge black crows were circling over the trees. Last night those pines had had dark sinister shapes of their own, their branches like phantom arms reaching out to hinder or ensnare him. Now, in the brilliant sun, silhouetted against a cloudless blue sky, it was hard to recall his fear and horror as he had groped his way through them to the safety of this monastery.

Far below he heard the heavy thud of the massive timbered front door as it swung on its huge iron hinges. Then Alex appeared, flanked by the Great Danes. She wore après-ski boots which were making deep dark imprints in the virgin snow covering the courtyard. The sun, glistening on the snow, sparkled like white fire all around her and the dogs.

The girl began to run, the dogs barking furiously as they leaped playfully at her side. She stopped, collected handfuls of snow and threw it at them. Then she slipped and fell, laughing, into the deep snow. Instantly the dog, Tristan, began to lick her face. She raised her arms to protect herself from the dog's excited caresses and Rory heard her laugh again, pure, childlike, entrancing.

He did not know it then, but this was the first time Alex had laughed in one whole year. He knew only that the sound made him feel happy, glad, as she was, to be young and alive and healthy in this perfect place on such a perfect day.

On a sudden impulse, wishing to join her in the courtyard below, he turned suddenly. His legs nearly gave way beneath him and he groped his way back and collapsed onto the bed with a weak grin. He was desperately stiff; his muscles and joints ached with fatigue. Remembering last night's efforts in the thick, wet, cloying snow, he understood the cause of this unaccustomed weakness. Gingerly, he stood up once more and found his way to the adjoining bathroom.

It was as luxurious as the bedroom. The floor was carpeted in the same green, white curtains covered the casement window. The bath was modern and made of white marble with silver-plated taps. Piles of green and white monogrammed towels were folded neatly over the heated towel rail. Bath oil, soaps, colognes, lotions were arranged on a bamboo vanity table, ready, no doubt, for the use of the Baroness's guests.

Rory lay in the bath, quietly contemplating the extraordinary place in which he now found himself, his surroundings as exotic as their fantastic owner, the Baroness. He wondered how old she was. It was difficult to be exact about a woman with her figure. He wondered, too, about the Baron whom he had yet to meet. Obviously one or the other had good taste. The modern had been perfectly blended with the antiquity of the abbey itself and, even to his inexperienced eye, he knew that a small fortune must have been spent on restoring the monastery if the little he had so far seen was typical of the whole.

He was soon to discover that his own guest room, the huge entrance hall and the octagonal ante-room in which he had been last night, were unremarkable in comparison with the *grand salon* to which he was directed ultimately by one of the servants. Inez Leyresse had sent a message to him by one of the maids, inviting him to join her there for mid-morning coffee. He had discovered his clothes, dry and neatly pressed, on a chair at the foot of his bed.

His hostess was awaiting him in one of the most beautiful rooms Rory had ever seen. He was to learn later that it had originally been a banqueting hall where the mediaeval monks had received their more eminent guests. Now he stood staring up at a marvellous curved and domed ceiling, which was hung with three great crystal chandeliers. He could imagine the effect when the lights were on and reflected by each of the perfect crystals.

Six tall windows opened out onto a terrace. The sun was pouring through them, filling the room with light and colour. Heavy white damask curtains, embroidered with gold and silver, framed the windows. The walls themselves had been panelled in the same white damask and were hung with Venetian mirrors and priceless oil paintings. Against one wall stood a long black chest of drawers with handpainted panels and gold handles.

'You are admiring my room?' Inez said, smiling at the unguarded astonishment and approval in the young man's eyes.

Rory turned to stare at his hostess. She was seated in a high-backed chair, looking like a queen on a throne. She had changed from the black trouser suit in which he had seen her earlier and was wearing a brilliant yellow hostess gown. It was of a jersey material which clung to every curve of her body. Yellow kidskin sandals had replaced the fur boots.

Her red hair was piled high on top of her head where it was held in place by a Spanish comb.

The whole effect was stunning, the woman and the decor perfectly complementing each other.

'I think it is one of the most exciting rooms I've ever been in,' he said, his artist's eyes still eagerly drinking in impressions. An ebony full-sized concert grand piano stood at the far end of the salon—away from the sunlight which might discolour the ivory keys. A massive vase of white and gold chrysanthemums, perfectly arranged, softened the harshness of the jet black lid. The three sofas and numerous armchairs were covered in yellow buttoned velvet—a tone deeper than the dress worn by Inez Leyresse. White bearskin rugs were scattered haphazardly over the polished parquet floor. Fringed silk cushions of every colour and shape had been flung with the same apparent casualness on sofas and chairs. The effect of the whole was of extreme elegance combined with warmth and colour.

Then Rory's eye was caught by the incongruous sight of a prie-dieu standing in a semi-circular alcove. Above it hung a carved wooden crucifix with a silver figure of Christ. Undoubtedly, he thought, this was one of the treasured relics of the old abbey.

Inez Leyresse laughed as she rose from her chair and came towards him.

'I can see you really appreciate the beauty I

have tried to create here,' she said softly. 'That is because you are an artist, no doubt. Now come over here and sit down and tell me about yourself. My guests will be arriving soon and I wish to hear all about you before they interrupt us.'

As Rory seated himself beside his hostess on one of the vast yellow sofas, Gilbert came in with a tray on which was a bowl of whipped cream, and silver pots of coffee, milk and hot chocolate.

'Come now, you must get back your strength,' Inez said smiling. 'What is it to be? Coffee or chocolate?'

She watched with an amused detachment as he drank two large cups of chocolate topped with generous helpings of whipped cream. There was envy in her eyes, too. She did not dare, at her age, to indulge in such fattening refreshments. Unnoticed by Rory, she drank only a small cup of unsweetened black coffee whilst she questioned him about his home in England, the reason for his visit to France and his plans to see Italy's art treasures.

'I suppose I'll have to throw up the whole idea now,' Rory ended his account ruefully. 'It hardly seems fair to go to Rome and Florence and Venice without poor Knut. We talked so often about making the trip together, I don't have the heart to go without him. I expect I'll pack up and go home. Maybe he and I can make it next year.'

Inez Leyresse listened with growing interest. The young man was becoming more and more attractive to her. Now that he was dressed and shaved, his resemblance to Michaelangelo's David was even more marked. She liked his quick, frank smile, the way it began in his eyes and ended with a wide boyish curve of the sensitive mouth. Her senses were very much alive to him, and deliberately she sought to make him equally aware of her. It was an art she had learned early in life and had used often to gain some advantage from a man who could be useful to her. They were legions in their numbers—the men she had attracted and intrigued. But this time there was no motive behind her projection of her feminine appeal. She wanted no more than that the young Englishman became an admirer.

'You will, of course, remain here at the Abbaye as my guest.' She spoke authoritatively. 'I could not permit you to return home whilst your friend lies alone in the hospital. He will naturally wish you to visit him and your presence will speed his recovery.'

When Rory began to protest that he would be outstaying his welcome, she laughed aside his objections.

'My dear boy, what is one guest more or less in this place? We have so many rooms, they are never all filled even when I am giving a big ball. The servants become lazy if they do not have enough to do, and I am in Paris with my husband so frequently they have almost forgotten how to serve efficiently. Of course you will stay here—and your friend too, as soon as he is well enough to be moved.'

She sensed Rory's weakening of resolve and added quickly:

'You would be doing me a kindness at the same time. Permit me to explain. I promised the mother of little Alexandra that I would try to find some young male companions for her. There was a tragedy, you see, and her fiancé was killed in a car accident. As an old friend of the family, I offered to have Alex here to live with me while she recuperated. I fear too much solitude has not improved her spirits and you could help me by trying to enliven her life a little, no?'

Rory nodded. He was strangely unsurprised to hear that there had been a tragedy in Alex's past. It explained that look of sadness he'd noticed even on so short an acquaintance. His heart warmed towards Inez Leyresse. Autocratic and dictatorial she might be, but obviously she was intrinsically kind.

'Of course I'll do anything I can!' he said. 'Alex struck me as a very pleasant girl. I'd be pleased to help.'

Inez lightly touched Rory's hand and let it linger there as if she was unaware of the contact.

'Then it is agreed you will stay,' she said. She smiled at him, once again surprising him by the youthful appearance the smile gave her. 'I think perhaps you are *très sympathique!*' she added, using the French words to express her meaning. 'But then all artists understand women very well, do they not?'

Rory laughed.

'I don't think any man would presume to understand you, *Madame!*' he said. 'You are different from any other woman I have ever met—unique!'

Inez looked pleased at the compliment.

'Gallant as well as *sympathique!*' she said teasingly. 'But not very friendly. I do not wish you to call me *"Madame"*. From now on you will call me Inez and I will address you as Rory.'

She had acquired the French habit of rolling her r's and Rory found his name enchanting on her lips.

'Inez is an unusual name, like its owner,' he said.

He was aware now of the strong femininity of this woman, of her personal appeal. At the same time, he was becoming more and more eager to catch her likeness on canvas—a far from easy accomplishment since her moods changed so rapidly. She was a curious combination of regality and of a primitive sexuality which was in direct contrast to the cold arrogance he had seen her display to Alex earlier that morning.

Without thinking he reached instinctively in

his pocket to search for a pencil. He found one and using the centre of a paper doily from the silver tray, began to make an outline sketch of Inez's profile as she talked about herself, about her marriage at seventeen, to the forty-two-year-old Baron; of her childhood in Brazil; of the birth of her only child, Eloise, and of the many influential friends who filled her life in Paris.

She gave no sign that she was aware of his actions, although she was intensely curious to see if he really had talent.

When finally they were interrupted by the Baron, Inez was genuinely surprised to find that the young Englishman had caught an astonishing likeness to her.

'Look, Bernard!' she said eagerly, handing the sketch to her husband. 'Is it not amazing? There could be no doubting it is I.'

The Baron smiled at Rory as he took the sketch and bent to kiss his wife's forehead.

'I congratulate you, *Monsieur*,' he said, his words and actions formal but friendly. 'I have also to congratulate you on your escape last night. I hope my wife and Alexandra have been taking good care of you?'

As Rory, in his turn, expressed his thanks formally for the hospitality extended to him, the Baron studied the sketch more closely.

'It is excellent!' he commented, returning it to its owner. 'Do you paint portraits, *Monsieur*? If so, I would be happy to have you

39

paint my wife. I agree this sketch captures an exceptional likeness.'

Inez stood up and, with unaccustomed vivacity, said:

'What a splendid idea, Bernard! Rory is remaining here as our guest for a few weeks until his Norwegian friend leaves the hospital. He was only just now expressing his embarrassment at what he felt would be an imposition. Now he can take the opportunity to earn his living! He shall paint my portrait.'

Rory drew a deep breath. He had made the sketch only because he felt the need to put Inez's likeness onto paper—not as an advertisement for his capabilities.

But before he could explain his feelings, Inez said, 'When Alex drives down to Valory you shall go with her and buy what you need . . . canvasses, oils, brushes. They can be charged to me. Now that the idea is conceived, I cannot wait for it to be put into effect. You will not refuse, Rory? You will paint me?'

Rory's face broke into a smile.

'I'm not sure if you would permit me to refuse!' he said laughing. 'Actually, I would be more than happy to have the chance to paint you. But I'm very inexperienced.' He turned to the Baron and added seriously, 'One day I would like to be a great painter—a portrait painter like Annigoni. But I'm still learning—only beginning. I doubt if I could do your wife justice.'

The Baron patted him on the shoulder paternally.

'I like modesty in a man. I also believe that it is wise to begin collecting the works of an artist before he has become established. That way, it is not necessary to pay a small fortune for a painting one takes a fancy to, such as this!' He indicated a painting on the far wall. 'That is a Sutherland,' he said. 'I paid a great deal too much for it but I like it. You see, your portrait of my wife will be in illustrious company!'

Rory felt a thrill of excitement. It was almost possible to believe that Fate had led him to this fabulous establishment where he had not only found safety but perhaps the one chance of a lifetime. If he could do a really good portrait of the Baroness, it could lead to further commissions from people who could afford to pay him well. It would mean the start of the career he'd dreamed about but had feared might be very difficult to achieve.

Inez was watching Rory unobtrusively through half-closed lids. She did not wish the Baron to sense her personal interest in this young man. Were he to do so, Rory's stay at the Abbaye St. Christophe would come to a very rapid end. Her husband, usually easy-going and compliant, would be coldly and ruthlessly adamant once his jealousy was aroused. He had no objection to another man's admiration of his wife. On the contrary,

41

he enjoyed being the possessor of something another man wanted. But if Inez herself returned the interest . . .

She shivered, remembering one occasion when she had permitted herself a mild flirtation with a French poet. Bernard Leyresse had arrived back at the Paris apartment to find Inez in the poet's embrace. She would never forget the icy expression in her husband's green eyes; nor the trembling fury in his voice as he had ordered her miserable admirer from the house. For a few minutes, she had been afraid Bernard might even intend to take his pistol from his desk and kill her would-be lover; or, indeed, kill her. In that moment, she did not doubt him capable of murder. Once her initial fear had abated, the thought had excited and amused her. It gave her a feeling of power that she could evoke such violence in the man she had married. She had wished that he were as passionate in bed as out of it, but the Baron had a very short-lived interest in this side of their marriage. For some time now he had ceased to come to her bedroom. She had not particularly cared about his disinterest. She had never loved him and her submission had been no more than that—a keeping of a contract she had made when she married him. Sex had had little meaning for either of them. But his jealousy was almost obsessive—no doubt inflamed by the knowledge that he could no longer hope to satisfy his young wife.

Seeking now to allay any further suspicion, Inez said, 'Rory will make a nice companion for our little Alex. You agree with me, don't you, Bernard, that some young company will be good for her?'

The Baron nodded.

'*Mais certainement, chérie.* It is an ideal arrangement,' he said.

Some sixth sense, engendered by an uncanny sensitivity to his wife's moods, had made him subconsciously aware of her inner excitement. But the first tiny seeds of jealousy were dispelled immediately by her words. The young man would be a perfect companion for Inez's little *protégée*. In his opinion Alexandra was too often alone and he felt Inez should have insisted that the girl should live with them in Paris, despite her protests.

He put an arm around his wife's shoulders, pleased with her behaviour and anxious, as always, to give her what she wanted.

Although the Baron spoke perfect English, as did Inez, both lapsed occasionally into French—a language Rory had studied at school but not too successfully. Rory decided that Inez's husband was a likeable old man. Clearly he was a collector of masterpieces and they would be able to share a common interest in art, if nothing else. From all points of view, he had every reason to suppose that he would be very happy and engrossed during his stay at the abbey.

The door opened and Alex came in. There was a charming, happy smile on her face, but as she approached them, the smile faded. It seemed to Rory as if she were staring not at him but through him. He felt suddenly cold and strangely uncomfortable.

'What is it, Alexandra?' the Baron asked. He, too, had noticed the girl's sudden change of countenance. 'You look as if you have seen a ghost!'

His words were ill-chosen. For as she stood rooted to the carpet, Alex was seeing not Rory Howes but David—David with blood-spattered hands held out as if in warning of a danger as yet unknown, unseen.

CHAPTER THREE

Alex recovered her composure so quickly that Rory was in some doubt as to whether he had really seen that fear and horror on her face or only imagined it. As they drove down to Valory together to do the necessary shopping, he hesitated before asking her directly if anything had upset her.

It was a moment or two before Alex replied. She, herself, did not understand why her mind had played tricks, turning the warm living body of Rory Howes into a pale injured ghost of the boy she had loved. How then, she reflected,

44

could she possibly expect Rory to understand. She had felt terrified with that same helpless horror experienced in a nightmare. Part of her fear had stemmed from an intense apprehension about the future; that Rory, in the person of David, was warning her of some disaster to come, rather than of one already past.

She supposed now that her mind had linked the two young men because they were both about the same age and Rory's figure had become confused with David's—nothing more.

Responding to the quiet sensitivity she sensed in Rory, she said:

'I suspect my active imagination was working overtime.' She forced herself to speak casually. 'Just for a moment you reminded me of someone I knew, someone who was killed in a car accident a little while ago.'

Rory noticed the clenching of her small square hands on the steering wheel and guessed what it cost her to speak of the past. He said encouragingly:

'The Baroness told me about your fiancé, David. It must have been a terrible experience for you. But time does heal most pain, Alex, no matter how corny the phrase may sound.'

Alex felt the tension go out of her body and leave her feeling strangely calm. She was grateful to the young Englishman for mentioning David so easily and naturally. Maybe in time she would be able to talk about him freely and without pain.

'I'm glad you are going to stay at the abbey for a while,' she said truthfully. 'Inez must have taken quite a liking to you!' she added mischievously. 'Especially since she is willing to sit for her portrait. You are indeed honoured!'

Rory glanced at her sideways and grinned.

'I'm taking the matter extremely seriously, even if you are not,' he said. 'It could be important for my future.' He was no longer smiling as he added, 'I've set my heart on being a professional artist but it isn't easy to begin. Some artists with far more talent than I, have spent half their lives hoping for just the kind of chance the Baroness has given me. She's very beautiful and from all accounts, very influential. If she likes my portrait of her, she might recommend me to her friends.'

Alex nodded. She did not wish to pour cold water on Rory's enthusiasm, but she was far from certain that Inez would have the patience or the sustained interest to sit for hours on end whilst Rory tried to capture her likeness. Inez was very much a woman of sudden whims and fancies. She was quickly bored and required the constant stimulation of friends, parties, concerts, the ballet, the opera, the theatre. Even a few days at the Abbaye St. Christophe, unless the place were filled with guests, were enough to make her irritable and anxious to get back to the bright life of Paris. Alex was certain the novelty of having her portrait painted would very quickly pall.

'I like the old Baron very much,' Rory was saying as they wound their way down the hairpin bends towards the valley.

Last night's storm had left in its wake over three feet of fresh snow but the snow plough had been out in the early morning and now great white walls lined the road on either side. Below them, in the valley, the town roofs were white and sparkling in the hot sunshine.

'I've always been a little afraid of the Baron,' Alex said. 'He is very reserved and quiet on the surface but I think underneath he is a man of considerable violence. I know it's wrong to pass on servants' gossip but Denise, the Baroness's maid, told me he had half killed a taxi driver who had driven carelessly and, so the Baron said, deliberately risked Inez's life. If the driver had not been young and strong, Denise said the Baron would have strangled him! No doubt she was exaggerating but it is not so hard to believe. He is passionately in love with his wife. When they are in the same room, he never takes his eyes off her.'

'Then I'll have to watch my step with the beautiful Inez,' Rory said, laughing again. 'I'm not sure she is as much in love with him as you say he is with her. She was being quite provocative with me this morning.'

Alex felt a little stab of annoyance. Rory Howes was of no importance whatever to her, yet somehow she did not care for the thought that Inez Leyresse was trying to attract him. At the same time, she knew that it was second nature for Inez to wish all men her adoring slaves and that it amused her to try to charm them, especially those who were initially less ready to fall at her feet. Rory was too nice a person to be one of Inez's playthings—as were most of the men whom she invited to the abbey as her guests.

They were now entering the little town of Valory. Alex went shopping there at least twice a week so she knew exactly where to go for her own requirements and knew the art shop where Rory might obtain his painting equipment. He also wanted to buy some books and magazines to take to Knut that afternoon.

Alex had promised to drive him to Geneva to see his friend and she was looking forward to the occasion. Apart from the break in the customary routine, it would enable her to avoid Inez's guests. The highly sophisticated, hard drinking, brittle socialites Inez chose to call her friends were alien to Alex. An afternoon with Rory would be wonderful in comparison.

'You're very quiet,' Rory remarked. He had been watching the changing expressions on her face with interest and not a little curiosity. 'I think you spend too much of your time inside your head. I'm sure you have very interesting conversations with yourself.'

Alex blushed a deep pink.

'I'm sorry if I seem rude!'

'Don't be so silly,' Rory chided her, feeling now quite at his ease with her. 'I wasn't being critical—merely curious. I'm interested in what people think about, and especially you. You're the very last person I would have expected to find in a place like the Abbaye St. Christophe. I think you've been using the place in the way people use convents or monasteries—as a retreat. Any ordinary girl your age would be screaming with boredom, shut away on a mountainside with only two great brutes of dogs for company.'

'I've not been unhappy,' Alex said defensively.

'Nor lonely?' Rory persisted.

'A little, perhaps. I haven't thought about it.'

'Then you should. No one has the right to run away from life forever and you are far too pretty to bury yourself in the Alps. I shall rescue you from your prison, Princess.'

Alex laughed. Rory seemed to have the ability to make her laugh often, ridiculous though some of his remarks might be.

'I'll take you down to the wine cellars in the abbey,' she told him as she found a parking place for the car. 'Then you'll see what a prison is really like.' She shivered. 'I only went down there once and it's horrible—dank, dark, scary . . . and huge. I believe the cellars run the entire length of the abbey. I can't imagine a more horrible death than to be entombed in a place like that.'

'Then don't think about it,' Rory said cheerfully. 'We're going to enjoy this beautiful sunny day without spoiling it thinking about dungeons. Now, what are we going to buy first—the flowers?'

He observed in shocked silence the fantastic cost of the flowers Alex chose to decorate the abbey. She explained that apart from being out of season, the flowers had to be transported from Geneva and in any event, the cost was irrelevant to Inez. The Baron and his wife could well afford such luxuries.

She was similarly reassuring about Rory's painting materials. Expensive though they might be, Inez would not wish him to economise by buying anything less than a full complement of paints and brushes. Alex told him that Inez would probably not even look at the bill. They then bought English and American newspapers and a few French magazines for Knut as well as two 'Get Well' cards with humorous messages.

When they returned to the abbey, Alex hurried away to do the flowers before lunch. Inez's guests were not arriving until later in the afternoon so Alex would have plenty of time to arrange the flowers.

The meal was served in the dining room—a room almost as vast as the *grand salon*. Rory estimated it must be about forty feet long.

Inez, obviously pleased with her own genius for interior decoration, told him it had once been the monks' refectory. But nothing now remained that was dark or gloomy. The original tall windows with their high sills were open to the brilliant blue skies. The sunshine poured through them, past sweeping curtains of claret-coloured velvet caught back with thick, golden ropes.

The stone walls were covered with tapestries, depicting in muted colours hunting scenes of the Vosges. Rory was instantly intrigued by the bluish shadow of the forests, the chestnut of the stags with their uplifted antlers, the greenish hues of the young men in their uniform of the Chasseurs riding on their satin-coated horses.

The tapestries dipped down to the deep red and gold of the rich Oriental rugs arranged on the dark polished floor.

The old refectory table was set with heavy plates of china, antique Venetian goblets, and big embroidered linen napkins. The velvet cushions on the high-backed walnut chairs were the same dark red as the low chrysanthemum centrepiece.

At one end of the room massive wrought-iron dogs supporting great pine logs stood in a stone fireplace.

'I have never seen anything so striking!' Rory told his hostess truthfully. 'I had imagined your drawing room to be the most

51

elegant and colourful I'd ever seen, but this is fantastic!'

Inez was watching the rapt expression on Rory's face with interest. His admiration was as obvious as his astonishment. She was pleased that here was no naive, uneducated boy but a young man, an artist, who could appreciate fully the craftmanship and beauty that she had so skilfully blended to create the final effect.

'Come and sit down here, Rory,' she commanded him. 'I wish to hear in detail what you like most about my dining room.'

The meal was served by Gilbert and a maid—a simple repast of soup, green salad and an assortment of cold meats. The big meal of the day would be served that evening when the vacant places at the long table were filled with Inez's guests.

Alex politely answered the Baron's remarks as she ate, but with one ear turned to Inez's and Rory's animated conversation. She knew very little about art, although she appreciated the better known paintings and sculptures and could recognise the most famous of the world's art treasures. She wished now that she knew as much as Inez Leyresse seemed to know, for the Baroness was succeeding totally in monopolising her guest. Alex could see the animation on Rory's face and guessed that he had no idea what he was eating as he launched into a further discussion with his hostess about the age of the tapestries on the wall. Alex felt gauche and uneducated, in comparison with Inez Leyresse.

If the Baron, too, was feeling a little jealous, he gave no sign of it, although his eyes never rested anywhere for long before they returned to the beautiful woman opposite him. There was in them a speculative look that probably only Inez would have recognised had she bothered to notice it, an expression in that green unwavering stare she might well have interpreted as a warning not to pay too much attention to the young man at her side.

It was, therefore, fortunate for Inez that immediately after coffee, Rory departed for Geneva with Alex.

'And what will you do with yourself this afternoon, my love?' the Baron asked his wife as the young people left the room.

Inez edged surreptitiously away from the gentle weight of his arm around her shoulders, her face enigmatic as she replied:

'I have plenty to do, *chéri*. My hairdresser is coming up from Valory and Denise has to alter the neck of the dress I am wearing tonight. I shall be busy until our guests arrive.'

'Then I shall retire to the study for a short nap,' the Baron said agreeably. He knew from past experience that this evening's entertainment would continue until the small hours and that at his age, if he did not manage a few hours' sleep in the afternoon he would be unable to last out the night.

In the car, very far from sleepy, Rory was voicing his opinion of the Baron's wife as they drove towards Geneva.

'Inez is really fantastic!' he said to an unresponsive Alex. 'Apart from being the most stunning woman I've ever seen in the whole of my life, she also has a remarkable brain. She's incredibly erudite—on the subject of art, anyway—and it wouldn't surprise me one bit to find she's equally knowledgeable about literature and politics. It must be quite an experience for you living with her.'

Alex tried to subdue the childish jealousy she felt. Pacifically, she said:

'I really see very little of Inez. She's away in Paris most of the time. She spent a month at the abbey last summer when Eloise was home for the holidays, but during that time she did a great deal of entertaining in which, as you know, I'm not included.'

Rory glanced at her, catching an inflection in her voice she had not realised was there.

'You mean, you're left out of the fun and games?'

Alex shook her head.

'No, I didn't mean that. Inez's friends aren't exactly my type, or my age. And even if they were, I am an employee and I think it's more tactful to keep out of the way.'

Rory grinned mischievously.

'I can't agree with the last part of your

remark. I'm sure all the middle-aged men would be more than happy to flirt with such a pretty girl.'

'Oh, shut up!' Alex said rudely, but suddenly happy again. 'I know you're only teasing. Anyway, you can play the gigolo tonight to all the middle-aged ladies and I hope you enjoy it. That is if you aren't too busy dancing attendance on your hostess.'

'Miaow!' Rory came back quickly. 'The kitten has claws. Seriously, Alex, I can assure you of one thing—I'm not attending this dinner party unless you do, and that's a fact. If her ladyship raises any objections, I shall say so.'

Alex's face clouded.

'I don't want to go—I really don't, Rory.'

'But I want you to go!' Rory overruled her. 'And so does Inez. And don't look so unbelieving. She told me herself she thought it was high time someone woke up "the sleeping princess". Moreover, she suggested I should be the one to do it. So you see, I'm only obeying orders. You will come to the dinner party and enjoy it, as I intend to myself.'

The happiness of a moment ago deserted Alex as quickly as it had enveloped her. Rory was being attentive because Inez had instructed him to be nice to her—out of pity. If he had really wanted her to go for his own sake . . .

'Now what is flitting around in that curious

mind of yours?' Rory broke in, cleverly divining her changed mood. 'A penny for them, Alex. Or should I say a franc?'

'Not for sale!' Alex replied.

Rory gave a mock sigh.

'Okay, be stubborn. See if I care! I tell you what I'm thinking—for free, too. I'm thinking that if ever a chap landed on his feet last night, Rory Howes is that man. I'm still finding it hard to believe that out of that dreadful storm, I've woken up to a fairy tale. At least when I tell Knut, he won't be able to disbelieve you— the fairy princess. Knut's crazy about blondes. He'll probably fall madly in love with you!'

He was pleased to see that Alex was smiling again. It was rapidly becoming a kind of game with him whenever he saw that look of sadness or loneliness on her face, to wipe it away and bring back the laughter. She was very attractive when she smiled. Knut really might fall in love with her. He, Rory, might even fall in love with her himself!

'What are you laughing at?' Alex asked. 'The thought of your friend falling in love with me?'

'No!' Rory said. 'And this time my thoughts are not for sale.'

They settled into an easy silence. Within a very short time, they seemed to have established a comfortable relationship with each other. On Rory's part he felt much as a brother might feel about a younger sister—

56

protective and affectionate. On Alex's part the feeling she had for Rory was more complex. When she first met David, they had fallen instantly in love. Romance had preceded friendship, the latter growing slowly as they learned to adjust to one another. But being with Rory was like being with a friend she had known for a long while. That she also found him attractive she was not yet ready to admit to herself. Nor did she recognise her irritation when Inez monopolised Rory at luncheon as tinges of jealousy. Yet she was very aware of him and self-conscious with him because of it.

The visit to the hospital turned out to be great fun. Alex had been secretly afraid that the sight of a hospital ward, of nurses, doctors, and the smell of antiseptics, would revive memories of those dreadful weeks she had spent recovering after the car accident. But as it happened she had little time to remember the past. The Norwegian, despite his ordeal and the pain his plastered leg must still be giving him, was bright and cheerful. He teased the young nurses who obviously already adored him, and flirted outrageously with Alex. He threatened Rory with unimaginable retribution if he took advantage of his immobility to 'court' Alex before he, himself, had a chance to do so.

'She's going to be *my* girl friend!' he informed Rory, his cornflower blue eyes twinkling beneath the fringe of lashes the same white-gold as his hair. His large, generous mouth widened still further in a smile. 'You understand, don't you, Alex, that you are to give Rory no favours, not so much as one little kiss'—he pronounced it 'kees'—'until I am well enough to fight him—how do you say in English—fair and square?'

'I'm not making any promises, Knut!' Rory warned his friend. 'We have another English saying—all's fair in love and war.'

'But not fair if I have the broken leg!' Knut argued, reaching for and holding Alex's hand. 'She is far too beautiful for you, my dear friend. All you will do is paint her picture, whereas I . . .'

'He won't be painting my picture!' Alex broke in smiling. 'He has been commissioned to paint the Baroness Leyresse.'

Rory told the Norwegian about this amazing piece of good fortune, but Knut pretended to be quite unimpressed.

'Enjoy yourself making likenesses of this exotic female. I am pleased you will be so occupied. When I am well again I shall have better things to do than make likenesses of the nobility. I shall flirt with Alex.'

A nurse came in to inform them that it was time for Knut to receive a further injection. Without it, the pain in his leg and in his frost-bitten hand would become extreme. But Knut would have none of it.

'My friends have only just come!' he

protested.

But Alex and Rory had both noticed the tiny lines of fatigue round the young Norwegian's eyes, and the occasional twist of his mouth as a spasm of pain engulfed him.

'We'll come again tomorrow,' Alex promised. 'I'm sure Inez will permit it and even if she wants Rory's company, I will be free to come.'

Knut grinned.

'All the better if you come without Rory,' he said, and pressed an extravagant kiss on Alex's hand. 'We will have things to talk about that do not need a third ear.'

'You old rogue!' Rory chided affectionately. 'Whether you want me or not, I'll come anyway, to chaperon Alex. I reckon a girl's not safe with you—even in a public ward with a broken leg.'

As they drove home, Rory asked Alex how she liked his friend.

'Very much!' Alex told him warmly. 'I know Knut was playing the fool, but underneath the clowning I'm sure he's very intelligent.'

'He's my best friend,' Rory said seriously. 'I've known him now for five years. I don't know what I would have done up there on the mountain . . .'

'Don't think about it,' Alex said quickly. 'Remember instead that he owes his life to you.'

'That's a nice thing for you to say,' Rory

commented softly. 'You played your part, too, in saving Knut's life. Not to mention those guides. I must stop by to thank them. Knut will wish to do so, too, as soon as he is better. Won't it be fun, Alex, when he can be moved from the hospital and we can show him the abbey? I can't wait for him to see the place. I want him to meet Inez, too. He won't believe his eyes! I know he thinks I have exaggerated her beauty.'

Alex was by now growing accustomed to that tiny nagging at her heart every time Rory spoke so enthusiastically about Inez Leyresse. She recognised it for what it was—a childish envy of the older woman with her fabulous clothes and jewellery and her exotic allure that no girl like herself could hope to emulate. Alex could well understand how a young man like Rory could become infatuated by her, might even fall in love with her!

'Why should I care, anyway?' Alex asked herself. Rory meant nothing to her. Superficially his friend Knut was more attractive. He was fun and amusing and although she had known he was flirting with her, she had responded to the flattery he had showered on her, instinctively aware that he meant quite a few of those compliments.

It was only after they had returned to the abbey and Alex was alone in her bedroom tidying herself before Inez's guests arrived, that she realised what a milestone this day had been in her life. She had actually and actively enjoyed it; enjoyed the morning with Rory; enjoyed the silly flirtation with Knut. She had behaved as she once used to behave—like any girl appreciative of the society of two attractive young men. She was even looking forward to this evening; planning which of her two evening dresses she would wear; contemplating piling her fair hair on top of her head to make herself look older, more sophisticated. She was participating again; living again. And most astonishing of all, there was no pain, no hurt, only an underlying excitement as to what the next few hours would bring.

CHAPTER FOUR

Inez's guests arrived in chauffeur-driven limousines or in taxis from the station. There were twenty-two in all. Rory was standing near Inez in the brilliantly lit *salon* as Gilbert announced each new arrival. He was secretly amused by Inez's *sotto voce* asides as her so-called friends came in.

'These two are the Count and Countess Wienborg–Austrian. She's a deadly bore but he's quite amusing. This couple are French. No title but she's a famous novelist and has a quick wit. He's *efféminé* but the Countess

61

fancies him and gets cross with me if I don't invite him when she is here.'

Seeing Rory's amusement, Inez continued her stringent commentary.

'These are a frantically dull couple—Swiss. He is a banker and very useful to my husband. I shall be very charming to him, of course. Now here is someone who might interest you—a Spanish princess, heiress to the throne I-can't-remember-how-many-times-removed, but she'll tell you! The man with her is known as her husband but he is only her lover and has been for twenty years. She has refused to marry him because he is a commoner, and if the monarchy is restored she wants to be free to drop him in favour of a more suitable husband . . . as if she would ever attract one with her looks!'

Rory was forced to agree. Inez's comments might be catty but they were very much to the point.

He began to lose count of the names and faces as Inez introduced him to more and more people. There was a well-known musician, a poet, a famous French film star whose beauty fell disappointingly short of her screen image. She had in tow a young blond Swedish actor, unknown according to Inez, except as the star's escort. Rory was amused to see that the young Swede made a beeline for Alex who was the only person in the room anywhere near his age.

62

Alex looked very pretty. She was wearing the forget-me-not blue gown he'd seen her in last night. It gave her an innocent little-girl look he found particularly endearing. One day, if there was time, he would like to paint her wearing that dress, he thought.

By five o'clock all the guests had arrived and dispersed to their various suites, whilst their chauffeurs and maids were despatched to accommodation elsewhere in the huge abbey. Inez and the Baron went to their own suite to bathe and change for dinner. Rory and Alex were alone except for the servants who came in to build up the fire with fresh logs and to set out plates of canapés.

'The lull before the storm!' Alex said, sinking gratefully into one of the large yellow sofas opposite Rory. 'They'll all be down again in about an hour and there'll be drinks served until dinner at eight.'

'I'm beginning to doubt I'm living in a real world,' Rory commented. 'It's like a film set. I suppose you've seen it all before.'

'Several times,' Alex assented. 'I felt like you do the first time. It's still impossible to imagine that at home Mother will probably be drinking a glass of sherry before dishing up chops for my father's supper!'

Rory laughed.

'Nor can I believe that a week ago Knut and I were cooking a rice dish on the gas ring in our digs at university, wondering if we could afford a bottle of cheap red wine to wash it down!'

He gave a sudden grimace.

'I've only just realised,' he said. 'I haven't got any evening clothes. I can't possibly turn up for a banquet dressed like this!'

Alex saw the look of horror on his face and laughed.

'It's a good thing someone thought about it sooner than you did. Inez had your clothes measured when you were still asleep this morning. One of the servants has found a dinner jacket for you. I checked before I came down and everything you need is in your room—white shirt, black tie, cuff links, studs, socks, patent leather shoes. I hope they fit!'

She smiled again at the look of incredulity on Rory's face.

'Inez never does anything by halves,' she said. 'You'll get used to it. I have!'

Almost philosophically now, Rory accepted the fact that the dinner jacket was a perfect fit. The shoes were a half size too large but definitely wearable. He was not even surprised when one of the valets came in to enquire if he had everything he needed; nor blinked an eye when the valet opened the wardrobe to show him his own few clothes which he had left in a rucksack at the youth hostel. Someone, during the day, had called to collect them and those that needed it had been laundered and pressed and neatly put away, as was his passport and other personal effects. Nothing at all had been forgotten. If this was due to Inez's thoughtfulness, Alex had been right in stating that the lovely Baroness never did anything by halves.

Almost as if she had been expecting him, Inez was alone in the great drawing room when Rory went downstairs, looking strangely different in his borrowed formal attire. He looked older but very slim and handsome as Inez was quick to notice and remark upon. She held out a hand to him and Rory felt it quite natural to take it in his own and kiss it lightly, as if the Baroness were a queen and he a courtier.

To him, she did, indeed, look like a queen. The yellow dress had been exchanged for a floating green chiffon gown which seemed to swirl around her beautiful body like a wave. With his artist's eye Rory pictured her as a sea goddess. He said eagerly:

'I would like to paint you in that dress. I think I will call the picture "Phryne". Will you wear it when you sit for me, Inez?'

The soft material was draped seductively across her white breasts, exposing the upper curves and revealing her shoulders. Around her throat was clasped a beautiful emerald necklace. Emerald pendant earrings hung from her delicate ears and her red hair was piled high on her head, an occasional tendril curling with seeming abandon above her ears

65

and in the nape of her neck.

Inez Leyresse felt a little thrill of pleasure. The look in Rory's eyes clearly revealed his awareness of her beauty. She had dressed tonight to enchant this young man who had so taken her fancy and she felt a quiet triumph at her success.

'You shall paint me exactly as you wish,' she said softly. 'But first I wish to know who Phryne is, since my picture is to be named after her.'

Rory sat down on the sofa beside his hostess and carefully lit the cigarette she held to her lips.

'Phryne was a Greek courtesan, celebrated for her beauty,' he told Inez. 'Praxiteles modelled his statue of Venus from her. She was, in due course, accused of profaning the Eleusinian mysteries but the judges acquitted her after she had appeared naked before them, because they felt obligated to preserve the image of divine beauty for all artists.'

Inez Leyresse gave a deep voluptuous sigh.

'Then I am flattered by the title of my portrait!' she told Rory truthfully. 'I hope you will paint a flattering likeness of me, too. Artists can be cruel, sometimes. I do not wish you to reveal my advancing age.'

As she had hoped, Rory was immediately indignant.

'You talk as if you are old,' he chided her. 'Surely you must know that no young girl's beauty could compare with yours?'

'Do you really believe that, or are you perhaps trying to please me?' Inez asked, looking at him provocatively from her fathomless dark eyes. She was sure now of her conquest and could enjoy these moments of listening to his compliments.

'On the contrary, I am always honest about beauty,' Rory said truthfully. 'A good artist does not lie. He paints what he sees, not what he wishes to see.'

'And does he not paint what he feels?' Inez parried. 'If he fell in love with a woman, would he not be blind to her faults?'

Rory shrugged his shoulders.

'I can't answer that since I have never been in love,' he laughed. 'At least, not really in love. I imagined once or twice that I had found the perfect girl but it never lasted long. I think my trouble is that I always find fault too quickly, too easily. So perhaps that answers your question—that an artist cannot blind himself.'

'Then I shall have to take care,' Inez said, the lightness of her voice belying the undertone of seriousness. 'I would not want a portrait showing the less admirable side of my nature!'

'I'm sure there isn't one!' Rory said gallantly. 'You are one of the most thoughtful and generous people I have ever met. I want to thank you for arranging to have my belongings brought here. It was very good of you. But then, you have shown me nothing but kindness.'

Inez remained silent. She had no wish to disillusion him by telling him that it had been Alex, not herself, who had thought of his clothes left at the youth hostel; Alex who had first suggested Inez should offer him her hospitality. Quickly, she changed the subject.

'Tell me about your Norwegian friend,' she said. 'I heard from Alex that he is making good progress. Also that he is a very charming boy. As soon as he is well enough to be moved, he shall come here to recuperate.'

'You really are too kind,' Rory said sincerely. 'You take in a couple of strangers as if it were a perfectly natural thing to do. And these . . .' he pointed to his borrowed clothes '. . . are yet another example of your thoughtfulness. I don't know how to thank you.'

'Then don't,' Inez replied. 'I am pleased to have you here beside me. The Baron and I see too much of the same people. It will be refreshing to have a change of conversation and company.'

Rory was on the point of thanking Inez further for the oils and brushes and canvas he had bought that morning, but the entrance of several house guests and the Baron put an end to his monopoly of Inez. He found himself engaged in conversation by the French film star, Louise de Montefort. He thought her exceedingly dull, although she did her utmost to make herself attractive to him. Her Swedish boy friend, Erik Neilsson, had discovered from Alex that Rory was an artist and passed the information on to Louise while they had been changing for dinner. He guessed, quite correctly, that Louise would be eager to have her portrait painted, since she copied Inez in everything. He hoped that Rory would direct Louise's attentions away from himself, thereby leaving him free to continue his pursuit of Alex. Louise was not only aging but boring and Erik remained with her only because he had not yet succeeded in making the grade either in the film world or socially, without her backing. He had found the English girl quite delightful and above all, young. The weekend had begun to take on an aura of excitement, sadly lacking in his life of late. So he was pleased to offload Louise upon the reluctant Rory.

Because Louise de Montefort was one of Inez's guests, Rory did his best to parry her advances politely. He explained that it might take several weeks for him to complete Inez's portrait and that he would undoubtedly be on his way either to Italy or England as soon as the commission was finished. He agreed to take note of Louise's address in Paris and was in the process of writing it down when Inez excused herself from the Baron's company and came over to Rory in time to see what he was doing.

She was instantly furious, not with Rory but with Louise. Her dark eyes stared at the Frenchwoman with undisguised venom and Louise was not so stupid as to be unaware of it.

'You have no objection to my having my picture painted by your young *protégé, chérie?*' she said sweetly, knowing that Inez would not choose to be at her most bitchy in front of this young man. 'After all, Inez dear, it is a compliment to your judgement, is it not? I understand *Monsieur* Howes is as yet quite unknown? Your own personal discovery?'

Inez forced herself to smile. Inwardly she resolved to find some way to punish this ridiculous middle-aged woman for presuming she could deflect Rory's attention from herself. At the same time, Inez felt a tiny shiver of apprehension. Silly though Louise might be—and really she did not have a brain in her dyed blonde head—she had somehow divined that her interest in Rory was not solely artistic. She, Inez, had let her guard down for a fraction of a second, betraying the jealousy she had experienced when she saw Rory noting down Louise's address. The emotion she had felt was so unexpected and foreign to her that she had not been able to conceal the expression in her eyes. Such lack of control could be dangerous and she resolved to be prepared and more careful. Louise was a gossip and the very last person she would trust.

Quite in control of herself now, she tucked her arm through Louise's, noting spitefully how plump she was getting although she was not much past forty. She said with a smile:

'I have every faith in my *protégé*, Louise, and as you say, I am most complimented that you should have such faith in my judgement. You see, Rory? I shall soon have you launched in Paris! Louise is a very famous film star and if you paint a beautiful picture of her, who knows what future lies in store!'

Rory caught the tiny flicker of Inez's eyelid as she stressed the word 'beautiful' and knew she was alluding to their earlier conversation on an artist's ability to flatter or to paint the truth as he saw it. Louise de Montefort's beauty was entirely due to the artifices of make-up and camera angles and both he and Inez knew it. It was perhaps a little cruel of Inez to draw his attention to it but he was also amused by her sharpness. He remembered her running commentary on her guests as they had arrived but since her sarcasm was not directed at him, the hints of cruelty in her character enhanced her fascination. He was beginning to see her now as a tigress with a kitten's claws.

Gilbert's announcement that dinner was served saved him from what might have been an awkward reply. He was far from sure whether Inez wished him to paint Louise's portrait or not! He was, therefore, happy to find Alex at his elbow.

'I've put your place card beside mine so we will be sitting next to each other during dinner. I hope you don't mind.'

'I couldn't be more pleased,' Rory said honestly. 'To tell you the truth, I'm a bit out of my depth with all these strangers. It'll be nice talking to a friend.'

Alex smiled at him.

'You seem to forget I'm a stranger, too. This time last night we'd never met.'

Rory stared down at her in astonishment. Her statement was true, yet the feeling he had known her for a long time made the brevity of their friendship difficult to credit.

Seeing his face, Alex laughed happily.

'I know how you feel. I could hardly believe it when I thought about it just now. Come on, everyone has gone in.'

Rory followed her into the dining room. The heavy claret-coloured curtains had been drawn and the room glowed with a warm light. Six silver candelabra, each with a trio of candles, sparkled down the length of the dark table. At the far end of the room whole sections of tree trunks burned in the fireplace, filling the room with an aroma of pine.

A stone archway led into an outer room through which the servants were bringing huge trays of food.

'This isn't a dinner—it's a banquet!' Rory whispered to Alex. A rich pâté with thin golden toast was followed by grilled river trout *aux amandes*. This, in turn, was succeeded by veal in a white wine sauce with a choice of four different vegetables.

'I won't be able to eat another thing,' Rory said as he consumed the last mouthful. But as Alex warned him, there was more to come—an assortment of pastries made by Inez's incredible chef; an enormous chocolate gâteau covered with a mountain of whipped cream and nuts; and finally, a huge basket of fruit—grapes, peaches, nectarines, pears, oranges, tangerines—all, Alex informed him, sent by train that morning from Paris.

With this repast were served the finest wines—delicate grape-flavoured Riesling, deep crimson Château Lafitte, sweet Château Yquem. To complete the meal there was port, cognac and every conceivable choice of liqueur and perfectly made coffee—black and strong, served in Limoges *demi-tasse*.

The Countess Weinborg, on Rory's right hand, seemed to find nothing very unusual in this lavish meal. She spoke to Rory only occasionally, preferring to eat stolidly through each course with a gourmand's silent satisfaction.

'I suppose this is nothing new to you, either!' Rory said to Alex after he had drawn her attention mischievously to his gluttonous neighbour.

'Sssh, she speaks good English,' Alex

warned him. 'And I'm no more used to all this than you are. You forget I don't usually attend these functions. I have a meal on a tray in the *petit salon* by myself! Besides, these weekend parties don't happen very often. As I told you, Inez spends most of her time in Paris.'

Rory sighed.

'One can't help wondering, if that is the case, if it isn't a ghastly waste of money keeping the Abbaye St. Christophe open—just to satisfy Inez's whim to come here once in a while. When you think of all the poor and the starving people in the world . . .'

'I know!' Alex broke in. 'But you can't think of Inez's life in terms of economy. She wouldn't know, far less care, what you were talking about. She has always had as much as she can possibly spend and poverty isn't a word she understands. The Baron has a better appreciation of what it means to be hard up. He's a strange man in many ways. He talked to me one evening about his family and their history and told me that he had grown up in the knowledge that it was his duty to marry a wealthy woman so that he could regain the Leyresses' land for his heirs. He believes that God compensated him for the fact that he had no son to carry on his name by giving him a wife not only rich enough to meet his financial requirements but one whom he could also love.'

'What I don't understand,' Rory questioned

74

Alex, 'is his purpose in restoring the abbey and, if you like, the family's former importance in the district, if he has no heir to carry on his name.'

'There is Eloise,' Alex reminded him. 'There is a will leaving her everything the Baron and Inez own on condition that her future husband adds the name Leyresse to his own. That way, the name and line will be perpetuated.'

'And is Inez's daughter as fantastically beautiful as she is?' Rory asked curiously.

For the second time that day, Alex felt a tiny stab of jealousy as Rory spoke so ardently of Inez's beauty. The moment passed and she said lightly:

'No! The girl is like her father, aristocratic looking but no beauty.'

The meal over, most of the men lit cigars. To Rory's surprise, so, too, did Louise de Montefort. Watching her with his ultra-observant eye, he was amused to see that she obviously did not enjoy it. It was an affectation—and effective enough, he thought not unkindly, since it attracted his notice.

During dinner the servants had tidied the *grand salon* so that when the guests returned after the meal, the big fire was ablaze with newly piled logs, the ashtrays were emptied and the remains of the cocktail hour drinks had been removed.

Inez came across the room to Rory and put her hand on his arm.

'Come and sit down beside me,' she said. 'I need a little light entertainment after that heavy meal, and you shall regale me with some stories of your youth in England.'

Obediently Rory sat down beside her. 'After that perfectly wonderful meal, I'd do anything in the world to please you, *Madame*,' he said with mock gallantry. 'Unfortunately, stories of my youth in England could only bore you. I've led a dull life. Compared with your world, I'm afraid mine would sound very mundane.'

'Not to me!'

The words were softly spoken—in a tone too low for anyone else in the room to hear and with an unmistakable meaning in them. Rory felt a moment of embarrassment. From a woman such as Inez Leyresse, flirtatious words might mean no more than a few minutes' after-dinner amusement. At the same time, there was an intense intimacy in her voice that belied frivolity.

He felt uneasy. One part of his mind refused to accept that a woman such as his hostess, beautiful, rich, emancipated, could possibly find him either particularly amusing or attractive. On the other hand, he knew very well that such women were frequently bored, spoilt, frustrated. Perhaps, he thought, he had the dubious advantage of being a 'novelty' to her. At the same time, he was flattered that she seemed attracted to him. And he was far from insensitive to her dynamic sexuality.

Rory did not look upon himself as different in any way from his contemporaries, but he did not agree with all aspects of the modern permissive society. He was at heart an idealist and a romantic. Sex for its own sake held no appeal for him. Nor did affairs with married women, although he knew several young men at university who had enjoyed such relationships.

Now, for the first time in his life, he found himself wondering if his morality had not been due more to lack of temptation than to the upholding of a principle. No man could be immune to Inez Leyresse's sex appeal, least of all an artist who could not fail to be drawn instinctively to such beauty.

'You are silent, Rory!' Inez spoke again in the same low voice. 'Will you not share your thoughts with me?'

Rory smiled.

'I was, as always, thinking how beautiful you are. I can't wait to begin your portrait. I think I know exactly how I shall paint you.'

Inez bit her lip in sudden exasperation. She had made the first tentative advances to this young man and somehow, accidentally or with a subtlety she did not expect from him, he had avoided a reply that gave her any indication of his feelings towards her. So far as she could elicit, his admiration of her was entirely that of an artist.

She controlled her impatience. It was, after

77

all, very much the start of a relationship and there would be all the time in the world when he was painting her for her to further her own desires. She was oddly disturbed to find herself so speedily and so unusually emotionally involved. Passion was a luxury she had coldly and deliberately avoided throughout her life. Now, without plan or intention, this young man had, in the short space of a day, made himself necessary to her in a way she could not explain. He had assumed an extraordinary importance to a point where she feared his rejection of her.

Even as the thought crossed her mind, she laughed at the utter ridiculousness of it. As if she, Inez Leyresse, could fail to charm any man she chose to put under her spell! There was no reason for her to doubt that if she wanted Rory Howes, she could have him. No reason, either, she told herself apprehensively, why she should suddenly find herself feeling like a young girl falling in love for the first time—nervous, uncertain, excited and intensely aware of him.

'I must go and talk to my other guests,' she said, standing up abruptly and with determination. 'You will excuse me, Rory.'

He stood up and watched her walk away from him with mixed feelings. He was very unsure of himself and of her. His senses warned him that Inez was more than a little interested in him, and his mind warned him that he would be wise to avoid any kind of personal involvement. He was both fascinated and afraid. He had seen a glimpse of her potential for cruelty and he could imagine she might be ruthless if she were thwarted.

With a sense of relief, he saw Alex. She was talking to the Baron, smiling at something he said to her. There was no hint of the sadness he had first remarked in her—only a soft shining innocence that for the second time, made him think of painting her as a Madonna. Then she turned and, seeing him, gave him a mischievous grin that was anything but ethereal.

'I've been telling the Baron about your friend, Knut,' she said as he joined them.

'I think I have one or two books in the Norwegian language in the library,' the Baron said to Rory. 'In the morning I will see if I can find them. It will be something for your friend to read whilst he's in the hospital.'

'That is very kind of you, sir,' Rory said warmly. 'In fact, you and your wife have been nothing but kind since I arrived here so inopportunely last night.'

The Baron stared at Rory for a moment, a speculative look in his green eyes that was somehow chilling.

'You are very welcome,' he said with slow formality, 'both as a companion for little Alexandra and as the artist who will paint my wife's picture.'

79

Rory felt a tiny shiver run up his spine. The room was warm with the many occupants and the heat from the blazing logs, yet he still felt cold. He was sure he was not imagining a look in the Baron's eyes that seemed to hold a very distinct meaning. Was the elderly man warning him that he would not tolerate any close friendship between him and his young wife, other than that of artist and sitter?

'My imagination is running away with me,' Rory told himself firmly. The effects of the exorbitant beauty and luxury of the Abbaye St. Christophe following so closely on his night of cold and terror on the mountain had obviously been too much for him.

'I think I should go to bed,' he said. 'I'm afraid I may still be suffering from the after-effects of yesterday. Will you both excuse me?'

The Baron watched Rory leave, his green eyes narrowed, the lids half closed. He was not aware of Alex's eyes also on Rory's slim young body as he moved with youthful suppleness across the room. He saw only his wife's face, unguarded, as she, too, watched Rory leaving. It held a look of angry disappointment that was clearly discernible to him, who knew her every expression. He had never yet been mistaken about that particular predatory look on Inez's face. It meant she wanted something. Only this time, it was not something but someone. And this time, he resolved with cold determination, she would not get her heart's

80

desire. He loved her far too violently, far too possessively to indulge this whim. He would give her anything else in the world that was in his power to give. But never, as long as he lived, would he let her have another man.

CHAPTER FIVE

Alex sat cross-legged on the bearskin rug with her back to the fire, Tristan's head heavy across her knees, the rest of his big body stretched out beside her. On the white onyx table between her and the sofa was a leather backgammon board. She was playing against Knut and had already beaten him twice. He was on the point of losing the third game when he paused and said reflectively:

'That dog is more attached to you than to his illustrious mistress. Not that I blame him one little bit!'

Alex laughed. She was accustomed now to Knut's continuous flirtation and, after ten days of constant companionship, she had grown very fond of him. She and Rory had been able to collect him from the hospital only a week after the accident. Although he could only hobble around on crutches, his cheerful presence had brought a wonderful atmosphere of gaiety and laughter to the abbey. He was always joking. He could make even the serious old Baron laugh when he set himself to do so. He teased Inez and managed to get away with it, and, of course, he and Rory were forever ragging one another like two schoolboys.

Alex was happy—happier than she had believed possible a few weeks ago. She awoke each morning with a fresh eagerness for the day to come and was not even downcast when yet another snowstorm swept the valley making skiing impossible and confining them all within the abbey walls. The bad weather seemed endless, continuing from day to day with yet more snow and biting cold winds driving down from the mountain summits. The skies were an ominous grey and darkness fell even earlier than usual.

Only Rory objected to the weather. He complained endlessly that he could not get the right light for his painting. Inez had given him a large room, once a huge attic, to use as a studio. All the lumber that had been in the room had been moved by the servants down to the cellars—great tin trunks containing who knew what bric-a-brac from the past. Inez had given Knut and Alex permission to go down to the cellars to open the locked trunks to see what was in them. But for the moment Knut feared he might not be able to negotiate the steep stone steps that led to the old vaults and it was a treat they looked forward to in the future when the heavy plaster was removed from his leg.

Rory was virtually lost to them now his portrait of Inez was started. He painted even when Inez was not sitting for him, eating his midday meal from a tray in his studio and appearing only after dark when he could no longer make use of natural light.

When Rory was not around, Alex missed him. But for Knut, she thought, Rory's absence would have been even more noticeable. Towards evening she would find herself looking again and again at her wristwatch or out of the window at the gathering dusk, aware that it would not be long now before Rory came downstairs, paint-stained, eyes red-rimmed, but usually smiling.

'And how's the masterpiece, Raphael?' Knut invariably asked.

Rory would give him a gentle push back among the cushions and reply:

'It's going well. I'm pleased with it!'

Alex listened with mixed feelings. She knew it was ridiculous to feel excluded but when Rory was painting, and for some hours afterwards, he was impervious to anything but his work—and the model he was working with.

'Inez is really fabulous!' he said again and again. 'She can recapture an expression, a gesture, in an instant. She seems to sense exactly what I want in the most uncanny way. I'm having difficulty with her eyes though. I don't seem to be able to get quite the expression I want . . .'

83

He talked on interminably in this vein until Knut stopped him.

'That's enough, Rory, old friend. Relax and have a drink!'

Then Rory would laugh and apologise and put an arm round Alex's shoulders, saying:

'Okay, so I'm boring you both to tears. Tell me what you two have been up to today.'

Such moments had become precious to Alex, for then Rory's attention was exclusively hers. He teased her about her relationship with Knut and seemed pleased that they were becoming such close friends. She would have been happier if he had felt just the smallest bit jealous.

Knut said now, bringing Alex's thoughts back to their game of backgammon:

'It's your move, Alex. Lucky old Tristan, I wish I could lie there with my head on your lap. If that's a dog's life, then I wish I were one!'

Alex smiled.

'I've never known anyone talk such a lot of nonsense as you do, Knut. Are you ever serious?'

To her consternation, his brilliant blue eyes suddenly sobered. His voice, no longer teasing, said quietly:

'I could be serious, little Alex, if I thought you wished me to be. I am afraid, though, that your heart is elsewhere, is it not? With my good friend, Rory, no?'

Alex bent her head over the dog so that her fair hair fell forward, hiding her hot cheeks.

'That's ridiculous!' she said crossly. 'You're teasing me again.'

But she knew he was not, and his words had brought to the surface of her mind something she had been trying not to think about.

'I am not teasing, Alex. I speak now what I think is the truth, although I wish very much it were not so. I am falling in love with you and you are falling in love with Rory. It is sad, is it not?'

With a great effort, Alex forced herself to look up directly into Knut's face.

'It would be sad if it were true,' she said. 'But it's all a lot of nonsense and you know it. Of course I'm not falling in love with Rory. I hardly know him.'

Knut sighed.

'You see now why I am not serious with you? You prefer I should be the clown. So I shall continue to be Pagliacci, and you will continue to like me and to laugh at me. It makes me happy to see you smile. Now, it is my move and I think I shall move this man here and remove yours from the board. So how is that, Alex? Maybe this time I win, eh?'

The awkwardness of the moment was gone and Alex felt herself relax. Knut was right. She did not want to know if he was falling in love with her. She hoped not. She liked him very much indeed but that was all. Nor did she want to fall in love with Rory.

Her uneasiness returned as the image of Rory came flooding back into her mind. If it had been Rory who was falling in love with her she would not have felt dismayed. On the contrary, she wanted Rory to notice her the same way as he noticed Inez Leyresse. In the logical half of her mind, she knew it was stupid of her to be resentful of Rory's endless praise of Inez's beauty; yet despite this reasoning it always hurt when he voiced his admiration.

Alex was far from vain. She could appreciate and share Rory's view of Inez and accept the fact that she herself had no claim to the adjective 'beautiful'. It was Rory's obsessive awareness of Inez that she found unsettling, an awareness that excluded her as totally as it did everything and everyone else in the abbey.

Alex continued the game of backgammon, playing automatically as her thoughts twisted and turned in unaccustomed malaise. Knut had put the thought into her mind that she might, if she were not very careful, fall in love with Rory Howes. A few weeks ago she would have said such a thing was impossible; that she would never, as long as she lived, be able to love anyone but David. Yet for a whole week, she had not even thought of David. She felt miserably disloyal and tried to evoke the memory of the thin, angular, dark-haired boy whom she had loved so deeply. But when she conjured up the image of his dark eyes, thickly lashed, and of that gentle sensitive mouth, the image became the face of Rory.

On an impulse bordering on panic, she said to Knut:

'I haven't told you about my fiancé, David, have I?'

Knut looked up from the game, his attention caught by the unexpected forcefulness of the girl's voice.

'No, you have not talked about him to me,' he said quietly. 'Although Rory told me about the accident . . .'

'Yes, he was killed,' Alex broke in in a cold deliberate voice. 'We were going to be married. David was an architect. We were to be married as soon as he had completed his final examinations. I loved him very much. He was a wonderful person.'

'If you loved him, he must have been wonderful,' Knut agreed calmly.

Alex felt as it she were on a flood tide. Now that she had begun to speak, she could not stop.

'David was everything any girl could want— good-looking, honest, fun to be with. He was twenty-four years old. That's terribly young to die, isn't it?'

Knut nodded. He sensed the rising hysteria in Alex's tone and decided to try to calm her.

'Yes, it is young to die. I thought I was going to die that night on the mountain. At first I was very afraid. Then I began to accept the possibility that my life might come to an end when I was only twenty-four. I realised that while I might miss a great deal, I would also be spared the possibility of disillusionment; of old age, of ill health. I'd had a good life, I told myself. In a way, it seemed reasonable that it should end before I reached the stage of regretting. I would hate to be old and regret things—things I did or said; things I didn't do. I think regret is one of the saddest words there is.'

While he was speaking, Alex managed to regain some control of herself. Knut's words were giving her a new viewpoint. For one whole year, she had regretted David's death and lived in sadness. Now, through Knut's eyes, she saw the emptiness of such a way of life. There was no purpose, no meaning to it. To regret the irreversible was a form of madness from which she was at last beginning to recover. Knut had made her see that although opening her heart once more might invite a measure of pain, even sorrow, it would be preferable to a continued negation of life itself.

'I'm glad I told you about David,' she said. 'I've never talked about him since . . . since he died.'

'You must do so whenever you wish,' Knut told her gently. 'Remember him with happiness, Alex. He would want that.'

It was an entirely new concept and one that Alex found herself hugging to her heart. She could see that she had negated David's memory. Now if she could talk about him, think about him, remember all the good things and be happy, his death might not seem so unbearable.

'I'm very grateful, Knut,' she said sincerely. 'You don't know how much you have helped me.'

'Then I'm happy,' the Norwegian replied. 'I want you to know at all times, Alex, that I am your friend. Whenever you need me for whatever purpose, I shall be there to help you if I can. I mean that. You won't forget? Promise me?'

'Promise you what?' a voice said from the doorway.

Rory stood looking at the couple in front of the fire with a strange sense of exclusion. He knew, because Knut had told him, that his friend was very much attracted by Alex. He knew, also, that Alex liked Knut a great deal. He was glad they got on so well and particularly glad to see Alex so happy of late. The sad remoteness in her face was a rarity now, and more and more frequently he heard her laugh—a carefree, joyous laugh that always made him smile when he heard it.

At this moment, however, he was sensitive to a new atmosphere in the room. He saw a seriousness in their faces and heard a warm intimacy in Knut's voice that was meant for Alex alone.

'Hullo, Rory!' Knut said, turning as Rory spoke and smiling in his normal way. 'How's the masterpiece?'

Rory frowned.

'Not going quite so well, if you want the truth.' He wiped at a daub of paint on the back of his hand with an oily rag and added, 'I spent all afternoon trying to get the bone structure of the wrist and I've still not succeeded. I keep making it too heavy. Inez has tiny bones and I don't seem to be able to get it right.'

'Come and sit down by the fire,' Alex said sympathetically. He looked cold and depressed and she forgot her own problems as she moved Tristan's head from her lap and pushed the big dog aside to make room for Rory. There was a smear of paint on his forehead and he smelt of turpentine. He looked very tired.

'You should take a day off,' she said thoughtfully. 'You've been working non-stop for a week. Surely like everyone else an artist is entitled to a day's rest?'

Rory put an arm round her shoulder, the gesture casual, friendly and impersonal.

'You may be right and I'm getting stale,' he said. 'But I'm really fighting against time. You see, Inez isn't sure how long she intends to remain at the abbey. She may go back to Paris soon and then it will be twice as difficult for me to work.'

Alex was surprised. Inez had shown no sign of wishing to leave. In the past, an occasional weekend here had been enough to send her rushing back to the bright lights and gay life of the city. But this time, she had seemed quite content to hibernate. When she was not sitting for Rory—something which usually took an hour or so in the morning and again in the afternoon—she remained in her bedroom suite, visited every other day by her hairdresser, a masseuse from Valory and a local dressmaker from whom she had ordered a complete new set of lingerie. The woman, a Belgian, sewed every stitch by hand, on delicate satins and silks, for Inez believed that nylon was unhealthy next to her sensitive skin.

It did not strike Alex as a very exciting life. Nevertheless, her employer had given no indication that she was bored and when Rory told them Inez had threatened to depart soon for Paris, the news came as a surprise.

Alex, of course, had no idea of the reason prompting Inez's threats. For seven days, the Baroness had used every feminine wile she could think of to make Rory aware of her. It drove her to a near frenzy that as an artist he could be so minutely aware of her, and yet remain oblivious to her as a woman. She was consumed with a passionate determination to force his attention to her that was rapidly threatening to get beyond control.

Rory's seeming indifference had served to

heighten her desire. The longer he remained aloof and withdrawn the more violent and frustrated she became. She was now caught in the deadly snare she had thought to set for him. He stayed objective, involved only as an artist with his model, whilst she could think of nothing else but that she wanted him.

The word 'love' haunted her mind. It was a word she feared. She was not yet ready to admit that she loved this young Englishman with all the pent-up emotion of a woman nearing middle age whom love had passed by. She was not even sure if she cared whether Rory fell in love with her or not, so long as he desired her as she desired him. His touch was wildly exciting to her. She would wait through long hours as she posed for him just for that one moment when he would leave his easel and come towards her, usually to correct her posture.

'No, that hand should be here, Inez,' he might say and lifting her hand, move it a little higher so that it partly cupped her breast. She wanted to believe that when he so touched her, it was deliberate. But her bitter angry heart forced her to accept that, if not accidental, such gestures were still totally dispassionate. He was passionate only about his painting—revealing an intense and violent love for the reproduction of her—but never for her, its inspiration.

For one so young, Rory was dictatorial when

he painted; even ruthless in his selfish disregard for her. Part of her responded to this domination—something she had never before experienced with a man. The other part of her hardened in her resolve to break him down—to make him feel, want, need her.

Whilst she modelled for the most part in silence, sitting for him as he painted with tireless concentration, she let her mind wander in dangerous fantasies. Like a schoolgirl in love for the first time, she enacted in her thoughts little plays in which Rory always discovered he was desperately in love with her. He, looking exactly as she could see him beside his easel at that moment, would say in a low vibrant voice:

'Inez, I cannot stay silent one minute longer. I love you. I've wanted you from the first moment I set eyes on you. I've tried to fight it but I cannot. I must have you, I must.'

Sometimes she would permit herself the luxury of keeping him at bay, tantalising him.

'I don't know if I feel as you do, Rory. Give me time to think about it.'

Or occasionally:

'Don't be such a silly boy. You are far too young. The difference in our ages cannot be overlooked!'

But far more often she simply closed her eyes and let him take her into his arms so that she could at long last feel the vital strength of that young body; feel her own long-dormant desires take control of her, carrying her to a state of total abandon such as she had never yet permitted herself.

Unfortunately for Inez, she was no schoolgirl who could dream happily and indefinitely of her idol. She was shrewd enough to appreciate exactly what was happening to her; honest enough to admit that it was certainly not happening to Rory. Attentive, gallant, friendly, charming though he was on all occasions, he had not given one indication that he would welcome her advances; nor even that he had noticed the subtle invitation in her eyes, her voice, her gestures. He behaved towards her with the utmost respect.

Her mention of the possibility that she might return to Paris had been no more than a gambit to discover if he would mind if she went away. As she had feared, his objections had been entirely impersonal.

'But, Inez, how can I finish my painting if you go now? I need you here.'

'Can you not paint me from memory?' she had asked him. 'You look at me often enough to have my image implanted in your mind.'

'But that is not the same!' Rory had argued impatiently. 'There is something in your face, your eyes, your expression, that I must capture if I am to paint you as you are and not as a photograph would show you. My memory could never do you justice.'

Inez smiled, momentarily content with the compliment.

'We'll see,' she said. 'But you will appreciate, dear Rory, that this is a little boring for me even if for you it is a great excitement.'

'I know and I'm sorry. I'm being very selfish,' Rory had said, laying down his brush. 'I really can't tell you how grateful I am, not just for all the hours you've sat here so patiently, but for giving me the chance to paint you at all. I can only hope that you will feel it is worthwhile when you see the finished portrait.'

'You are pleased with the way it is going?'

Rory sighed.

'I think so. Sometimes I am not sure. I've had so little experience. Maybe an artist needs years before he can realise his full potential. I am a little afraid I may not do you justice. You have some indefinable quality no other woman has, Inez. I can't explain it. I just know it is there, if I can only capture it on my canvas.'

'Perhaps you would find what you are searching for if you knew me better,' Inez suggested softly. 'Surely any artist must have a close rapport with his subject—a special feeling inside his head or his heart?'

Rory nodded eagerly.

'I do know what you mean and I do have that feeling about you whenever you come into a room. I can't stop myself looking at you, wondering if I have quite caught the tilt of your chin or the curve of your arm. You have an elusiveness that would challenge any artist.'

'You flatter me,' Inez said archly, but Rory remained innocently factual.

'Indeed I don't, Inez. I am telling you only what I see.'

She had wanted to lose her temper with him; to shout and scream at him that he was blind if he could not see what must be obvious to any other man; that she desired him; that the look he could not define was the look any woman has for the man she wants, and only for him. It was a hungry, basic, animal look; yet softened by tenderness and the wish to caress and fondle as well as consume.

Inez had no way of knowing, nor even of suspecting, that Rory was not so blind as he feigned. He felt her eyes following him, had seen the invitation in them and in the way she moved her body when she knew he was looking at her. But he was afraid of what he might unleash if he gave her the slightest hint that he was aware of her as a man as well as an artist. He was, after all, young, healthy, human. Inez was the epitome of temptation and he knew that every artist has always to be a little in love with his model if he really means to capture her beauty. It would be very easy to fall under Inez's spell. It was impossible to ignore the woman herself as he painted her body, her skin and muscles and flesh and bones; the delicate neck, the small hands with their brilliant crimson-tipped fingernails. At night he would find himself unable to sleep, conjuring up her image as he waited impatiently for the dawn so that he could return to his painting of her.

But fortunately for Rory, there were two factors helping him to keep a firm hold on reality. First, the Baron, who never lost an opportunity to warn Rory, in the most subtle of ways, that Inez was his wife and his most treasured and exclusive possession. He made it clear to Rory that he trusted him, that if Rory should abuse that trust, however lightly, he would regret it. Such warnings were never actually voiced yet somehow the elderly man managed to convey a threat that was chilling. Rory could understand now why Alex had once told him she was frightened of the Baron because of that underlying violence beneath the façade of aristocratic indifference.

Rory's other life-line was the end-of-the-day companionship he shared with Knut and Alex. They teased him, laughed with him and brought him back to reality—a world in which Inez Leyresse had no real importance. Knut made no bones about the fact that he heartily disliked Inez. As if uncannily aware of Rory's wavering emotions, he seldom let an opportunity slide to point out her arrogance towards the servants, her selfishness towards her husband, her indifference to the feelings of others. Although Knut conceded that she hid this well beneath a show of kindness and generosity, he had little doubt that it was feigned.

Alex remained aloof from the violent arguments Knut would pick with Rory about Inez, Rory defending her as heatedly as Knut argued against her. The more Knut attacked Inez, the more strongly Rory seemed impelled to support her.

'You don't know Inez the way I do!' Rory usually ended by saying and Knut's face would dissolve into a mischievous grin as he replied, 'And don't let the Baron hear you say that, my friend, or it will be kaput for you, huh?' and he drew his hand across his throat, making such a realistic noise of a man in his death throes that Rory and Alex inevitably burst out laughing.

Knut, also, had begun to use his talents as an artist. But unlike Rory, he had chosen soft crayons instead of oils as his medium. He covered sheets of heavy drawing paper with outline sketches of Alex, nearly always with Tristan. Sometimes the Great Dane could be seen lying as he did now with his heavy head across her lap. In others, he was behind or beside her, but always there, so that Rory had begun to call him Alex's familiar. He knew she loved the dog and that Tristan was no longer happy if she left the room or the abbey. He knew, also, that Inez deeply resented her dog's defection, as she chose to call it.

'You English are all so sentimental about

your animals,' she had said to him that morning. 'It is not good for Tristan to be so spoilt. I must tell Alex not to make such a stupid fuss of him.'

She had spoken lightly but with an undertone Rory sensed very clearly. But he hesitated before relaying the warning to Alex. He felt certain she would be upset and justifiably resentful. It was not her fault that the dog had decided to devote himself to her rather than to the mistress who was so often away for months at a time and who, even when she was at home, demanded that Alex take him for walks and feed him. Inez's caresses were spasmodic according to her mood and though Rory was not aware of it, there were times when she lost her temper and kicked Tristan for no greater fault than that his big frame was in her way.

Rory decided, literally and metaphorically, to let sleeping dogs lie. Tristan looked so content, eyes closed but one huge dark ear twitching occasionally whenever Alex spoke.

'Lucky dog!' he said, as Knut had done an hour or so earlier. 'Wish I could put my head on your lap and go to sleep. I am tired!'

He noticed the sudden change of colour in Alex's face and was momentarily surprised. He had not thought his teasing remark would embarrass her. The three of them were such easy companions now and spoke without restraint. He was not to know that only a short while ago Knut had suggested to Alex that she might be falling in love with him, Rory. He was far too engrossed in his own private problem of Inez to wonder about Alex's feelings. So long as he saw her laughing and happy, he was content and could forget her.

Seeing Alex's embarrassment, to ease the moment Knut said:

'Isn't it about time we changed for dinner? I need a bath. How about it, Rory?'

Without Rory's assistance he could not manage to bath himself with one leg in plaster which he must not get wet. The floor on Knut's 'bath night', as Alex called it, was always submerged in water and the two young men would emerge soaked and laughing like a couple of schoolboys.

'Time I fed Tristan and Isolde!' Alex said, looking at her watch. 'Thanks for the game, Knut. You can have your revenge tomorrow.'

She left Rory to assist Knut up the stone staircase and went through to the kitchen quarters to give the two dogs, ambling behind her, their evening meal of veal and rabbit. Someone had once told Inez that Great Danes were liable to kidney trouble and from that time onward, the dogs had been given an exclusive and expensive diet of white meat only.

But tonight, although the dogs' bowls were filled and ready as usual, Gilbert looked at Alex with an apologetic smile and said:

100

'The Baroness wishes to feed the dogs herself in future, *Mademoiselle*. She asked me to inform you.'

'Yes, of course!' Alex replied, puzzled by Inez's orders.

She walked away, Isolde remaining hopefully behind, her big dark eyes set greedily on her food, but Tristan, as always, followed Alex.

As she went upstairs she tried to shrug off her feeling of uneasiness. This could be no more than one of Inez's strange whims. By tomorrow she would quite likely be reprimanding Alex for not feeding the dogs as usual. But it did seem strange that Inez had left one of the servants to tell her of her wishes.

She had forgotten the incident when she went down to dinner. She was wearing the forget-me-not blue dress Rory seemed to like so much and she felt relaxed and happy. Although usually sensitive to Inez's moods, this evening she did not notice at first that the Baroness was furiously angry, although doing her best to conceal it.

'I'm afraid Tristan is off his food,' she said to Alex across the dinner table, her voice sharp and icy. 'No doubt this is because he has become so devoted to you, he will not now condescend to eat from the hand of his mistress. I doubt if you realise, Alex, when you make such a silly fuss of him, that you are doing him a disservice. After all, you will not always be here, will you, and then if he refuses to eat, he will die.'

'That is not likely, my dear,' the Baron broke in soothingly. 'Dogs may go off their food but they will eat when they are starving. It is human nature.'

'Tristan is not human!' Inez snapped, her dark eyes flashing. She was wearing a black dress tonight, made from a shiny satin that reflected the light, relieving the sombre effect. Round her white throat like a collar, were coil upon coil of tiny jet beads, held together with a gold clasp. The only colour about her was her red hair, falling to one shoulder in a single shining red flame. She looked beautiful and dangerous.

'Tristan is probably not hungry,' Knut put in tactfully. 'After all, the dogs have had no exercise for three days with this terrible weather. Tell me, *Madame*, how is the portrait going? Rory says he is pleased with it.'

The subject of the dogs was dropped. But Inez's mood was still far from relaxed. Her nerves felt like taut wires and her emotions were see-sawing between hate for Rory because of his rejection of her, and a love for him that was totally obsessive.

'I am not allowed to look at my picture,' she replied in a cold voice. 'It is very tedious of Rory but he insists I shall not see it until it is finished.'

'That decision is the prerogative of the artist,' the Baron said calmly. 'After all, it is his painting until he gives it to you.'

'I'm no longer sure I shall want it!' Inez said, avoiding Rory's eyes, as the servant put a plate of grilled salmon in front of her. 'To tell you the truth, I am becoming very bored with so many sittings.'

'I'm afraid I've worked you too hard,' Rory said with genuine concern. 'Alex was telling me only this evening that we should have a break. We'll take the day off tomorrow, both of us. Would that make you feel happier?'

Inez shrugged, giving the appearance of disinterest.

'I cannot think what I shall do with this day off you have so kindly permitted me. What can one do in such weather? Certainly not ski. It is so dull here, Bernard. Maybe I will go to Paris for a little *divertissement*.'

'Whatever you wish, *chérie*. You know, my dear, I have been thinking, it is a long time since we had a ball here at the Abbaye. You know how you love to give a really big party. It would entertain the young people also. Why not a masked ball? That might be amusing.'

'Sounds very exciting!' Knut said with his usual good humour. 'Do say "yes," *Madame*. I could go as Captain Hook!'

'He was a pirate with one arm, not one leg!' Alex said laughing. 'Anyway, it's a masked ball, not a fancy dress.'

103

'I haven't been to a fancy dress dance since I was a kid,' Rory joined in, laughing at the memory. 'I think I was a cowboy.'

Inez had been listening, at first with a refusal on her lips, but as she watched Rory's enthusiasm rise to match that of his friend and Alex, she suddenly warmed to the idea; a fancy dress ball; a chance to wear some really fabulous, glamorous outfit that would finally convince Rory that no other woman could outshine her. It would be a night with candles and music—with dancing and drinking; a night made for seduction; so many people in so many guises, that she could slip away with Rory unnoticed, be alone with him . . .

'Well, my dear, I see that you are considering my idea. What is your opinion?' the Baron enquired, glad to have averted one of his wife's bad moods.

'It is an excellent idea, Bernard. We will go to Paris tomorrow and telephone all our friends. It is too late for written invitations if we are to have the ball soon—next weekend perhaps. I will choose a costume to wear and, of course, one for you, too, Bernard.' She warmed to the idea still further. 'We will invite about a hundred and fifty guests—no more, I think. We can accommodate about fifty. The rest can stay at the Hotel Montagne. Alex, you can book it for the weekend and tell the manager I shall require all his rooms.'

Her mood now swung from low to high. She

felt a little drunk with excitement. Two spots of red on her high cheekbones and the brilliance of her eyes enhanced her beauty.

The Baron, watching her as always, said quietly:

'You are so lovely, my dear, you should attend this ball as Cleopatra.'

Inez laughed, her eyes sliding towards Rory.

'Oh, no, Bernard, I should go as Phryne!' she said.

To Rory's embarrassment, he felt himself begin to flush a dark red. He feared that the Baron, an erudite man, might well know the story of Phryne appearing before her judges naked.

But if the Baron did so, he gave no sign, his face remaining impassive.

Rory managed to stammer:

'Whatever fancy dress you choose, you are bound to look beautiful.'

Later, after the customary *demi-tasse* of coffee and cognac had been served in the *petit salon* and Inez and the Baron had retired, Knut asked his friend who Phryne might be.

'I'm not much up in Greek mythology,' he said. 'But there was some meaning that was over my head. You looked scared out of your wits, Rory. Do tell us what it was all about.'

His voice was teasing, as always. Rory tried to laugh but his earlier embarrassment returned.

Alex noticed it and said quickly:

105

'Rory doesn't have to tell us if he doesn't want to, Knut.'

'Then I shall have to get a book from the library and look up this mysterious Phryne,' Knut insisted.

Rory managed to smile but his voice was halting as he told them the story. Alex looked astonished but Knut was grinning.

'So our lovely Baroness will appear at the fancy dress ball quite naked!' he said. 'I can't wait for the night. May I be one of the judges?'

'Shut up, Knut!' Alex chided him. 'It's not really funny at all. It must have been very embarrassing for poor Rory.'

'And no doubt intended to be,' Knut said shrewdly. 'Inez is after you, my friend, in no uncertain terms.'

'Don't be an idiot!' Rory's tone was sharper than he had intended. He felt thoroughly upset by the turn the conversation had taken—the more so because it was in front of Alex. Somehow it seemed all wrong to be discussing Inez in her presence. She looked as embarrassed as he felt.

'Look, Alex,' he said, trying to put the record straight. 'I'll have you know this is all Knut's nonsense. Inez is no more interested in me than she is in him.'

'I don't see what it has to do with me anyway,' Alex said in a small, tight little voice. 'I'm tired and I'm off to bed. Come on Tristan, I'll let you and Isolde out for a last run before

I go.'

Suddenly she remembered Inez's reprimand about the dogs.

'Someone has to let them out,' she said frowning. 'If Inez doesn't, I'll have to. That's not spoiling them.'

'Of course it isn't,' Knut reassured her.

Alex stood for a moment in uncertainty. Then she went out, Tristan close against her side, Isolde bounding ahead.

Knut looked across at Rory with raised eyebrows.

'Something tells me there is a storm brewing,' he said without a trace of his usual humour. 'And I don't mean the weather. There's an atmosphere in this house this evening that I don't like. Have you felt it, Rory? Inez was really unpleasant to Alex about the dogs.'

'Oh, I don't think it's anything much. Inez's just a bit bored,' Rory parried the question. He had been as aware as Knut of Inez's strange and variable moods.

In the silence that followed they could hear the dogs barking, then the faint sound of Alex's voice calling them. The heavy front door banged shut and Alex's footsteps faded into another part of the house.

Knut watched thoughtfully as Rory went over to the fire and kicked one of the logs inwards. It crackled and smouldered as it touched the hot ash and then burst into flames.

'Maybe we should leave here, Rory,' he said softly. 'Maybe it was a mistake to stay on as we have. Things seem to happen in this house over which one has no control.'

Rory essayed an uncomfortable laugh. He did not want to be made aware of Knut's uneasiness.

'You're not trying to make out the abbey is haunted?'

'No, but seriously, Rory, I think we should go. Don't ask me to explain. I have the strongest feeling we should go now, before we become more deeply involved.'

'And leave my painting half-finished? Not on your life, Knut!'

The Norwegian sighed.

'I was afraid you would say that. Couldn't you take it with you and finish it from memory? I mean it, Rory. Let's go.'

'And what about Alex?'

'She can come back to England with us.'

'But she might not want to leave. Besides, what reason could you give her? You can't even explain to me why you want to run away.'

Knut sighed.

'I suppose it does sound crazy. I just feel sure we should go, and take Alex out of here, too.'

'You're in love with her, aren't you?' Rory said flatly.

Knut met his searching gaze.

'If you insist on knowing, then I think I am. But she is not in love with me, nor likely to fall in love with me. We have had so much time alone together that if it had been there—that feeling, she would have discovered it by now. Just as I have discovered it. She is the nicest of girls, Rory, and very, very vulnerable. Don't you find her attractive, too?'

'Yes, I suppose so,' Rory said. 'I haven't thought too much about it. I like her enormously. I feel . . . well, like an older brother. I wouldn't want anything to hurt her.'

'Or anyone?'

Rory bit his lip.

'And what's that supposed to mean? You think Inez would hurt her? You've got an obsession about Inez, Knut. You can't see anything but evil in her and she has been damn good to you as well as to me. I don't understand it.'

'I'm not getting into an argument about Inez tonight. I'm too tired,' Knut said quietly. 'Forget what I said. We'll stay until the portrait is finished—then off. Is that agreed?'

'Agreed!' Rory said at once. 'That's all I'm interested in, Knut, despite your insinuations.'

He sounded so sincere that Knut was reassured.

'I believe you,' he said as Rory helped him onto his one good leg. 'The trouble is, I think Inez Leyresse is beginning to realise it, too.'

'So what!' said Rory, as he handed him his

109

crutches.

'So that's what I am scared of!'

Knut was smiling as he spoke, but Rory noticed that the smile never quite reached his eyes.

CHAPTER SIX

'I must have been mad ever to suggest we leave this lovely place,' Knut said.

He was sitting with his leg propped up before him as Rory and Alex dragged the sledge across the frozen crust of snow towards the abbey. The weather had taken a sudden turn again. The hot sun was beating down on them as they returned from their walk through the pine forest, the dogs leaping, barking and racing around them, as happy as the three young people to be out of the house and in the open air again.

Inez and the Baron had been in Paris for the last week. Rory had abandoned his studio and the portrait was covered with a cloth, untouched since Inez's departure. With the absence of its owners, the abbey had taken on a new guise. Without the restraining influence of their elders, Rory, Knut and Alex had begun to talk in louder voices, to laugh more, to play the radio, to run instead of walk, reverting to behaviour that was almost childlike.

Alex was even happier than Knut, who still suffered the restrictions of his plastered leg. Her pleasure sprang from her awareness that Rory had at last begun to notice her. Frequently he would take her hand and hold it, sometimes playing with her fingers as if it was the most natural thing in the world to do. He had lost the look of strain and, of the three of them, laughed the most, although Knut had the monopoly on teasing.

They rose early each morning, and drank cups of rich hot chocolate topped with whipped cream, sitting in the sun on the terrace. Then Rory and Alex went off for an hour's skiing together, leaving the dogs with Knut for companionship. After lunch they took Knut out on the sledge, stopping for a rich tea at the village patisserie. Then they would walk home slowly, tired but content as the sun began to go down. In the evenings, comfortably attired in their jeans and old sweaters, they sat in front of the log fire in the study playing backgammon and poker and occasionally 'Cheat' at which Knut excelled.

'It's been such fun!' Knut went on, as Rory threw a snowball at one of the dogs, missing the target and nearly hitting a passer-by.

'You talk as if it was all coming to an end,' Alex chided him. 'This fine weather can last for weeks once it sets in.'

'Ah, but our proxy parents return tomorrow,' Knut reminded her. 'The children

111

will have to behave themselves!'

'Oh, nonsense!' Rory laughed. 'You try to make Inez out to be a kind of ogre, or is it ogress? You forget she is the one who is arranging a fancy dress ball to entertain us kids!'

'As well as to amuse herself,' Knut put in.

'What are we going to wear?' Alex asked. 'We've never given it a thought.'

'Inez may bring back costumes for us,' Rory suggested.

'I think Alex is right and we should think up something for ourselves,' Knut argued. 'Something we can wear as a trio—The Three Wise Men or Three Men in a Tub—something for all three of us together.'

They were still making ridiculous suggestions when they arrived back at the abbey, each idea a little sillier than the last so that they were weak from laughing.

It was Alex who thought they might find costumes in the trunks that had been moved to the cellars when Rory took possession of the attic for his studio.

'Maybe some of the old clothes Inez said were in them will give us an inspiration, even if we have to adapt them,' she said and then shivered. 'Not that I really want to go down to the cellars. It's dark and horrible there.'

'How are we going to get Knut down there?' Rory asked practically. 'We'll have to go without him, Alex. Poor old Knut!'

'I wish Knut were going with you and not me,' Alex said as they sat round the fire in the study, sipping hot tea in the tall, silver-framed glasses that Gilbert had brought in to them. With sugar and spices and a slice of lemon, this was a wonderfully warming drink. 'I'm sorry I ever mentioned the cellars.'

'You're not really scared, are you?' Rory asked, noting Alex's dubious expression. When she nodded he laughed gently, saying, 'I'll take care of you, silly!'

True to his word he held her hand tightly in his own when they descended the worn stone stairs leading from the kitchen quarters. They twisted in almost a complete circle far beneath the main floor of the abbey. The air rising up to meet them was icy cold, dank and stagnant.

In his other hand Rory held a torch which he flashed round the walls in search of an electric light switch. The massive boulders that formed the sides of the huge cellars were green with damp and covered with a slimy moss.

'I agree it's not exactly pleasant down here,' Rory said with a half-hearted laugh. 'Moreover, I imagine any clothes we found here would be rotten or mildewed or both.'

'The trunks the servants brought down from the attics were tin ones,' Alex reminded him. 'I suppose they would be impervious to the damp. Besides, they have only been here a short while.' She shivered. 'Let's forget it,

113

Rory. Let's go back upstairs.'

'Oh, nonsense! There's nothing to be frightened of,' Rory chided her. 'Here, hold my hand!'

He shone his torch around him. Along the walls at regular intervals were rusty iron fixtures which, Rory suggested, had once held lighted tapers. His voice echoed eerily as though they were in a tunnel. Alex held back as Rory attempted to urge her forward.

'It's really horrible down here,' she said in a small scared voice. 'The Baron calls it the crypt but Inez says it's a vault.'

'I agree, it's a bit dungeon-like. But look over there, Alex, beyond those wine racks. That must be the crypt.'

They walked further into the darkness and he shone the torch above him. They both gasped at the sight of a huge carved roof, timbered with mighty beams that had withstood the weight of the abbey for hundreds of years.

'They must be rotten with the air being so damp,' Alex whispered fearfully.

Rory grinned. 'You sound as if you're afraid of your own voice!' he teased. 'Look, Alex!'

His light picked out a row of partitioned walls in low narrow catacombs. Then its beam came to rest on a strange figure.

Alex cried out and Rory paused, feeling a moment of panic. Then he stepped forward for a closer look and said excitedly:

'It's a knight's armour. That would make a splendid fancy dress, Alex. Knut could wear it and nobody would notice his plastered leg!'

Alex let out her breath.

'For one horrible moment, I thought it was a ghost! Don't touch it, Rory, please! It looks so . . . so lifelike!'

But Rory was already detaching the dusty sword and waving it above their heads in a boyish enthusiasm Alex could not bring herself to encourage. Despite Rory's presence she had a sensation of terror and an ever increasing reluctance to stay down there.

Rory put down the sword and lifted the visor of the knight's armour.

'Alex, look!' he cried excitedly. 'There's a black and white effigy inside.'

He tried to remove the headpiece but the steel had rusted with age and damp and creaked ominously.

'Please, Rory, don't . . .' Alex began, but at that moment Rory dropped the flashlight.

For one long minute she stood in total darkness as he searched for it. Her vivid imagination flooded her mind with the possible consequences. The flashlight might be broken and she and Rory might never find their way upstairs again. They could be entombed here, hopelessly lost as they crawled around the damp darkness trying to find a way out and stumbling further and futher into the vaults until even Knut could not find them.

She was sure she heard the knight's armour creaking.

Then the flashlight went on. Rory swung it around and gave an exclamation of satisfaction.

'There's a light switch over there,' he said. 'I'll turn it on.'

Unthinkingly he moved away from Alex's side, taking the flashlight with him. He was gone only a few seconds before the cellars were illuminated with a dim light.

'That's better!' he said, turning to Alex reassuringly. But to his dismay her face was white and terrified and her eyes wider than ever with fear.

'You let go of my hand and left me!' she accused him, almost in tears. She had been truly frightened when Rory had rushed away so suddenly and left her standing in the semi-darkness alone.

'I was only turning on the light, you silly goose,' he said softly. As if it was the most natural thing in the world, he put his arms around her and drew her close to him. 'You can't believe I'd try to scare you on purpose. It was thoughtless of me, Alex. I'm sorry. Forgive me.'

Alex felt her heart turning over at the tender concern in his voice. Her body was trembling violently, no longer from fear but from the awareness of Rory's body so close against her own. As her eyes closed, she knew this was where she wanted to remain. Beyond that she had no other thought at all.

Rory, too, was experiencing a rush of inexplicable emotion. When he had put his arms round Alex he had had no other thought but to comfort and reassure her. But the feel of her soft, warm young body melting against him had roused in him all the dormant desires that Inez had skilfully awakened. If Alex had drawn back from him, he might have had the will to control himself, but she remained pressed against him, small, supple, her face buried in his shoulder.

He bent and kissed the top of her head. Her hair felt soft and silky. As she lifted her face he began to kiss her urgently, her eyes, the tip of her nose and then, at last, her lips.

It was some few moments before he could stop kissing her. He was increasingly excited by the ardent manner in which she responded.

For weeks now, Alex had meant little more to him than a delightful and charming friend, his little sister, he had often thought. Now, as he held her, this image of her ceased to have any credibility. Alex was a woman—a young, attractive, quite adorable and enchanting young woman.

'Oh, Alex, darling!' he said breathlessly, as he finally drew away his mouth, though still holding her tightly. 'I think I ought to apologise or something, but I'm not sorry, not one bit. Are you?'

Alex stared back at him from eyes that seemed to Rory to be shining as brilliantly as two blue stars.

'No, I'm not sorry,' she said, her voice little more than a whisper.

Rory felt himself relax with pleasure at her reply. A wave of happiness engulfed him and his face broke into a grin.

'Then let's do it again!' he said. 'Properly!'

He kissed her a second time, but as his fervour mounted, his mind sent a small belated warning into his consciousness.

Alex was not the kind of girl who would be casual in her relationships with others. She was vulnerable, and understandably so after that terrible accident in which her fiancé had been killed.

Reluctantly, he drew away from her, his face serious.

'I'm not sure if this is such a good idea,' he said with difficulty. 'Trouble is, Alex, you rather knocked me off balance for a moment. I'm sorry if . . .'

'Please, don't be sorry!' Alex broke in. 'I'm not. If you didn't mean it, then we'll just forget it happened. Okay?'

Her voice sounded lost, a little bewildered. Her eyes were averted now from his and Rory felt suddenly miserable, as if he had betrayed her. He said sincerely: 'But I did mean it, Alex. I wanted to kiss you and, to tell you the truth, to go on kissing you. I'm not sorry I did.

118

Alex . . . about you and me . . . all this has taken me a bit unawares, as they say. I simply never thought that we . . . that I'd feel this way. Am I making sense?'

Gently, Alex withdrew her hand. She was very confused. She wanted Rory to find her attractive, to want to kiss her, make love to her. But at the same time she knew quite clearly that Rory was still a long way from falling in love with her. Perhaps it would never happen. She was not even certain that she wanted it to, or if she was in love with him. She knew only that she was glad he had kissed her and that she wanted him to be glad, too.

'I think I understand what you're trying to say,' she said in a quiet level voice that gave Rory no inkling of her inner tension. 'It would be stupid for either of us to take this seriously. After all, what's a kiss or two between friends?'

Rory did not reply at once. Alex's casualness confused him still more. He did not wish her to dismiss those moments as if they had had no significance. Didn't she realise how attractive she was? How intensely he had wanted to go on making love to her?

At the same time, he felt a sense of relief. Since Alex was not taking those passionate kisses seriously, he was in no way committed to a future relationship he might find he had no wish to continue. As Alex said, they could forget all about it. They could remain platonic friends.

His feelings for her underwent another rapid change. He now felt grateful and happy and very, very fond of her.

'You *are* a nice person!' he said softly, regaining her hand and pressing it tightly. 'Nice is such an inadequate word but I can't honestly think of a better one. I really do like you!'

Alex smiled. She, too, felt strangely happy.

'I like you, too,' she said. 'But I think we've wasted quite enough time down here. If we're going to find those trunks, then it's about time we started looking. Poor Knut will be wondering what on earth we're up to!'

'And probably making a good guess at the truth!' Rory laughed. 'Not that I should be joking about it. He's really fond of you, Alex. I think he's in love with you.'

'Well, I'm not in love with Knut nor am I likely to be,' Alex said firmly. 'So you haven't spoiled any budding romance between me and your best friend. He knows how I feel, too, because I told him so.'

Rory felt a little stab of jealousy. 'So, Knut has admitted he's in love with you?'

'That's his secret,' Alex replied loyally. 'Now do let's find those trunks, Rory. I'm getting cold down here.'

They were back to normal, or nearly so. But beneath the casual exchange of words, both were still a little shaken by the turn of events.

Rory, in particular, was finding it difficult not to think about Knut being in love with Alex. Knut was an extremely attractive young man and immensely popular with women. Alex was alone with Knut for a very large part of the day when he, Rory, was in the studio painting. If propinquity counted for anything, she might well succumb to Knut's charms . . . a thought he found vaguely disquieting. At the same time, he felt he ought to be happy at the idea of his best friend winning for himself a girl like Alex. They might be very happy together and Alex deserved a break.

But the discovery of the tin trunks put further thoughts of Alex out of his mind. There were three of them, stacked one upon the other against a stone pillar.

'You'll have to help me, Alex,' Rory said as he tried to move the top one. 'I can't lift it by myself. Think you can manage?'

Together they half lifted, half tipped the topmost trunk on to the floor.

'It's padlocked,' Rory said, examining it more closely. 'And as rusty as an old nail. Give me that sword, Alex. I'll see if I can force the lid.'

Alex hesitated. She felt a renewal of her earlier terror. But Rory was oblivious to her fears and said impatiently: 'Come on, Alex! I can't wait to see what's inside!'

She handed him the sword. But over the centuries rust had eaten so deeply into the

121

metal that when Rory tried to use it to pry open the lid of the trunk, it bent and then snapped.

'We'll have to find a crowbar,' Rory said. 'There must be something of the sort down here. I'll have a look around.'

Alex remained by the trunk, shivering. She was both cold and frightened. The knight in armour seemed to be watching them disapprovingly, as if he were on guard and forbidding them to pry into the locked trunks.

But when Rory returned triumphantly with a long iron bar, he swept aside her objections.

'Even if he were alive, your knight can hardly object since we don't intend to steal anything, silly!' he said. 'Anyway, Inez said there were only a lot of old clothes in the trunks, probably rotten at that.'

There was a sudden screech as the padlock snapped open and Rory lifted the lid. A not unpleasant aromatic odour rose from the interior.

Alex sniffed.

'It smells like incense,' she said doubtfully.

Rory peered into the trunk and removed the top covering of heavy black velvet. The material was musty but there was no sign of mildew or rot. Then he gave a cry of horror. Beneath the velvet was the unmistakable skeleton of a hand. On the middle finger, shining brilliantly as if it had been newly polished, was a twisted silver ring, the black stone in the centre of it engraved with a crest.

He was too late to conceal this macabre relic from Alex, but to his surprise, she was staring down at it with considerable interest.

'*I know what that is* . . . or what it was!' she said with a shaky laugh. 'The Baron gave me a book to read on the history of the abbey and it has a story in it about the first abbot of St. Christophe . . . !'

'Well, go on, tell me more,' Rory prompted as she hesitated.

'The abbot was supposed to have been a saint,' Alex continued, her voice trembling with excitement. 'He committed only one sin in his life and that was when he lied to the Brothers of the Community, but I can't remember what the lie was about. Anyway, to prove his remorse, he struck off his own hand—the hand bearing his signet ring—calling upon God to forgive him as he did so. I remember distinctly the description of the ring—silver, engraved with his crest.'

Rory let out his breath.

'That is some story! And if this is the abbot's ring, it must be fantastically valuable.'

Alex shuddered as he reached towards it.

'Don't touch it!' she said, closing her eyes so that she could no longer see the long, thin bones of the skeletal fingers.

Rory hesitated. He had no wish to touch the skeleton either. But when, after a moment's thought, he used the iron bar to try to lift it, it crumbled instantly. The joints separated and the ring rolled into a corner of the trunk out of sight.

'Let's leave it,' Alex suggested. 'We'll tell Inez when she comes home and she can empty the trunk. The ring must be in there somewhere.'

But Rory would not be stopped from his exploration.

'One of the servants might come down here and, finding the trunk unlocked, steal the ring. We must find it now, Alex.'

He removed the layer of black velvet, revealing a neat row of wax corpse-candles.

'I think they've been handmade,' he said. 'They look like tallow to me. And see how rough the wick is—a kind of twine. They must be hundreds of years old!'

Beneath them was an exquisitely embroidered altar cloth; below that, a priest's lace-edged surplice, the lace handmade; a satin embroidered cape and a scarlet cassock.

Finally Rory drew out two monks' robes of fustian brown, each with a white rope girdle, and a length of huge black rosary beads.

Rory looked up at Alex with an excited grin.

'Knut and I could wear those for our fancy dress!' he said. 'And look, Alex, there's a white robe in here on the bottom of the trunk.'

He drew out, surprisingly, a nun's habit. It was creamy-white, hand-woven and complete with a delicate wimple and coif and a long fine white veil.

'And you can wear this!' Rory was almost shouting in his excitement. 'These clothes are exactly what we've been looking for. They might have been put here especially for us, Alex. I can't wait to show them to Knut. What a magnificent find! Aren't you pleased now that we opened the trunk?'

He noticed Alex's hesitation and frowned.

'You're not going to suggest we don't use them!' he said. 'They'll be perfect. You'll look absolutely stunning in that nun's outfit.'

'I think we ought to ask Inez's permission before we remove them,' Alex said slowly. 'She might object. After all, these are religious garments, Rory. I think we should put them back.'

'Oh, nonsense, darling!' The endearment was quite unconscious but it affected Alex instantly. Her resolve weakened. No matter what Rory asked her to do, she could no longer refuse him. Let Inez cool his enthusiasm if she wished. She, Alex, would not be the one to do so!

'The ring is here!' Rory told her, as he reached down into the corner of the trunk. 'And some kind of paper.'

He handed the ring to Alex and then held up a scroll of parchment tied with a leather thong.

'The last of the mysteries!' he said as he untied the thong and the stiff parchment

125

slowly unrolled itself.

'Well, what does it say?' Alex asked as Rory's enthusiastic impatience communicated itself to her.

'I don't know,' Rory said slowly. 'I think it must be some kind of mediaeval Latin. I can't make out one word of it. What a disappointment!'

He looked so dejected. Alex smiled.

'I think I know someone who could translate it,' she said. 'The old Curé in the village. He's a Latin scholar. I'm sure he'll help us. He has been up to the abbey several times and I know him quite well. We could show it to him.'

Rory stood up and hugged her.

'You're brilliant!' he said, laughing. 'Come on, Alex, let's go and show all these things to Knut. He'll be getting impatient.'

'What about the other trunks?' Alex asked as Rory began to gather up their finds.

Rory shrugged.

'We can come and explore those tomorrow,' he said. 'They'll keep for a rainy day. We've got quite enough for now.'

With a feeling of intense relief, Alex agreed. The moments of fear she had experienced in the cellars had been very real and she could not quite rid herself of them even when she was back in the *petit salon*, sitting by the fire, listening as Rory announced their discoveries to Knut. In the warmth and the soft light of the room, the boys' voices were happy and excited. Tristan was snoring lightly against her legs, the pine logs were spitting and crackling in the fireplace, yet she still felt that strange uneasiness at the thought of the knight standing in the shadows and the skeleton hand disintegrating in the trunk.

Knut, having experienced none of this atmosphere, was as excited as Rory. He whistled appreciatively when he saw the ring and congratulated Rory on finding the perfect solution for their costumes. The two of them continued talking throughout dinner and were still discussing the parchment document when they returned to the *petit salon* for coffee.

'Let's take it down to the Curé tomorrow,' Knut suggested, 'immediately after lunch.'

'Don't you think we should wait till Inez returns? She'll be back at teatime,' Alex reminded them. 'That's not so long to wait.'

But the young men would have none of it.

'I can't think why you feel Inez or the Baron will object to what we're doing,' Rory said. 'After all, the old boy is always on about his family history. All we've done is discover a bit more of it for him. I wonder why no one has opened those trunks before. It seems extraordinary when you think about it.'

'Inez said they had been in the attics for years,' Alex told them. 'I know she thought they contained nothing but a lot of old clothes. She can't possibly have known about the hand.'

Knut grinned.

'I'm not surprised Alex was scared. You must admit, Rory, it's a somewhat grizzly relic. Maybe Inez did know but was too scared to touch it!'

For once Rory did not rise to her defence.

'I'm sure she would never have left the ring there,' he said. 'She's very keen on antique jewellery.'

'Perhaps the keys to the padlocks were lost years ago so no one has bothered about the trunks,' Knut suggested. 'If the locks were as rusty as you say, they can't have been opened in years.'

Alex looked up at the mantelpiece. The china bon-bon box which always stood there now contained the silver ring.

'No one can have suspected it was there,' she said more to herself than to the others. 'It must be very valuable.'

'And the Baron would have kept the parchment with his other records,' Rory agreed. 'I can't wait to find out what it says.'

They were trying to guess the meaning of the writing on the scroll when Alex drove them down to Valory the following morning. The perfect weather of the last few days had disappeared and the skies were heavy again with leaden clouds. Alex had slept badly and the memory of those brief intimate moments with Rory in the cellars only partly held her

128

growing depression at bay. She knew that with Inez's return, Rory would no longer be free to spend the days with Knut and her. He would go back to work and the happy, carefree companionship the three of them had shared would no longer be possible.

Rory and Knut, however, were in the best of spirits as they drove up to the Curé's little stone house. The old man had retired many years ago when his advanced age and ill health had made it impossible for him to continue his religious duties. But his mind was unimpaired. He greeted Alex warmly and was clearly interested when they explained their mission. Having offered them all a glass of wine, he took the parchment from Rory and disappeared with it into another room.

It was a full fifteen minutes before he returned. He surveyed their excited young faces, his own unsmiling, as he said:

'The Latin is of the fifteenth century. I have had some difficulty in the translation. It is a letter from a Seigneur François de Valbanon— a nobleman whose lands adjoined those of the Seigneur Pierre Leyresse. He wrote it after the death of his daughter, Sister St. Cecile, in a fire that partially destroyed the Abbaye St. Christophe. The charred remains of his dughter, a novice of the Convent Sacré Coeur, and those of a lay preacher, Brother St. Vincent, were found in the vaults of the Abbaye and were buried in the crypt.'

'But what was a nun doing at the abbey?' Rory asked. 'Does the letter explain?'

The Curé spread his hands and shrugged.

'The letter says nothing but there is an old legend concerning this matter, *Monsieur*, that I have heard many times. The Baron has an account of it in his family history. The legend relates that Cecile, daughter of the Seigneur de Valbanon, fell in love with a young man who was not of noble birth. He was reputed to be a bastard son of a member of the Leyresse family. The girl refused to marry the man of her father's choice and he consigned her to a convent. The young man she loved was ordered to the monastery, thereby, it was hoped, effectively separating the lovers for all time. But there was a secret passage between the convent and the Abbaye and the girl discovered it. Whenever possible she used this passage to visit her lover and had many secret assignations with him. They might never have been discovered but for the fire in which they perished together.'

'What an incredible story!' Knut exclaimed. 'And sad, too.'

'But we still don't know what is in the document,' Rory reminded the Curé.

'I am arriving at this point,' said the old man. He crossed himself as if in the presence of evil; then picked up the parchment and read slowly from it:

'I hereby lay a curse upon the family of Leyresse and upon all its descendants; and may God have mercy upon the Lord Abbot, François Leyresse and upon the Reverend Mother of the Sacré Coeur, upon whom lies the ultimate responsibility for my daughter's death in sin, for I shall never pardon them.'

The Curé looked at Alex over the gold rim of his spectacles.

'You must understand that as both the young novice and the lay brother had broken their vows of chastity, they could not have been buried in holy ground,' he explained. 'Their souls would not rest in Heaven and this would have been a great torment to the Seigneur de Valbanon. He is said to have idolised his daughter, his only child.'

Alex shuddered.

'Is there more to the Seigneur's curse?' she asked.

The Curé nodded.

'He damns their souls and those of their descendants to be consigned to the flames of Hell for all Eternity and he adds:

'May the sins of the fathers be visited upon their sons now and forever more, Amen.'

The Curé laid down the parchment and crossed himself a second time.

'As a man of God it does not behove me to

131

believe in superstition,' he said. 'Nevertheless, this document is curious in that it could be said that the curse redounded on its author. God cannot be mocked with impunity. No doubt it is purely coincidental,' he added quickly, 'but the de Valbanon family were wiped out in their entirety by the plague. The deadly disease was carried from England by one of the sons who was a page at the English court. It spread through the Château with such rapidity and effectiveness that not even a servant remained alive.'

Rory gave a soft whistle.

'And the Leyresses?' he asked. 'Has the curse touched them?'

The Curé shrugged.

'The family has had its misfortunes through the years. As you may know, the father of the present Baron was rendered penniless and lost all his estates. However, they have been partially recovered now and, but for the fact that the Baron Bernard Leyresse has no male heir, the family fortunes have been successfully restored. I pray they may continue to prosper.'

'Let's hope neither Inez nor the Baron is superstitious,' Knut said after they had thanked the Curé and were driving slowly back to the abbey. 'Otherwise they aren't going to thank you, Rory, for unearthing that particular relic from bygone days.'

'It sounds positively horrible,' Alex said. 'I wish we'd never found it.'

Rory laughed.

'You don't seriously believe any of that mumbo-jumbo, do you? As the Curé pointed out, the de Valbanon family were unlucky but the plague killed thousands of other families who hadn't been cursed. As to the Leyresses— they seem to be doing very nicely indeed. So stop worrying, Alex.'

Alex felt the tension ease from her body. Rory was perfectly right. It was silly to be frightened by something that could have no possible substantiation in fact. Ignorant people living centuries ago believed in witchcraft and curses and if she allowed herself to do so, she would be as ignorant as they!

'That's better,' Rory said softly, watching her. 'You look much prettier when you smile. Don't you agree, Knut?'

'I think she is pretty all the time, happy or sad,' said the young Norwegian, whereupon Rory gave him a friendly push sideways and Alex had to tell them both to behave like adults lest she drive the car over the side of the road.

'Which,' said Rory laughing, 'would mean that the curse of the Grand Seigneur de Valbanon would have pointed its ghostly finger at us, too?'

'Don't tempt Fate!' Knut chided him. 'Or you'll frighten Alex again.'

But her fear subsided completely as Rory reached out and gently squeezed her hand.

CHAPTER SEVEN

Inez took exactly ten minutes to reach the conclusion that going to Paris had been a very big mistake. She had hoped, by her absence, to force Rory into the realisation that the abbey was a dull and lifeless place without her. Erroneously she had imagined that Rory, eager to get on with his painting, would have counted the hours until her return. She had missed him and the welcome she anticipated he would give her was to have compensated her for the days she had lived without sight of him.

She had rushed round Paris like any other woman in love, looking for new clothes that would appeal to her beloved; she had had her hair restyled so that Rory would notice her anew; selected the most seductive gown she could find to wear at her fancy dress ball, so that he could not fail to succumb to her beauty. He had never been far from her thoughts.

Now, as she stood proudly but nervously fingering a white onyx table lighter, Rory appeared totally indifferent to her. He was vying with Knut to be the first to tell her of their adventures and discoveries. She barely heard their words. Her one thought was that she had been wrong to leave Rory. He had renewed contact with his friend. He had become young and carefree again. She had only to look at his tousled hair, his rough jeans and torn shirt to see that for the moment, anyway, she had lost the man she wanted. Rory had reverted to boyhood. If he even noticed what she was wearing, which she doubted, he was far too excited about his 'discovery' to pay her one of his usual compliments. The perfectly tailored, madly expensive tangerine-coloured pants suit she had chosen might never have been bought for all the attention Rory gave her attire. Edged at collar and cuffs with black ermine, the suit made her look younger and showed off her figure to perfection. But it was three thousand francs wasted.

She felt her patience evaporating.

'When you all talk at once, I cannot understand one word you are saying,' she broke into their chattering with cold authority.

It seemed they had been 'exploring' and the 'treasure hunt' had revealed a ring and a skeleton hand and an ancient parchment document which was causing their excitement. It sounded improbable and juvenile.

'What is this all about?' she asked. She took the ring Rory held out to her and frowned. 'Who does it belong to? Where did you find it?'

'That's what we've been trying to tell you,' Rory said. Inez's mood was far from encouraging and he felt the first warning of trouble to come. In a quieter tone he told her of his visit to the cellars with Alex and how they had found the ring when they opened the trunk. 'We thought you'd be pleased to have it, Inez,' he added finally. 'It looks very old and valuable.'

To his surprise, Inez crossed herself. She looked as white and scared as Alex had done.

'You should not have touched the hand!' she said. 'It could bring bad luck. You and Alex had no right to remove anything from the trunk without asking me.'

'Alex didn't want me to. It was not her fault!' Rory said quickly. 'I did so against her wishes.'

He turned to Alex and put an arm round her shoulders as if to protect her from Inez's anger.

Instantly Inez's senses were alerted. She felt physically sick with jealousy. Something had gone on between these two in her absence . . . she would find out in due course. Whatever it was she would not permit it to continue.

Her eyes lingered on the young girl in a moment of pure hatred. Alex's hair was straggling untidily across her face, her shirt was hanging out over her jeans. She looked a 'gamine' but a very attractive one at that.

'Oh, no, *ma petite*!' Inez thought. 'You will not have Rory as long as *I* want him. Do not think that a little nobody like you can take him from me!'

'We found this, too,' Rory said, handing her the parchment.

Inez now had her feelings under control. Feigning an interest she did not have, she said:

'I can't read Latin, Rory. You had better tell me what this is all about.'

Obediently, Rory translated the document and handed it to Inez. Mistakenly, he took her silence for approval.

'We think the Baron will be especially interested,' he told her enthusiastically. 'It is hundreds of years old and the Curé says it is quite authentic.'

Inez flushed an ugly red. Her eyes, inscrutable, looked blacker than ever. To the dismay of the three young people staring at her, she was trembling with anger.

'You had no right at all to touch this—this idiotic thing!' she said in a low, fierce voice. She threw it on the sofa. 'No one gave you permission to remove it from the trunk, far less take it to the Curé for translation. In future, kindly leave alone the things that do not belong to you.'

It was Rory who faced up to her anger.

'I am entirely to blame,' he said. 'Alex and I were looking for costumes. You had said we could search the trunks. When we came on these things, I truly believed you'd be interested, Inez. I'm sorry if we've displeased you but I don't understand why. Surely such a document as this is of interest to your family? I mean, it is part of the Baron's family history!'

While he spoke, Inez managed once more to regain her self-control. She was, in fact, not so much angry as frightened. Somewhere deep within her lay the unalterable belief in superstitions of her own forebears. She reacted to the terrible words of the curse with a fear that was instinctive rather than logical. Such warnings, she felt in her bones, should not be ignored. But Rory's sincere young voice, expressing surprise in her disinterest in Bernard's ancestors, restored her reason and common sense prevailed. She must disregard such a ridiculous idea that a curse could possibly reach across those hundreds of years to touch her, Inez Leyresse, Baroness, in the year 1985. It was absurd.

'I daresay Bernard will be interested,' she said with an effort at normality. 'But I am not. Such stupid beliefs belong in the nursery, which, I may add, is where all three of you look as if you still belong. Should you not be changed for dinner? It is already seven o'clock.'

Rory, Alex and Knut looked at each other sheepishly. Inez had successfully reduced their status to that of errant schoolchildren and dampened their enthusiasm for their discovery. They were also aware that without the Baroness there to correct them, they had let the high standards of the Abbaye St.

Christophe slip alarmingly. Each saw the other as hopelessly untidy and dishevelled.

Alex jumped to her feet with a murmured apology. As always, Tristan rose beside her and made as if to follow her out of the room. Inez called him back sharply.

'You, at least, might give your mistress a welcome,' she said pointedly.

'Inez, that's not fair. We all welcome you back,' Rory said, and added quickly, 'and looking, as always, fantastic. Is that a new get-up, Inez? It suits you. That tangerine colour with your red hair . . . I'd never have thought of combining them but the effect really is stunning!'

He spoke with genuine admiration and Inez softened. As Rory helped Knut out of the room, she looked down into the fire through half-closed eyes. Perhaps, after all, she had jumped to the wrong conclusions about Rory, she thought. However belated, his compliment had been genuine. As for Alex, he was probably just trying to be nice to her as she, herself, had instructed him.

She turned to look at the dog. Tristan was lying just inside the closed door. He was whining softly but irritatingly, asking to be let out. Inez's mouth curled.

'You will not go to her. You will remain here with me! she said. 'Come here at once when I tell you. *Come here!'*

The dog turned his head to look at her but

did not move. Her mood changing again, Inez's face whitened with fury. She went across the room and jerked at the silver chain collar round Tristan's throat. He gave a low growl and remained where he was.

'You will do what I tell you!' Inez said, her voice close to a scream. She jerked once more at his collar with such viciousness that Tristan whined and rose to his feet, his ears flat against his head, his hackles rising stiffly.

Inez tried to drag him across the room but the dog was too strong and resisted.

'We'll see which mistress you are going to obey in future!' Inez shouted, no longer caring who heard her. She gave him a violent kick. Tristan yelped, pulled away from her trembling grasp and hunched himself up against the door.

Inez went back to the fireplace. Leaning against the mantel-piece, she lit a cigarette and watched the dog as he returned to his soft whining. Her mouth curled and her eyes narrowed. This was all Alex's doing. It was time Alex, as well as Tristan, was taught a lesson. She, Inez Leyresse, was not going to be put in second place, not by a chit of a girl, nor by a dog. Both would discover that to their cost.

She put her hand on the bell rope and pulled it impatiently. Gilbert came shuffling in apologetically, carrying the usual tray of drinks.

'They should have been put out long ago!' Inez reprimanded him coldly. 'Pour me a whiskey and soda. Then go and get the dog bowls. They can be fed in here this evening.'

When the manservant entered the room Tristan had escaped through the open door. Inez could hear him now padding swiftly up the stairs. She smiled as she took the big cut - glass tumbler from the old butler. Tristan's defection did not matter for the moment. He and Alex would in due course pay the price. And neither of them, she told herself with satisfaction, would have to wait long.

*   *   *

As Rory helped Knut change for dinner, he was unusually quiet. Inez's homecoming was a disappointing anti-climax. He had fully expected her to feel the same excited interest in the ring and the document as had the three of them.

'Don't let Inez get you down,' Knut said wisely when he discovered why Rory was so subdued. 'I, personally, think she reacted that way because we stole her thunder. She probably intended to make a grand entrance— and one has to admit she did look stunning— but instead of noticing her, we all wanted her to notice us!'

Rory shrugged.

'I suppose we were a bit rude. The fact is,

we're both so used to living here now we take Inez's hospitality for granted. I'm not surprised she was put out.'

'Then you'd better be especially attentive this evening,' Knut said grinning. 'But not too attentive or you'll give her ideas.'

'Oh, for heaven's sake, Knut!' Rory snapped. 'Don't start that nonsense again.'

Knut fastened his tie, then shrugged his shoulders.

'You only object to my teasing you about Inez because you know there is some truth in what I say. I think our Baroness is crazy about you. I think she'll stop at nothing to get you. I think if she were to guess that you and Alex were becoming attached to each other, she'd pack Alex off without hesitation. So watch it, for Alex's sake if not for your own.'

Rory fidgeted with the objects on Knut's dressing table. He felt uneasy, although far from convinced his friend's warning was justified.

'You make Inez sound horrible!' he parried. 'I'm sure you're not right about her. As for Alex, it was Inez's idea, not mine, that I should try to cheer her up, to be nice to her.'

'And is that why you,do it? Not because you want to?'

Rory sighed.

'No, of course not. You know how I feel about Alex.'

'No, I don't!' Knut replied in the same

serious tone. 'I do know that Alex is on the point of falling in love with you. She hasn't said so but I can see it. What I don't know is how you feel about her. I don't want her hurt.'

'And what makes you think I'd hurt her?' Rory countered angrily. It was the nearest they had ever come to a real quarrel. 'I suppose you think because you're in love with her, it gives you the right to dictate to me.'

'Come off it, Rory. I'm not dictating. I'm only trying to find out if . . . well, if you really care about Alex.'

'Of course I care about her. But if you mean, am I in love with her, I don't know.'

'Well, you would know if you were.' Knut then said more gently, 'I expect you are right—you've not known her all that long, have you? I've spent a great deal more time with her than you and I think I do know and understand her. We talk a lot while you're closeted in your studio with Inez.'

'Whatever you may think, I'm not making love to Inez when she's alone with me. I happen to be sweating my guts out, trying to paint her,' Rory said sarcastically.

'Or wasting your time wondering what it would be like to make love to her?'

'That's a damn silly remark!' Rory said furiously.

But even as he spoke he knew that Knut was not so far from the truth. He had wondered what it would be like to hold Inez's incredible body in his arms. He had wondered if after all he was not just a little in love with her. She was beautiful, desirable, a temptation to any man. He could not be expected to stare at her hour after hour and not be affected. But Knut should know him better than to believe that he would ever permit himself to become involved with Inez, if for no other reason than that she was someone else's wife. Moreover, Rory respected the old Baron and had no intention of abusing his hospitality.

Besides, Rory thought, there was Alex. He had seriously asked himself if he was not, like Knut, a little in love with her. She might not be as exotic, as exciting as Inez, but she was great fun. Her nature was sweet, unselfish, generous, kind. He liked everything about her.

In other circumstances he might well have fallen head over heels in love with Alex. But while Inez's image haunted his dreams . . .

'There's the dinner gong!' Knut said. 'We'll be late.'

To Rory's relief, Inez seemed in a very good humour during the meal. She wore yet another new dress—this time a simple floor-length white wool caftan, heavily embroidered with coloured braid. Her hair was caught back at the nape of her neck in a shining coil and she looked like an Eastern princess, dark eyes sparkling, her crimson mouth the only colour in her white face. She looked strange—and very lovely.

Rory could not take his eyes from her. He longed to rush upstairs to the studio to look at his portrait, fearing that his painting of her was not really like her at all. She was different, in a tantalising and mysterious way. Perhaps, he thought, he would have to begin his painting all over again. He had not even been to look at it these last few days. Now his obsession to continue with it was back in full force.

Alex was very quiet. She was miserably aware that Rory's eyes never left Inez. She herself no longer existed for him. Since that moment in the cellar yesterday evening, Rory had stayed close beside her, sometimes holding her hand, smiling at her often and clearly showing his happiness at being with her. He had always been friendly but she was sure their friendship had changed subtly and taken on a new dimension. He was at last aware of her. She had slept peacefully, without dreaming, and woken with a feeling of intense joy. She had even been able to think of David without pain, knowing he would have been pleased to see her happy again.

Now everything had changed once more with Inez's return. Rory was once again impervious to her existence. He seldom took his eyes away from Inez and the moment dinner was over, he sat himself beside her in the *salon* and was lost in conversation with her.

Alex was not alone in noticing Rory's attentiveness to his hostess. The Baron, also,

145

was aware of it. During their stay in Paris, Inez had been fractious and irritable, impatient unless her commands were instantly obeyed. He had attributed this high state of nervous tension to excitement over her prospective party. His erstwhile suspicions with regard to his wife's interest in the young Englishman had been fully allayed when she, herself, suggested they go back to Paris. But now, watching Inez surreptitiously, he noted her heightened colour, her animation, her softened expression as she looked at her young admirer, and his senses quickened with reawakened jealousy.

He gave no indication of his fears. Politely, as always, he replied to Knut's questions, discussed with him the parchment document and recounted some items of the family history of the era when the letter was thought to have been written. But all the time, one ear was tuned to his wife's low, sensuous murmur in the background; to Rory's young excited voice in reply.

The Baron's thin, gnarled hands with their light scattering of brown freckles, began to tremble. The brandy glass he was holding shook slightly, disturbing the amber liquid.

Suddenly, without warning, he dropped it.

The sound of breaking glass stopped all conversation. Alex rose at once to her feet and began to collect the fragments.

Inez said sharply:

'What are you thinking of, Alex? That is the

servants' job. Ring the bell for Gilbert. Rory, pour Bernard another brandy, will you?'

If anything, she seemed amused by the incident.

'You must be tired, Bernard,' she said sweetly. 'It is unlike you to be so clumsy. The long journey was obviously too much for you. Would you not like to retire?'

Subtly, cruelly, she pushed him into the category of the elderly, near-senile, the incapable. It was an unwise self-indulgence. The Baron's mouth tightened imperceptibly.

'I am feeling remarkably wide awake,' he said dryly. 'I could not possibly sleep if I went to bed so early.'

'Oh? Well, just as you like, dear.' Inez nodded and turned back to Rory. 'Do continue, Rory. If Van Gogh was really insane, how did he come to paint the way he did? His earlier pictures show no sign of madness, do they?'

The Baron remained seated. Gilbert came in and cleared up the broken glass. Alex returned to her tapestry stool by the fire. Tristan lay with his head on her lap, whining occasionally in a way that made Alex uneasy. He had been strangely restless all evening.

'I think there is something wrong with Tristan,' she said eventually. 'He has got up and walked around three times now, as if he has a pain. I'm sure something is wrong with him.'

147

'You fed him yourself before dinner, remember?' Inez commented, without moving from her place beside Rory on the big sofa. 'Gilbert brought the dogs' bowls in here; Tristan refused to take his food from me so you gave it to him. I hope there were no rabbit bones in the meat? Perhaps you overlooked one and it is stuck in his intestines?'

A small white string of saliva formed and dropped from the Great Dane's mouth. It was followed by another.

'He is ill!' Alex said in a small, frightened voice. She knelt on the floor and cradled the dog's head in her lap, impervious to the froth now coming from his mouth. 'Poor Tristan. What's wrong with you? Have you got a pain?'

The dog's tail thumped weakly on the floor as she spoke but then he whined again and Alex said to Inez:

'Don't you think we should telephone the vet? I'm sure something is very wrong. May I telephone, please, Inez?'

Inez sighed.

'You do make such a fuss of that dog, Alex! He has probably eaten his meal too fast and is suffering from indigestion. Leave him alone. He is all right.'

'But he isn't. I know he's not!'

Alex looked appealingly at the Baron, hoping he would countermand Inez's opinion. But the old man was too involved in his own gnawing suspicions to bother about the dog,

148

and in any case, he had never had the slightest interest in either of the animals.

For half an hour, Alex sat helplessly nursing Tristan who was now so obviously in pain that Rory intervened.

'I think Alex is right. Tristan really is ill,' he said. 'Maybe it would be best to call the vet.'

He stood up and went across to the dog. Alex stared up at Rory from huge, scared eyes. Instinctively, he put a hand on her head and said softly:

'Don't worry, Alex. He'll be all right.'

Inez heard the tender, protective note in his voice and her mouth tightened.

'It's nearly eleven o'clock,' she said tersely. 'We can't ask the vet to come up from Valory at this time of night. We'll see how Tristan is in the morning.'

Knut spoke up for the first time. He was in no doubt that Alex was justified in her fears.

'Tristan is obviously very ill. Doctors expect to be called out at all hours, why not vets, *Madame*?'

'I agree with Knut,' Rory said. 'Why don't we telephone anyway and see what the vet says. If he refuses to come, then that's that. But if he is willing . . .'

Inez's mouth tightened still more. She was not used to having her orders questioned. But she shrugged her shoulders, not wishing to appear callous or indifferent in front of Rory. She knew the reputation of the English. They

149

were animal mad. If Rory knew . . .

'Ring the vet by all means if you really think it is necessary,' she said. 'I, myself, am sure it is nothing serious.'

'I hope you're right,' Rory said quietly. He was now as concerned as Alex about Tristan's condition but, for her sake, he tried not to show his apprehension.

Alex went to telephone the vet, returning with a look of relief on her face.

'He's coming at once,' she said, kneeling down again to stroke Tristan's head.

'I shall not wait up,' announced the Baron, rising stiffly to his feet. 'Are you coming to bed, my dear?'

'But of course not, Bernard!' Inez's voice sounded reproving. 'How could I possibly sleep if my poor Tristan is really ill?'

Rory's heart warmed towards her. He had begun to think her behaviour callous with regard to her dog. Now he believed she was as concerned as Alex but, like himself, trying not to show it too obviously.

Monsieur Govin, the vet, arrived half an hour later. Tristan was by then so obviously in great pain that no one was surprised by the prognosis.

'He has eaten poison of some kind,' the tubby little Frenchman announced when he had completed his examination. 'I cannot administer an antidote unless I know which poison. He is a very sick dog.'

150

Alex looked so stricken that once again Rory forgot Inez and reached for Alex's hand.

'He's not going to die, is he?' he asked the vet tentatively.

Monsieur Govin gave a typically Gallic shrug of his shoulders.

'It is possible. It depends which poison and how much the dog has had.'

Alex drew in her breath sharply.

'There must be something you can do for him?' she pleaded.

Monsieur Govin patted her hand paternally.

'I will give him a mixture of castor oil and linseed oil. This will line the walls of the stomach and help to clear out the poison. If he seems to become worse, you can give him a little brandy as a stimulant. Someone will have to remain with him during the night in case . . .'

'I'll sit with him, I want to!' Alex cried. She dropped to her knees and bent her head over Tristan's. 'You're going to be all right! I won't leave you!'

'Pull yourself together, Alex. You're becoming hysterical!' Inez spoke coldly from across the room. 'By all means stay up with the dog if you wish but do try to be a little more calm. We are all concerned about him, but it won't help the dog to be so emotional!'

When the vet had done what little he could for Tristan and left, Inez announced that she was going to bed.

'Since Alex will obviously not sleep if she

151

does go to bed, there is little point in my offering to sit up with Tristan,' she said to Rory. 'I only wish I could understand what has happened. You fed him, as always, Alex. How could he possibly have eaten any poison?' She gave a helpless little sigh. Then, as if the idea had just now occurred to her, she added, 'Where has he been today? Before I arrived home? Have you let him wander off on his own? You know I do not permit the dogs to leave the grounds of the abbey.'

Rory heard the faint note of criticism in Inez's voice and spoke quickly in Alex's defence.

'Apart from our visit to the Curé, when we did not take the dogs, none of us has been out and you know Tristan never leaves Alex's side,' he said.

'Exactly!' Inez replied. 'That's why Alex is the only person who can clear up this mystery. Only she could know where Tristan picked up the poison. Try to remember while you are sitting up with him tonight, Alex. Then we can avoid repetition. The gardeners do sometimes put down arsenic to kill rats. One must suppose Tristan found some when Alex was otherwise occupied!'

Alex looked up, her cheeks flushed, but Inez left the room before she could speak.

Knut spoke up, his voice holding no hint of its usual light-hearted humour. It was hard and cold.

'That woman is trying to put the blame on you, Alex,' he said. 'It was both a cruel and a dishonest thing to do. She knows you adore Tristan and wouldn't knowingly let him come to any harm. Even if he had picked up poison in the garden, it wouldn't have been your fault. You can't watch him every minute of the day.'

The tears dripped slowly off the end of Alex's nose and plopped one by one onto Tristan's head.

'I was responsible for him,' she said helplessly. 'But I can't think where he could have picked up any poison. He's been with me all the time. He was never out of sight even when I took him round the garden for a walk.'

'Well, it's certainly not your fault, Alex,' Rory said. 'And you're to stop thinking it might be. Knut is right. Inez ought not to have inferred you could have prevented it. I can't think what made her do such a thing.'

'I can,' Knut said quietly.

'Oh, dry up!' Rory looked very angry. The sight of Alex in tears was distressing him. 'You'll be saying Inez poisoned the dog herself in a minute!'

'Maybe that's not such a wild idea,' Knut replied, equally angry. 'She'd be capable of it. She'd do it just to spite Alex.'

'Now you're both being silly,' Alex said, sniffing. 'Inez loves Tristan. Whatever happened was an accident. Inez would no

153

more allow harm to come to him than I would.'

Rory's heart warmed towards her. She had no cause to defend the woman who had been anything but generous to her over this tragedy.

'Look, Alex, I'll sit up with you,' he said. 'I'd like to. I'm not leaving you here alone all night.'

'No, I'll stay with Alex,' Knut argued. 'You won't be at all popular if you do, Rory.'

Rory shot him a look of hatred.

'If you make one more of those insidious suggestions, I'll push the words down your throat, Knut, broken leg or no broken leg!' he said warningly.

'Don't quarrel; please don't,' Alex said. 'I don't need either of you here. I'd really prefer to be alone with Tristan. Go to bed, both of you. If he gets worse, I'll wake one of you.'

Rory frowned.

'Why don't you want me to stay?' he asked. 'I really meant it when I said I'd like to. You can't stay here alone.'

'I'll be perfectly all right. You'll be working tomorrow and you'll need a good night's sleep,' Alex said sensibly. 'You can't paint well if you're tired.'

It was true that Rory needed sleep if he was to paint; true, also, that he intended to get back to work as soon as Inez was willing to sit for him. She had promised she would make herself available the first thing in the morning, though he could not think how Alex had guessed this.

'Why not me, then?' Knut asked.

'Because I'll feel even more guilty about the whole incident if you had to stay up all night as well as poor Tristan and me!'

The two young men were finally persuaded reluctantly to leave her. Before doing so, Rory put more logs on the fire and brought a rug for Alex to put round her shoulders if she became cold. He also brought in Tristan's big tartan dog blanket and a bowl of water and towels so that Alex could wipe the saliva still dribbling from his slackened jaws.

He went up to bed, assisting Knut who was as silent as he, and then undressed and climbed into bed. But he could not sleep. The thought of Alex sitting alone with the dog she loved, who might be dying as she watched over him, precluded sleep. Two hours later he put on a dressing gown and slippers and went back downstairs.

As he opened the door he saw Alex silhouetted against the glowing red embers of the dying fire. The dog's head was on her lap, his eyes shut and Rory felt a stab of fear that Tristan was indeed dead. But as he tiptoed into the room, Alex looked up and smiled.

'I think he's sleeping,' she said. 'The pain seems to have gone.'

Her face was so radiant, her eyes so brilliant with relief and happiness, Rory could do nothing but stare. He knew then that one day he would paint Alex just as she was now, the red fire behind her, the thick white bearskin rug beneath her, her soft fair hair in tendrils around her. And the golden dog, peaceful, trusting, his great noble head lying across the flower-patterned skirt of Alex's dress, the firelight casting flickering shadows over both of them.

'I'm so glad!' he said, the sound of his voice breaking his trance. He went over to her and added happily, 'He's breathing much more easily. I really am glad, Alex.'

He knelt down beside her and as if it was the most natural thing in the world to do, pulled her head gently against his shoulder.

'You must be tired,' he said softly. 'In a minute, I'll go and make you a cup of coffee.'

Alex's head settled more comfortably into the niche of his shoulder. She felt his cheek against the top of her head and said:

'Thank you for coming down, Rory. I know it's selfish of me, but I am pleased to see you!'

'Silly girl! Of course it's not selfish!' he said. 'I couldn't sleep anyway.'

They sat in silence for a few moments. Then Alex asked:

'What time is it? I thought I heard it strike one just now but perhaps it was a quarter past some other hour.'

'I should think it's about half past one now,' Rory told her. 'It doesn't really matter much, does it?'

'No!' She smiled and said dreamily, 'I think if I don't have that coffee, I might fall asleep, I'm so comfortable.'

'Then why don't you,' Rory said, liking the idea. 'I'm very comfortable too.'

Alex closed her eyes, permitting herself the luxury of relief and contentment. She let it last a little longer, then sat up, stretching her arms above her head, and said:

'We can't fall asleep here, Rory. I think Knut was right—Inez wouldn't like it if she found us both down here with Tristan.' She sighed. 'I know she thinks I'm stupidly sentimental about Tristan. I suppose I am. Sometimes I wonder how I'm going to bring myself to leave him when I go home. It's silly to love a dog so much and I know it isn't really fair to let him become so fond of me but . . .'

'When *will* you go home?' Rory asked curiously. 'Somehow I cannot imagine you anywhere else but here. What will you do when you go back to England?'

'Return to work, I suppose,' Alex told him. 'I've not thought about it. Until recently I've tried not to think about a future of any kind. I was too unhappy knowing David wouldn't be there to share it. But I'm all right now. I can talk about David, remember him, without pain.'

'I'm glad,' Rory said truthfully. 'You were such a sad little thing when I first saw you. You

157

were not made for sadness, Alex. You are at your most beautiful when you smile, you know. You should always be happy.'

Alex felt her heartbeat quicken. 'Nobody is happy all the time,' she said. 'Maybe because moments like this are so rare they are all the more perfect when they do occur.'

Rory raised his eyebrows.

'That was a cynical remark from one so young! But true, I suppose. All the more reason not to break up this happy moment. Come back here and let's make it last a little longer!'

He patted his shoulder, holding out his arms. But as Alex moved towards him, Tristan stirred, opened his eyes and whined softly.

'He wants to go out, I expect,' Rory said practically. 'We'll have to help him up, Alex. He's pretty weak!'

Together they struggled to get Tristan upright. His legs trembled and but for their strong arms, he would have fallen over. Slowly they guided him outside onto the snow-covered ground. Then they waited for him, shivering in their thin clothes in the freezing night air.

A brilliant moon hung over the top of the mountain, turning the white snow to silver. The sky was a velvet black, glittering with stars.

'It's like fairyland!' Rory said through chattering teeth. 'I never realised how beautiful moonlight is at this altitude.'

'It will be a lovely day tomorrow,' Alex forecast. 'It always is when you can see so many stars the night before.'

They helped the dog indoors and he staggered back to the fire, sinking gratefully down on his blanket. Alex brought him some warm milk while Rory made coffee. By the time they had finished drinking it, Tristan was asleep.

Rory said:

'I honestly don't think either of us need sit up with him any longer, Alex. If he had been going to get worse it would have happened long before now. That's what the vet said and it makes sense.'

Finding Alex in agreement, Rory tucked his arm through hers and switched off the light.

'Then off to bed. You look exhausted,' he said as he led her up the stairs. 'Promise me you'll go straight to sleep?'

She nodded, smiling. He bent his head and kissed her.

High above them on the landing, hidden by shadow, Inez Leyresse stood watching them. Her face was ugly in a way Rory had never seen it—ugly with frustration, anger and hatred.

Her plan to make Alex and the dog suffer for offending her had redounded on her. Alex was happy and she, Inez Leyresse, had been thwarted yet again. She had known exactly how much poison to put in Tristan's food—

enough to make him ill but not to kill him. Alex's subsequent distress and that of the dog had satisfied her vindictive nature. She felt quite justified in hurting them. But she had not taken into account Rory's reactions. His sympathies had been aroused and were directed entirely toward the girl. She felt sick with jealousy.

The sight of Rory kissing Alex good night was like a poison in her own veins.

CHAPTER EIGHT

Rory did not see Alex the following morning. He slept late and by the time he went down to breakfast, she had already left for the village with the Baron. The Baron intended to spend a few hours with the old Curé discussing the document Rory and Alex had found in the trunk. Alex had a long list of orders to carry out for Inez.

Her first task was to arrange for six extra maids and two waiters to cope with the vast number of guests expected to stay at the abbey for the ball. There were flowers, too, and food, fruit and drink to be ordered. Alex had also to visit the director of the hotel where Inez intended to house the overflow of guests, and then hire cars to transport them to and from the abbey.

Normally Alex would have enjoyed these jobs, but she knew that Monsieur Govin, the vet, was calling at the abbey to see Tristan during the morning and naturally she wished to be there when he came. Tristan was recovering but he was very weak and his back legs trembled violently whenever he tried to stand up. Inez, however, had made it quite clear to Alex that she, herself, would see Monsieur Govin and attend to Tristan's needs.

During the drive down to the village the Baron was unusually talkative. Normally a silent, reserved man, he seemed intent upon discovering the exact state of Alex's relationship with the two boys.

'You find them amusing?' he asked, as he sat beside her, his green eyes unobtrusively studying Alex's every expression.

Alex smiled.

'They are great fun to be with, *Monsieur,*' she told him. She had never reached the same state of informality with the Baron as she had with Inez, nor had he invited it.

'I am sure you enjoy the companionship of young men your own age,' he pursued the matter. 'And which of the two boys do you like the most, Alexandra?'

The question sounded teasing and Alex had no reason to guess the ulterior motive behind it.

'Rory, I suppose,' she replied shyly but truthfully. 'Although I like Knut very much, too.'

'Ah!' The Baron sounded pleased. 'And which of the two young men is most interested in you, my dear?'

Surprised but not really embarrassed by these personal questions, Alex said:

'I suppose Knut is, although one cannot take him too seriously. He is always joking. He pretends he is in love with me but he is probably just teasing as usual.'

The Baron's eyes narrowed.

'But you wish he were serious?' he asked carefully.

Alex's reply was quite unguarded.

'Oh, no! I don't want Knut to fall in love with me. I could never feel that way about him. I wish it were . . .' she broke off, realising where her impulsiveness was leading her.

The Baron finished the remark for her.

'You wish it were Rory who was falling in love with you, eh? Do not deny it, *ma petite*! I can see that it is the truth. And what is wrong with this wish? Rory is an eligible young man, handsome, attractive, and very charming. I approve of your good taste!'

Alex bit her lip.

'I don't think Rory notices me. He is too preoccupied with his painting. Besides, I am not at all sure I want to fall in love again.'

The Baron looked away, his eyes suddenly sad.

'Alas, it is not always possible to prevent

oneself from loving,' he said. 'The heart can so often betray our wishes. When love strikes, it takes no account of reason.'

Alex was silent. The tone of the Baron's voice was so wistful that she forgot herself in an intuitive sympathy for him. It could not be easy for him married to a woman like Inez, younger than himself, spoilt, beautiful, and— as far as she could judge—no longer in love with her husband, if she had ever been.

'For the moment Rory is enrapt in his painting,' the Baron interrupted her thoughts. 'Soon the portrait will be finished and he will leave the abbey. You, too, will probably very soon decide to return to England. Then you will meet again and things will be different.'

His words were surprisingly comforting. Rory was fond of her—of that she had no doubt. Away from Inez . . .

'All men fall in love with my wife to a greater or lesser degree,' the Baron spoke again as if he had divined Alex's thoughts. 'But they very soon recover their senses once they know they can never take her from me. I understand their admiration. My wife is the most beautiful woman in the world.'

Alex remained silent. Surely, she told herself, the Baron could not be so certain of Inez that he never felt a single pang of jealousy! Old as he was and far from attractive, it would seem unnatural if he did not from time to time question his power to keep Inez's affections from straying elsewhere. If she, herself, resented the way Inez monopolised Rory, the Baron must resent it a hundred times more.

Alex could not know that Bernard Leyresse's apparent unconcern concealed a jealousy far in excess of any emotion she could feel. He guessed that Inez, herself, had poisoned her dog. He alone knew how vindictive was her nature; knew from past experience that she would go to any lengths to hurt another human being if she believed they had hurt, insulted, or neglected her.

He had no doubt that his wife had decided—coldly and cruelly—to injure her own pet in order to revenge herself upon someone. But upon whom? It was possible that she had turned against Tristan because the dog clearly preferred Alex's company to that of his mistress. But equally possible was Inez's intention to hurt Alex—her only rival for Rory's attentions.

Watching and listening last night as was his custom, the Baron had been aware of the carefree friendly companionship that had grown up between the three young people during his visit to Paris with Inez; he, too, had noticed the new attentiveness to Alex in Rory's behaviour. He had seen that Inez had noticed it and been irrationally displeased.

When Alex dropped the Baron at the door of the Curé's house, he was still in a state of uncertainty as to Inez's motives in harming Tristan. Of one thing only was he in no doubt whatever—that if his wife were intending to take her flirtation with Rory Howes to its ultimate conclusion, he would kill him with as little compunction as Inez had poisoned her dog. The feelings of the young girl, Alex, were of no consequence. There would be other young men to console her. The Norwegian was there at hand to do so. But for Rory there would be no mercy. There would be an 'accident'—fatal, of course—in which Inez's lover would be removed once and for all from temptation.

Throughout his married life, the Baron had learned to endure his wife's cool indifference towards him; her occasional cruel jibes about his age and infirmity; her restlessness. That her nature was anything but admirable made no difference to his obsessive and possessive love for her. He tolerated her flirtations and with one exception, Inez had sensibly kept these affairs within the prescribed limits. Only one man had made a cuckold of him, and he had all but strangled that man. He would have done so but for the intervention of a servant. His own possible death and disgrace had meant nothing to him in the heat of that moment of intolerable jealousy and anger. He had cared for nothing but the removal from life of the man who had dared to make the Baroness Leyresse his mistress.

The incident had been a timely warning to Inez. To his knowledge there had been no repetition of such an affair and the marriage had continued on the unspoken understanding that he would indulge her every other whim but this one. He could endure the absence of her love for him but, as long as Inez was his wife, he would never accept her infidelity. Inez knew very well the danger of taking a lover.

For some years past she had apparently accepted without question this one restriction on her way of life. Until the advent of Rory Howes, there had been no man in whom she had shown any pronounced interest. Now she had betrayed her feelings by poisoning her dog. The Baron knew she would not have gone to such lengths unless her emotions were deeply aroused, and Rory Howes was the only person who could have aroused them deeply enough.

As it happened, the Baron liked Rory. He considered him well-bred, well-mannered and intelligent. The boy seemed to behave in a conventional way—unlike most artists and unlike the majority of Inez's friends. He was far from convinced that Rory was the type to take advantage of his host, whether from moral scruples or from a sense of fair play. But of this he could not be certain, and he knew Inez could succeed in seducing Rory if such was her intention.

The quickest solution to the problem, he

166

thought wearily, was to tell Rory and his Norwegian friend to leave the abbey; that they were no longer welcome. But to do so would be to alienate Inez to such a degree that she would make the ensuing weeks, if not months, intolerable. It was also possible that on some pretext or another she might pursue Rory to Italy or to England, or to any other country where he chose to go.

It was preferable, the Baron thought wryly, to have the enemy beneath his roof where he could watch developments and deal with the situation if and when it arrived.

He had decided to pay this visit to the Curé this morning, leaving Inez alone in the studio for several hours with Rory with the knowledge that he was safely out of the building. If she intended to make use of this brief freedom from fear that he might walk in on them, then she had every opportunity to do so.

On his return to the abbey at lunchtime with Alex, he would know from one glance at his wife if she had achieved her desires. Inez never failed to show her satisfaction when she succeeded in getting her own way. Her voice would become softer, her eyes warm and glowing, her whole body relaxing from its customary taut posture into a lazy torpor. On such occasions she reminded him of a well-fed lioness. But of late she had resembled a tigress on the prowl and, knowing her so well, he was on the alert.

His manner gave no indication of his feelings as he was shown into the Curé's shabby little house. His voice gave not the slightest hint of his inner tension as they exchanged greetings. With cold, superb control, he accepted the offer of a glass of wine and made suitable apologies for the absence of his wife.

The two men discussed at length the exploration of the trunk and its contents. The Curé agreed to retain the documented letter to make an accurate verbatim translation. They further agreed that the remaining two trunks should stay padlocked until the Curé could be present at their opening. Since they might also contain religious relics, it could do no harm to have his blessing, the Curé suggested. He believed very firmly in the devil as an existing force of evil, and who could tell, he said to the Baron, what evil lay behind the storing of such relics. The letter itself, from the Seigneur de Valbanon, was certainly not a godly epistle!

'You will carry out a form of exorcism,' the Baron remarked, as much to himself as to the old priest. It could do no harm. If the old man wished to pay a visit to the abbey, there was no reason why he should not do so. It would mean yet another 'donation' but the poor old fellow looked as if he could do with a gift of money. His black cassock was almost green with age!

The Baron, himself, had no superstitions,

no fear of the devil, nor of the curse upon his family contained in the letter. As an historian, albeit non-professional, he looked upon historical relics as a scientist might do, proven or non-proven. The letter from de Valbanon was of interest to him only in so far as it added to the authenticity of the legend surrounding his family at the time. He could now reasonably include it in his history of the Leyresses. It would make an interesting chapter. The compilation of the book had been his life's work. It had required much research and a painstaking piecing together of facts, many of which had been missing. Now, at last, the volume was nearing completion and he was already thinking in terms of arranging for its publication. To see it at long last in print was the only ambition he had and this he was determined to do before he died.

He was silent as Alex drove him back up the winding road to the abbey. The thought of his own death had unsettled him. Although still some years from seventy, he did not anticipate that he would survive much longer. A heart specialist had warned him of high blood pressure and the necessity to lead a quiet life. As if such a thing were possible with the restless Inez at his side!

She, of course, would be a comparatively young woman when he passed on, young and extremely rich in her own right. He had long ago faced up to the fact that she would not mourn him longer than convention demanded before she remarried. Had he been the one with money, he would have tied it up legally so that if she remarried after his death, she would forfeit all of it.

But he had no hold over her fortune or her future and the thought rankled, making him even more determined to possess her totally whilst he still could. His physical impotence had become a lesser irritation these days. He had never been able to satisfy Inez from the first years of their marriage. His inadequacy, of which Inez left him in no doubt, was a humiliation he had found intolerable. A man of great personal pride, he had preferred not to attempt at all rather than to attempt and fail. When Inez moved to a bedroom of her own, he was grateful, if bitter, that the one woman capable of arousing him was justified in her rejection of him as a lover. His inability to possess her body made him even more possessive of her in other ways.

He allowed her to dominate him. She decided the mode and venue of their daily life. Knowing she would not accompany him where he wished to go, he was forced to accompany her. Her independence was total. He knew that she remained with him as his wife only because she enjoyed being the Baroness Leyresse with all that the title entailed. For that she had married him, and for that she put up with the shortcomings of her elderly husband. He had no illusions about her or about himself.

Inez's thoughts that morning were as far removed from him as his were concentrated upon her. She could think of nothing but that she was alone once more with Rory.

She had slept little the previous night. The memory of Rory kissing Alex on the stairs tormented her. It was small consolation that he had appeared to be kissing her gently, as a father might kiss a sleepy child, rather than with the fierce passion of a man in love. But she clung to this interpretation because she could not face the thought that Rory might be lost to her before she had won him.

Dozing fitfully, she had awoken with new determination. She convinced herself that Alex could not possibly compete with her, Inez Leyresse. If Rory had paid the girl some attention, it was only because she, herself, had been unavailable. Now she was home again Rory would have eyes for her alone.

To her satisfaction he was as eager as she was to go up to the studio after breakfast and begin work. She had not yet changed into the green dress of Phryne as she followed him upstairs. Rory hurried past her as they went into the room, going directly to the easel to remove the cloth covering his portrait. She watched him as he stood frowning at it.

'I've missed some vital nuance,' he said, shaking his head despondently. 'It's you but it isn't all of you, Inez. I must re-do the eyes. Go and change your clothes quickly. I'd like to start at once.'

Behind him Inez smiled. She always liked it when Rory used that dictatorial voice.

'You still won't let me look at my picture?' she asked softly. 'After all, *chéri*, I might be able to tell you what is wrong with it!'

Rory turned impatiently and said crossly:

'Do stop talking and go away and change, Inez, I'll get it right eventually.'

She smiled enigmatically and reached into the large tapestry bag she was carrying.

'I do not need to "go away and change",' she said. 'I have my dress with me. I can change here.'

Rory's mind was too engrossed in his painting to give much thought to her remark. He merely nodded his head, not bothering to answer her.

Inez stood silhouetted against the window. Slowly, she removed all her clothes. When she was completely naked, she gave the necklace round her throat a quick tug. It broke at once, the coloured beads scattering over the floor.

'Oh, Rory, help me!' she cried. 'My beautiful necklace. It has broken!'

Rory stepped from behind the easel, totally unprepared for the sight of Inez's nudity. Her body, white as alabaster, but warmly rounded, was shadowed by the bright sunlight streaming through the window. She was breathtakingly beautiful.

'Don't just stand there! Help me!' Inez commanded, as she bent to retrieve the coloured stones. She seemed quite unaware of her nakedness. But Rory had grabbed a pencil and a large sheet of paper and he began feverishly to make quick outline sketches of her.

Inez looked at him over one white shoulder, her eyes mischievous.

'I have not given you permission to draw me in the nude,' she said with mock severity. 'Come here at once and help me find my beads!'

'Inez, please, don't move. Stay like that one moment longer,' Rory pleaded. He worked as a man caught in the grip of inspiration. His model's flawless beauty made him impervious to anything but his desire to capture it on paper.

As if unconsciously, Inez changed from a kneeling position to a full length pose. Her white body was now outlined even more sharply against the crimson rug on which she lay. Both arms were outstretched as if she were searching for a lost bead beneath the chair. Her breasts, tautened by this position, curved upwards in perfect symmetry.

She waited impatiently for a few minutes whilst Rory sketched. Then she stood up. Holding out her hand, one or two beads balanced on the palm, she said to him:

'If you are not going to help me, I might as well get dressed. Really, *Monsieur l'Artist*, you are not very gallant!'

Rory looked up apologetically. The last of his sketches was finished and he was delighted with it. But as he met Inez's eyes, she suddenly ceased to be his model, but became Inez the woman, her every gesture inviting, provocative. There was no misunderstanding the smile in her eyes. He stared at her as if he were seeing her for the first time.

'Anyone would think you had never seen a naked woman before,' Inez teased him gently. 'You do stare!'

Rory stood rooted to the spot, his thoughts and feelings in a turmoil. His voice was husky and tense as he said:

'You are very beautiful!'

She took a step towards him. 'Am I? It is in the eye of the beholder, no?'

She came up to him and put her hands on either side of his face.

'You, also, are very beautiful, Rory!' she said softly. 'At least in my eyes.' She ran her hands down his body and felt him trembling. 'Of what are you afraid, Rory? There is no need for you to be shy with me. How young you are!'

Rory tried to calm his whirling thoughts.

'It isn't that I'm shy—or frightened!' He was annoyed to hear his voice wavering. 'But you cannot realise what effect you are having on me, Inez. Please—go and get dressed!'

Inez gave a low, deep laugh.

'Silly boy! You do not really wish me to put on my clothes, do you? You like to see me like this. And I would like to see you without clothes. I know you would be beautiful to me.'

'No, Inez . . .' The half-spoken cry of protest died on his lips as her arms encircled him. Her mouth pressed hard against his own as she began feverishly to kiss him.

'Inez, don't!' Rory said weakly, trying to draw away from her. He was only just in command of himself and knew that control would not last much longer.

She pouted, certain now of victory.

'Do stop being afraid. Don't you know that Bernard has gone to the village with Alex? They will not be back until lunchtime. We will not be interrupted.'

She could have bitten off her tongue as Rory reacted instantly, drawing away from her embrace. Her words had reminded him of the existence of her husband.

Inez must be out of her mind, he thought. She could not possibly mean to betray the Baron as her words and actions implied.

'Please, I want you to get dressed!' he said in a new, firm voice. 'I mean it, Inez. If not, I shall have to leave.'

Inez's face turned an ugly red. To be thwarted and rejected at this moment of near triumph was almost more than her mind could accept. But with an extreme effort she controlled her nerves. Except for the heightened colour of her cheeks, she gave no sign of her anger. Instinctively she adopted the right tactics.

'Don't be so serious!' she reproved him, lightly tapping the back of his hand. 'I am sure you are not so naive as to treat a little harmless flirtation as if it were a sin. We were not hurting anybody by stealing a little kiss or two.'

She began to put on her clothes. Only the trembling of her hands betrayed her true emotions. She went on:

'Perhaps I was mistaken in you, Rory. You are not as experienced with women as I had imagined. When you are a little older, you will know when such moments are serious and when they are no more than a little amusement.'

She saw the tension leave Rory's face. Slowly, he relaxed, and she knew that she was achieving the desired impression. Avoiding his eyes, she continued in the same vein:

'If I had thought you would react in such a way to a naked body, I would certainly not have allowed you to see me without my clothes. I only did so because you are an artist and, so I believed, would be indifferent to such lack of modesty. For one so young, you are really most provincial in your outlook, are you not?'

Rory fiddled with his pencil uneasily. Inez

had managed to make him feel like a gauche schoolboy. Yet he was sure he had not imagined the genuine passion behind those kisses. If that was Inez indulging in a harmless flirtation, what would she be like when she was serious!

'I'm sorry if I am a disappointment to you,' he said pompously. 'I dare say I am a bit out of my depth. I apologise.'

Inez was now fully garbed in the green dress. She came over to him and with well-feigned casualness, touched his face for the second time.

'There is no need to be sorry, Rory. I am very fond of you and I like to think you are fond of me. So what is a kiss or two between friends?'

Rory nodded. Inez was right. He had been really stupid to take her seriously—to have imagined she was inviting him to make love to her.

'So, I will kiss you again to show I am not angry with you!' Inez said, planting a kiss on his lips that Rory felt obliged to return. She smiled. 'Now we will begin work,' she said, and with a sideways glance at him, added, 'Maybe you will find that missing essence now, Rory. Who can tell?'

But although Rory picked up his palette and began to mix the colours he required, his desire to paint had gone. His hand was trembling and he found it hard to look across the room at Inez, now sitting demurely in the high-backed chair, smiling enigmatically at him as if nothing untoward had happened between them.

Rory's thoughts were in total confusion. It was all very well for Inez to change moods as often as she changed her clothes, he told himself. One minute she was the proud Baroness, the next a wanton, the next a Mona Lisa. He, himself, did not feel able to adapt so quickly to this chameleon behaviour. He still held the vision of Inez's marble white body before his eyes and although it was now fully covered by the green dress, he could see her nakedness beneath the soft material. The man, not the artist, was predominant.

He was about to confess that he was no longer in the right mood for painting when an instinctive caution made him hesitate. To make such an admission to Inez was to reveal the effect she had had on him, and somehow he knew that he would be making a mistake if he did so. Knut's oft-repeated warning that Inez wanted him as a lover no longer seemed irrational. Rory was forced to admit to himself that, on the contrary, it was highly probable. The suspicion alarmed him more than it flattered him, for he knew himself capable of succumbing to Inez's overwhelming allure. Were it not for Baron Leyresse, he might very easily have lost control himself. He did not believe that Inez was given to mild flirtations, no matter how hard she had tried to convince him that this was the case. She was not one for half measures in anything. She was prevaricating now only because she was unsure of his reactions. He strongly suspected that if he allowed her to know how desperately he desired her, she would once again reveal her passionate nature and invite his response.

It did not occur to Rory, his mind occupied as it was with his own immediate problem, that Inez could see she had managed to upset him sufficiently to render him unable to work; that she had forced him to think first of her, the woman, and to forget his portrait of her. At this moment he could not forget what he had seen, desired and felt obliged to reject. And if the memory should fade, she thought triumphantly, he had those sketches to remind him of her.

Her returning confidence in herself became tinged with uneasiness. If Bernard were to see the nude drawings there would be a terrible scene. She must warn Rory to keep them secret from Bernard's eyes. Yet to mention Bernard was to remind him that she had a husband. She was reasonably sure now that this was the reason Rory had rejected her advances. He had clearly forgotten Alex. Only her own marital status stood between her and what she wanted, she concluded.

For the first time in her life, Inez found herself wishing her husband dead. Until now, though she had no love for him, she had been willing to put up with him. Indulgent, aristocratic, cultured, erudite, Bernard was a social asset, without impinging in any way on her personal freedom. She did as she wished and he never stood in her way, often easing her path and always compliant. He demanded only one thing in return, her absolute fidelity. This had not really inconvenienced her in that she had never fallen in love. She had quickly tired of the few men she had briefly permitted to make love to her. The paraphernalia of secrecy that Bernard's jealousy necessitated had made the rewards from such episodes not worth the trouble. But Rory had aroused in her emotions she had never before experienced. Although young and without sophistication, he had somehow captured her heart and she wanted him as she had never before wanted a man.

Now, however, she sensed that Rory was going to elude her grasp. He, unlike her other lovers, was not going to be drawn into a hole-and-corner affair. She had offered herself to him and he had rejected her, not because she was undesirable to him but because she was another man's wife. Therefore Bernard was directly responsible for Rory's attitude and she wished him dead.

For days now Inez had been aware of her husband's eyes following her every move, watchful, suspicious, warning. The danger of the situation had enhanced her enjoyment of it. It required skilful acting to monopolise Rory's attention without appearing too personally involved. But Bernard was not deceived and Inez knew she must tread very warily. *Rory must be warned about the sketches.*

'If you don't feel like painting this morning, why don't we relax and talk?' she suggested, moving her chair so that she destroyed the pose he needed to continue working. 'In any case, I cannot model for long, since soon I must go downstairs. Monsieur Govin is coming to see Tristan. I'm so relieved he is better, poor dog. Come and sit down here, Rory.'

Rory was now in control of himself.

'No, while you are here I want to paint, Inez. Turn your head back. Your position is all wrong. We can talk as I work.'

He had recovered his composure and with it, his desire to paint.

Inez heard the renewed note of authority in his voice. As a rule she welcomed his dominance but now she bitterly resented it. She resisted the desire to voice an angry refusal and said, sighing:

'So autocratic! I think I must go to live in America where women are fully liberated and give all the orders!'

Rory's face relaxed into a smile at the preposterousness of her remark.

'You must be the most liberated woman I

know, Inez, if giving orders is the yardstick. You run this place like a general in charge of an army. Nobody would dare to defy you.'

Inez quickly saw her opportunity.

'That is what you think, Rory. *It is not so.* I appear to be in command but really it is Bernard who has complete control. I am only his mouthpiece. He is a very dominant man. I should also warn you, Rory, that he is sometimes a very narrow-minded, bigoted man. He has old-fashioned ideas and I fear he would object very strongly if he saw those sketches of me. I would advise you not to exhibit them.'

Rory glanced down at the white sheets of drawing paper and suddenly the sight of his nude sketches made him feel uneasy. He had portrayed Inez just as he had seen her, voluptuous, passionate, enticing. She looked exactly as she had been when he drew her, a woman inviting love with every line of her face and body, with every gesture and pose of her beautiful limbs. If anyone with any degree of sensibility should see these, they would know exactly how Inez was feeling at that moment. His work had been inspired. Unconsciously, he had captured in a few bold strokes her sensuous mood, her underlying passion.

He bit hard on the end of his paint brush, his mind a whirlpool of thought. He understood now why Inez had told him he would never reproduce her likeness in his

182

portrait successfully unless he really knew her. He had until now missed that particular expression in her eyes, her body, because he had been trying so hard not to see it. He had deliberately blinded himself to the truth until Inez had forced him to see her as she really was—not the proud, imperious queen of her domain, but a wild, wanton hot-blooded woman of the jungle, taunting, tempting, inviting. Through the media of his own sketches, he saw her now as Knut had seen her from the beginning.

Angrily, he looked back at his oil painting. It was empty, meaningless. True enough, he had captured the delicate transparency of the green chiffon; captured, also, the flashing flame of Inez's shining red hair. But the face and the body beneath were like those of a statue. He might as well have painted it from the picture he had once seen of Phryne—an imaginary, unreal figure. If he could now put Inez's real body, her real face, into his portrait, he would truly capture the likeness.

Feverishly he began to scrape at the canvas.

'What are you doing, Rory?' Inez cried. 'What is wrong?'

'Everything!' Rory shouted. 'That is, everything I have done of you. I shan't touch the dress or your hair, but you . . . I have to re-do your face, your body, your limbs. It was all wrong—*all of it!* Now I know how to do it—if I can. I know how it should be!'

183

Inez smiled.

'All that time wasted,' she said softly. 'Now it will be a long while before the portrait is finished.'

Rory missed the note of satisfaction in her voice.

'I can't help that!' he cried impatiently. 'I've got to get it right and I can now, I know I can. These sketches will help enormously.'

'I am glad!' Inez said. 'For your sake as well as my own, I want your portrait of me to be a masterpiece. It will make us both famous, no?'

But Rory did not hear her. He was once more totally absorbed in his work. When much later, the gong sounded for lunch, he refused to leave the studio.

'Send something up—anything. I'm not hungry,' he told Inez.

No longer entirely displeased with the outcome of her morning's work, Inez went down to join her husband and the two young people for lunch. When the meal was over, she ordered Gilbert to have a tray sent up to the studio. As she followed Knut and the Baron into the *salon* for coffee, she was unaware that Alex, with her usual thoughtfulness, was telling Gilbert that as she, herself, was going upstairs to the linen room, she would take Rory's tray with her to save the old servant from climbing the stairs.

Glad of the opportunity to see Rory for the first time that day, Alex knocked on the door of the studio and went inside with a happy smile of anticipation on her face. Last night Rory had kissed her on the stairs; this morning Tristan was pronounced out of danger; the sun was shining and she was radiantly happy. She paused for a moment, looking at Rory's back as he stood in front of his easel, too preoccupied even to turn his head.

She knew, then, that the Baron had been right when he had declared that wishing could not prevent love from striking where it would. She was in love with Rory—as deeply in love as she had ever been with David. More than anything in the world she wanted Rory to turn his head and seeing her, put down his brushes and take her in his arms. She wanted him to kiss her as he had done last night, tenderly, lovingly. She wanted to kiss him and tell him, 'I love you, Rory, I love you.'

But all she said was:

'I've brought you some lunch.'

Rory turned and smiled at her.

'That's nice of you, Alex. Shove the tray down somewhere. I don't want to stop even for a moment.'

Obediently Alex put the tray down on the table near the easel. She was about to move some sheets of drawing paper to one side when the subject of them suddenly hit her. The sketches were of a naked woman— unquestionably Inez. Rory had caught the likeness brilliantly.

Instinctively, she turned her eyes away. But the images continued to burn inside her head, unforgettable. They were artistically magnificent but the very intensity of the subject made any doubt impossible. If Rory had had to put a title to them they could have but one name—Desire.

Sick with an emotion she did not understand, Alex put down the tray and without speaking again, quickly left the room. She went to the linen room and leaned against the wall, the strong sweet smell of lavender, which perfumed all Inez's bed linen, making her feel dizzy and faint. She closed her eyes, trying to shut out the memory of those drawings.

Her revulsion was not from prudery. Nakedness had never seemed anything but natural and beautiful to her. Nor was it from envy. Her own body was every bit as perfect as Inez's, as slender and as shapely.

She tried desperately to define her feelings. At the back of her mind the word 'lustful' became the predominant adjective for the sketches. Had Rory satisfied Inez's desires? The idea of physical intimacy between them was totally abhorrent to her.

Standing there alone, confused, Alex sought to keep her thoughts rational. All artists want from time to time to draw from life, she told herself. Many, like Rory, would be inspired by the very earthiness of Inez's sensuality. If only

186

she could believe that Rory had made those drawings entirely dispassionately, Alex thought. But how could he have failed to react to Inez? He had been alone with her in the studio all morning. He could have made love to her and no one would have been any the wiser; he could have responded to the sexuality he must have sensed in her since he had been able to capture it so realistically on paper.

Knut had been saying for weeks that Inez was determined to seduce Rory. Rory had laughed at the idea, even been angry with Knut. She, Alex, had refused to think too seriously about it. Rory, though attentive to Inez, had not behaved like a man in love. If he had occasionally seemed enslaved, she had told herself that his obsession was with his painting. Deep inside, Alex had never taken Knut's remarks seriously until now.

She covered her face with her hands, feeling cold despite the warmth of the little room. She did not wish to see in front of her the neat rows of satin sheets, each bearing the family crest, that were waiting to adorn Inez's bed. Deep violet, soft blue, crimson, palest ivory— all in turn would add to the luxurious beauty of the giant four poster. This, with its diaphanous pink draperies, dominated Inez's bedroom, together with her fantastic dressing table. Covering the length of one wall, entirely mirrored in bevelled panels, was the custom-made Italian dressing table, painted with garlands and touched with gilt. On the glass-covered top stood matching sets of scents and cosmetic jars from the famous beauty salons of Paris; different perfumes to match Inez's changing moods; make-up to create the desired effect of the moment. The jars and bottles were in themselves so beautiful, it looked like a display shelf in a *parfumerie*.

Two walls of the room were covered from floor to ceiling with built-in cupboards containing Inez's vast wardrobe. Only her personal maid knew just how many dresses, shoes, gloves and handbags Inez owned. But not even the maid had access to the cleverly concealed safe containing the Baroness's jewels. Only Inez and the Baron knew the combination of that safe and as far as Alex was aware, the Baron never went near his wife's room. His bedroom was some distance down the passage, by contrast austere in its simplicity. He did not care for satin but insisted instead on sheets of the finest Irish linen. These, too, lay in neat rows in the linen cupboard, each with its individual crest.

The linen sheets used for the guests were of slightly inferior quality but still wonderfully smooth and hem-stitched to match the varying colour schemes of the guest rooms. It was these Alex had come to collect for the maids who would make up the beds the following morning. Every bed had its own electric blanket and these would be checked at least two days before the guests arrived. Inez's friends lacked no physical comfort.

Nor did Alex herself lack for anything that money could buy, she thought, as she began to sort through the linen. She had grown used to living in luxury since she had arrived at the abbey. Yet she had never known any real happiness here. At first her grieving for David had dulled all other feeling. And now, just when she was beginning to find not only peace of mind, but real happiness again, there were ominous signs of a storm gathering that might shake the very foundations of this great establishment.

Once again Alex shivered. In this mood it was all too easy to remember the sensation of horror she had experienced in the cellar; the sinister warning in the yellow parchment document that the house of Leyresse would never know peace.

Without understanding why she did so, Alex buried her face in the sweet-smelling linen in her arms and whispered aloud:

'Don't, Rory, please, please don't!'

But she feared that her prayer had come too late and the storm was already under way.

CHAPTER NINE

'Something is wrong with the Baron,' Knut said as he stood beside Alex in the butler's pantry where she was busy arranging flowers in preparation for the weekend.

'What do you mean?' she asked him. 'Do you think he is ill? He did look a little pale at breakfast.'

Knut shook his head as he lifted a great bunch of carnations from the bucket beneath the sink and put them on the draining board beside Alex. He had had his plaster-cast removed the previous day and was mobile once more, an elastic bandage helping to support the muscles weakened by weeks of inactivity.

'I wasn't suggesting he is physically ill. But he has been behaving very oddly these last two days. He hardly says a word to anyone.'

'But he's never very talkative,' Alex reminded Knut. 'In fact, it would be more remarkable if he was being chatty!'

'I know that,' Knut said impatiently. 'It's hard to explain exactly what I mean but he has been so morose. There's a strange brooding expression on his face that I have noticed more often lately. I don't like it. For some reason or other, it is a sinister look.'

'Now who is being imaginative!' Alex said

with a forced little laugh. 'I'm the one usually accused of seeing things that aren't there.'

In fact, she had been so busy with preparations for the weekend that she had had little time to notice anything but the next task to be done. Inez, closeted with Rory in the studio, had told Alex that on this occasion she was leaving in Alex's hands the supervision of the servants and the responsibility for seeing everything was correctly prepared for her guests. All the spare beds were now made up; the bathrooms supplied with toiletries, soaps, towels; the furniture dusted and polished; the carpets vacuumed and windows cleaned. Now there remained only the flowers for Alex to arrange; a bouquet in each bedroom and two dozen or more downstairs in every available niche in the hall, the dining room, *salons*, library and billiard room. The task had already taken up the morning, even with Knut's help. It would be many hours yet before she would be finished.

'I think the Baron is brooding about Inez and Rory,' Knut said quietly. 'And I'm not joking, Alex. Without it being obvious, he listens to every word they say and his eyes are always on one or the other. I tried to warn Rory last night but he won't listen.'

'Warn him about what?' Alex asked, her heart thudding uncomfortably at Knut's words. Since she had taken Rory's lunch to the studio two days ago, she had barely exchanged a word with him. He worked from first to last light with a feverish excitement he could not conceal. For several hours each day, Inez was in the studio with him. At meal times their conversation related entirely to the portrait and how well Rory's second attempt was progressing. Neither seemed aware how excluded the other three people at the table felt.

Alex had not told Knut about the nude sketches. But now she wondered if he knew about them; if perhaps Rory had told him.

'I warned him that he was monopolising Inez and that her husband doesn't like it,' Knut went on. 'Not that it did the slightest bit of good. Rory merely replied, "Rubbish! How can I paint his wife if she isn't allowed to sit for me when I need her! . . ."'

'That makes sense,' Alex argued. She had used the same arguments on herself.

But Knut was shaking his head.

'So long as an artist has a few sittings it should be sufficient. Imagine if I were painting the Queen! I could hardly insist she give up three weeks of her time to model for me. There's a lot of work Rory can do without Inez there.'

Alex put the last of the carnations in place and handed the vase to Knut.

'That one can go on the hall table,' she instructed him. 'I'll use the roses next.'

While Knut was gone she began to arrange

some of the blooms from the vast bunches of red, pink and yellow roses. Their perfume was beautiful. It reminded her of the garden at home. She felt a sudden longing for England, for her house, her parents, and the comparatively simple life she had once led with them.

As if in telepathic understanding of her thoughts, Knut said on his return:

'I wish you'd let me take you away from this place, Alex. I know you think I'm a little crazy to be afraid, and even I think I am being unreasonable. But each day we stay here, the three of us, I feel more and more anxious. There's something in the atmosphere . . . I don't know . . .'

His voice trailed off, his face serious and perplexed.

'Rory won't leave until he has finished his painting,' Alex said after a moment's silence.

'I know that. But you don't have to stay here any longer, do you, Alex? Neither do I, for that matter. Let me take you back to England. Or come with me and visit my home in Norway. You'd like it there and my parents would be very happy to receive you.'

He was so obviously in earnest that Alex felt his fear increasing her own. But she could not bring herself to admit this, lest by doing so the fear became even more tangible.

'And leave Rory to face the possible dangers alone?' she said in a light, bantering tone. 'We can't desert him, Knut. Besides, it would seem so rude and ungrateful if we just walked out without one good reason for doing so. I, in particular, am indebted to the Leyresses.'

Knut broke the thorns off a rose stem and handed the flower to her.

'I know you don't want to leave Rory, Alex. Nor do I. But nothing I say to him makes him realise the danger he may be in. Perhaps if he knew we believed there was a risk and intended to go, he'd change his mind and come with us.'

Alex sighed.

'You don't really believe that. Anyway, Knut, what is this danger you keep talking about? Even if the Baron suspects Rory of having an affair with Inez, he can't do worse than throw Rory out of the house. I think you're exaggerating the whole situation.'

Knut frowned, his blue eyes narrowed and uneasy.

'Nevertheless, I am afraid, Alex. The Baron might do worse than expel Rory. It depends what provocation he and Inez give him. I think he could be a very dangerous enemy. I don't believe he is entirely sane—not where Inez is concerned. He is violently jealous beneath that quiet restrained exterior and it is the quiet characters who are often the most dangerous. He is too controlled. Believe me, Alex, I've been watching him closely.'

When Alex made no reply, he went on:

194

'Rory is so tactless. He sits at the table never taking his eyes off our lovely Baroness. If you speak to him, he gives the briefest of replies and then turns back to stare at her again. He's obsessed with her.'

Alex gripped the cut-glass vase with both hands. Her face was white.

'Are you trying to say Rory is in love with Inez?' she asked.

There was a quiver in her voice and Knut's eyes softened. He put a hand on Alex's shoulder and replied gently:

'I suppose I am, in a way. But you must remember, Alex, that Rory is primarily an artist. He may not be so much in love with Inez as with his painting of her. Do you understand what I am trying to say?'

'I don't think so!'

'Rory is confusing what he is creating with what actually exists. Inez means everything in the world to him at this moment because she is the inspiration for his Phryne. No other woman could replace her . . . she's unique for him, all important and utterly necessary. This is a kind of need akin to being in love, is it not? Yet it is not being in love in the way that you or I might mean the phrase.'

'You said "at this moment". Are you suggesting that when Rory's portrait is finished, he won't need Inez any more?'

Knut heard the note of hope Alex had been unable to keep from her voice. He tried to be

195

reassuring.

'I imagine not. Sometimes a painter goes through a phase of needing one particular model to inspire him. I could give you many examples. But others need fresh faces, new ideas.'

Alex's grip on the vase tightened.

'And that could depend on how personal the relationship was between artist and model? If they were lovers?'

Knut did not reply. He had hesitated to use the word for fear of putting an idea into Alex's mind. Now he knew that she, too, was afraid Rory might succumb to Inez's desire—might already have done so. Knut was familiar with Rory's views about married women and his resolve never to become involved with one. But Inez Leyresse was a forceful, determined woman, and Knut was in no doubt whatever that she intended to involve Rory. Each day she became a little less able to conceal her feelings. In Knut's opinion, the Baron would have had to be quite blind not to see the look of longing in her eyes when they rested on Rory; not to notice the way she used every excuse to sit beside him, to touch his hand or his arm, to cater to his needs. She was that most dangerous of all women—at the end of her youth, unsatisfied by her husband, consumed by desire for a love that had passed her by until it was almost too late. In a few years' time that fabulous beauty would begin

196

to fade. And Rory's very reluctance to become involved would be the biggest spur of all. Inez was not accustomed to denial and would see it as a challenge.

As for Knut himself, whilst he could appreciate Inez's unusual looks, he had never felt attracted by them. As he had grown to know her as a person, he had felt an increasing dislike for and distrust of her. The reverse was true of his feeling for Alex. Though far from beautiful in the strictest sense, she was more than just attractive. With her large blue eyes and soft, sensitive mouth, she aroused in him the most protective instincts. He wanted to hold her, guard her, kiss her, take care of her. He wanted to make her happy, to bring back the laughter in her eyes, to hear her voice happy and excited. He loved her. Had she reciprocated his feelings, he would have asked her to marry him, although he was in no position financially. He had not yet begun his career and could barely support himself.

Perhaps it was fortunate, therefore, that Alex was not within his reach. He guessed that she was in love with Rory and although the knowledge hurt, he understood it. Rory was his best friend and Knut admired as well as liked him. There were no ugly traits in Rory's character. He was a good friend and Knut would have been happy to see him involved with someone like Alex. The two of them would have made a wonderful pair. It could still happen if only he could persuade Rory to leave the Abbaye St. Christophe before it was too late!

'I'll talk to Rory again,' he said to Alex. 'He must be on the point of finishing the portrait. Maybe he'll agree to leave after the fancy dress ball. We'll all have to stay for that no matter what! I can't wait to see you in the nun's outfit, Alex. I'm sure you will look quite adorable!'

As he hoped, Alex's face relaxed into a smile.

'And I can't wait to see you as a monk, Knut. I don't think you'll look the part—not unless you remove that twinkle in your eye. I'm sure monks weren't permitted to be teases!'

Knut grinned.

'What about our friend, the lay brother, who met his lady love, the novice, for fun and games in the cellar? He must have been quite a bad boy one way and another!'

'Stop it, Knut!' Alex ordered, laughing nervously. 'You don't know how spooky that cellar was. I can't bear to think of those two young people being burnt to death. They should have been allowed to rescind their vows and marry if they loved each other so much.'

'And live happily ever after!' Knut agreed. 'Though I doubt Seigneur de Valbanon would have permitted it. No bastard son of the Leyresses would be good enough for his daughter. Obviously he was a violent man. Vindictive, too, judging by the curse he put on the Leyresses.'

Alex gave a little shiver.

'I can understand people living in those days being superstitious enough to believe in the effectiveness of a curse or a spell put on them. Even now, knowing it's a lot of nonsense, I still feel a twinge of fear when I think about it. In a way, part of it came true, didn't it? The Leyresse family never really prospered until this last generation—when Inez's money made it possible for the Baron to re-establish himself.'

'But at what a price!' Knut said. 'I doubt the old boy can have had a very happy life married to Inez. He is certainly not a happy man at this moment. I just hope his anger is directed at Inez and not at Rory.'

'You don't really think Rory is in any kind of danger, do you?' Alex asked. She had begun to feel some of Knut's anxiety about the Baron.

'I honestly don't know. It's probably a good thing the guests start arriving tomorrow. With the house full Inez can't disappear off to the studio for hours on end, can she? She simply won't have time. It will give us a chance to try to divert Rory. See what you can do, Alex. He's very fond of you. Make him notice you. You could if you wanted.'

Alex smiled.

'You're wearing those rose-coloured spectacles again,' she said. 'Rory hasn't noticed me for days and you know it.'

'Then we'll begin making him tonight. We haven't tried on our costumes yet. We'll drag Rory upstairs after dinner and leave the Baron the field. Inez won't like it if we take Rory away from her but we've got an excellent excuse. So let's use it.'

When that evening Knut announced that they would probably be absent for the next few hours, Inez was furious.

'I don't see the necessity for a dress rehearsal,' she said coldly. 'And what are these costumes you will be wearing? You have not told me about them, Rory,' she said accusingly.

'It's a secret!' Knut said firmly before Rory could speak. 'Half the fun of a fancy dress ball is not knowing what everyone else will be wearing. *We* don't know what costume *you've* chosen, Inez!'

'You have had plenty of time to try on your clothes during the day!' She looked back at Rory and, in a soft persuasive tone, said, 'You must be dead tired, Rory, after so many hours standing at that easel. Would you not prefer to relax?'

'He can't do that,' Knut argued. 'We need Rory with us.'

'Is it really necessary to rehearse now?' Rory asked. He really was tired and he sensed Inez's disapproval at the idea of them absenting themselves.

'Yes, it is!' Knut said at once. 'Alex is going to be busier than ever tomorrow and won't

200

have time to play around with costumes. If she can make the effort, you can, Rory. I'll bet she has been on her feet just as long as you have today.'

Rory stood up.

'Yes, of course!' he said at once. 'You will excuse us, Inez? Baron Leyresse?'

The Baron nodded but Inez merely shrugged, her face distorted with annoyance.

When the door closed behind them, the Baron spoke:

'It is natural the three young people should wish to be alone occasionally,' he said, watching his wife's face closely. 'It may interest you to know the little Alexandra is in love with Rory. I think he returns her affection, or might do so if he spent more time with her. They are very well-suited, do you not agree?'

Inez's eyes flashed dangerously. With an effort she managed to control her anger.

'You don't know what you are talking about!' she said rudely. 'Alex may have a schoolgirl crush on Rory but he most certainly is not interested in her.'

'Alex is not a schoolgirl, my dear. She is a young woman who has already been affianced. As for your artist, I see no reason why he should not be just as susceptible to Alexandra's charms as is our young Norwegian friend. She is a very attractive young woman. Moreover, she has a sweet disposition. She would make an excellent wife for an artist.'

'I doubt Rory is looking for a wife!' Inez said through clenched teeth. 'What stupid ideas you do have, Bernard. Rory is an artist and needs a great deal more than "a charming disposition" to make him fall in love.'

The Baron poured himself a brandy and sat gently swirling the amber liquid round the bowl of the glass. If Inez had not been too angry to notice it she would have been warned by his smile.

'You interest me, my dear. What would you say, from your apparently vast knowledge of this young man, would be likely to appeal to him in a woman? Alexandra has other advantages beside charm—her youth, her innocence, for instance. Are you implying Rory would prefer an older, more experienced woman?' He stressed the two adjectives with cold irony.

Inez saw the trap and succeeded in controlling herself in time. She managed to shrug her shoulders as if indifferent to the subject of Rory's taste in women.

'How should I know what an artist requires in a woman to make him fall in love. I merely doubt Alex is the type to inspire a man of his talent. And he is talented, Bernard. Wait until you see the portrait. It is magnificent!'

'So you have already seen it?'

Inez nodded.

'He forbade me to look but I managed to get a glimpse of it when he left the room for a few minutes. It is quite astonishing—like looking into a mirror. You will like it, Bernard.'

The Baron sipped his cognac and, without looking up, said:

'Perhaps I shall not see you with the same eyes. Perhaps he has a different impression of you, my dear, from the one I have.'

Inez said quickly, nervously:

'What is that supposed to mean? You don't make yourself clear, Bernard.'

'I think I do!'

Inez felt unable to break the uneasy silence that followed. It was the nearest her husband had ever come to voicing his feelings. He was admitting his suspicion. And he was right to be suspicious, Inez told herself with cruel satisfaction. If Rory were willing, she would not have the slightest hesitation in being unfaithful to her husband. She no longer cared about the possible consequences. If Bernard chose to divorce her, she would not care if she had Rory beside her as her lover. Bernard's religion did not allow divorce but that, too, made little difference. She would not care what the world said or thought if she ceased to be Baroness Leyresse and became Rory's mistress. She had enough money for both of them to live in luxury for the rest of their lives; enough money to open the many doors that might otherwise be closed to them because of such a liaison.

Such a liaison was possible, she thought for the hundredth time, if only Rory would forget his ridiculous scruples and give way to the passion she was sure he felt. She had convinced herself that Rory returned her feelings but was refusing to reveal them only because she was Bernard's wife. She attributed the fact that he had refused to allow her to pose again for him in the nude to his fear that he could not trust himself to live up to his principles under such conditions. She knew he still had the sketches he had done of her because he looked at them frequently when he was working.

Because Inez could not bear to face the possibility that Rory was not in love with her, she did not permit herself to accept that there were alternative reasons for Rory's behaviour. She did not wish to consider that he was using the sketches only as reference for his work. She preferred to believe that he derived an erotic satisfaction from looking at them.

So successful was her self-delusion that Inez felt it was only a matter of time before Rory succumbed to his desperate need for her. She even managed to admire him for fighting this lone battle for moral rectitude. He had a lot to learn—and she would be his teacher. She would show him that conventional behaviour was unacceptable to an artist; and that he owed it to himself to live life to its fullest, regardless of whether the world said it was right or wrong. She would love him as no other woman could—no *younger* woman could. She would be all things to him, mistress and model, lover and inspiration. She loved him enough to throw away everything she had hitherto valued—her title, her beautiful abbey. Her home in Paris was her own and she could continue to live there if she wished.

When the idea of living with Rory in Paris had first occurred to her, she began to talk to him of the home she had made there and of the city itself. It was, she told him, the true home for an artist. She cited the great men who had lived and worked there. Rory seemed only mildly interested and Inez once more convinced herself that he would not admit to an intense desire to go there only because she was another man's wife.

If another woman had admitted these private dreams to Inez, she would have told her she was deluding herself. She would have said, quite logically, that even if Rory were willing to indulge in an affair, he would not be likely to tie himself up to a woman nearing middle-age, if, indeed, to any woman. She would have said that it could lead only to desertion and disaster for the woman who loved Rory. She would have said it was madness for a woman of her social standing to take such a risk.

But because her dream was so violent and vivid, Inez could envisage nothing but the sweet rewards of being in Rory's arms. There was no room in her heart for logical argument. Her real life had become the dream and Rory the only reality. But he was not yet her lover and until he was, she knew she must use caution with Bernard.

She had not lost interest in the fancy dress ball for she had convinced herself that this would be the night when Rory succumbed. It was her intention to look so magnificently seductive that he could no longer resist temptation. The scene would be set with candlelight and champagne and dancing. She had engaged two different bands, one Italian and one South American. Rory would not refuse to dance with her and would hold her in his arms. If Bernard retired to bed early enough, she might dance the flamenco. She had learned to do this in her childhood; but perfectly though she could perform it, her husband considered it improper for her to do so and only on the rarest occasions when Bernard was absent could she display her talent. She knew that Bernard was shocked by the wild abandon of the dance although that was part of the romance and excitement of flamenco music. Inez was well aware that it aroused most men's passions, and her intention was to dance for Rory, expressly for him, so that he could not fail to be affected. He would probably want to paint her again . . . this time as a gypsy, she mused. He would see that she could be all women. Her first costume would be graceful, regal, superbly dignified and aristocratic. She would show herself to him first as a queen and then as a gypsy.

'You are very quiet, my dear.'

The Baron's voice jolted her from her reverie. She had forgotten his existence. Remembering now that he and he alone stood between her and the fruition of her dreams, she looked at him coldly.

'That is hardly my fault, Bernard. I did not find your conversation particularly attractive. If we cannot find something a little more pleasant to talk about, then it is better we de not talk at all.'

The Baron gave an imperceptible shrug of his shoulders.

'Then let us discuss something that will interest you, *chérie*,' he said quietly. 'No doubt you have not forgotten the ring the young people found in the cellar? I sent it to Paris the day before yesterday. The curator of the museum telephoned me in person this afternoon to inform me that it is genuine thirteenth-century, quite unique and immensely valuable. He asked me if I would consider lending it to the museum but I told him I would not as I intended to have it made small enough for you to wear. He was very shocked at the idea. However, I imagine you will be delighted to have such a rare jewel to display to your women friends.'

Now he did have Inez's full attention, but not in the way he had anticipated. Her face had paled and she looked angry and frightened.

'Nothing in the world would make me wear it!' she said in a small, shocked voice. 'It was on a skeleton hand, Bernard. Even to touch it would appal me.'

Her husband looked at her in surprise.

'There are times when I simply do not understand you, Inez. Every piece of antique furniture once belonged to someone now dead. Much of the jewellery you wear belonged to my ancestors—to some woman long since dead. Why should you object to wearing this ring?'

Inez tapped her foot nervously on the floor.

'It is directly associated with violence and death,' she replied. 'You may call me superstitious if you wish, but I will not wear it—ever. I am certain it would bring only bad luck, as it did to its original owner.'

The Baron shrugged. He had expected to earn her gratitude but as so often happened, his plan had misfired.

'As you wish, my dear. I thought the gift would please you. However, perhaps it is as well under the circumstances. The ring is too big for you at present and to alter it might reduce its value as an antique. I shall wear it myself.'

'No!' Inez's voice rang out shrill with fear.

'*You must not wear it, Bernard. I know it is evil.* Get rid of it. Give it to the museum on permanent loan. They want it and I don't want it kept in this house. The parchment too. Can't you burn it? Destroy it. Every time I think about it, I am afraid.'

'I think you are hysterical,' the Baron said coldly. 'You cannot be so ignorant as to believe a piece of parchment can carry evil in it! Nor, unless it had poison concealed in it, could the ring itself possibly do anyone the slightest harm. To believe such nonsense is to admit to having the mind of a servant girl, an uneducated peasant.'

Inez's face, hitherto devoid of colour, now flushed an angry red.

'You are insulting!' she said. 'It is your wife you are speaking to, please remember.'

The Baron remained unmoved.

'And I consider your remarks insulting both to my intelligence and your own,' he said coldly. 'Moreover, I hardly think this is the correct moment to remind me of your marital status. It is I who should be reminding you that you have a husband.'

His words momentarily shocked Inez into silence. But she recovered quickly and gave a scornful little laugh.

'Why, I do believe you are jealous, Bernard!' she said in a bantering tone. 'Life is going to become unbearably dull if in your old age you are going to object to my harmless little flirtations. If you deny me these, what other *divertissements* have I left? I must amuse myself somehow. Do tell me, *chéri*, of what I am accused. Do you object to my interest in our young portrait painter? Is that why you are behaving so strangely?'

The Baron looked away from her challenging gaze. He had not expected her to mention Rory.

'I am not accusing you, Inez—merely reminding you that you are my wife, the Baroness Leyresse. It is quite possible that you are only amusing yourself with your aspiring artist, but he does not strike me as the type of young man who is accustomed to the permissive behaviour of the society in which you usually find your amusement. If it were one of your usual admirers, well . . .' he shrugged his shoulders, '. . . they understand the rules of the game, if that is the correct terminology for your flirtations. I believe myself to be a tolerant man, a lenient husband, but I do not wish you to forget, my dear, that there are limits even to my tolerance. That is all I have to say.'

He put down his now empty brandy glass and rose stiffly to his feet. The conversation had required a great effort on his part. He disliked revealing his feelings and had only done so as a last resort, when he believed Inez's monopoly of Rory had become so obvious that even the servants must be gossiping about it. He was reasonably certain that Inez had not yet taken the boy as a lover. Her manner was still too tense and high-pitched to be that of a satisfied woman. But every day that passed she was less and less able to conceal the fact that she wanted Rory; and he, her husband, had no intention of making it easy for her to achieve her aims. On the contrary, he would go to any lengths to stop it. His warning this evening was only the first of those steps.

'Are you coming up to bed, my dear?' he asked courteously with a return to his customary tone of voice.

Inez did not bother to turn her head as she replied:

'At this hour? It is not yet ten o'clock! I shall stay down here and play some of my records . . . the Dvořák symphony, I think. I am in the mood for it.'

The Baron nodded. Had he felt less exhausted, he, too, would have enjoyed the music.

He walked slowly up the great staircase, his hand on the massive polished bannister steadying him as he climbed. He touched something sticky and looked at his hands with fastidious distaste. It was a daub of blue paint.

As he wiped at it with a silk handkerchief, his mind was drawn towards the painting up in the studio. Was it really the masterpiece Inez claimed? he asked himself. He wanted suddenly very much to see it.

He stood perfectly still, listening. There was a faint murmur of voices from the servants' hall. Above him, from the landing, he could hear the sound of pop music and knew that Rory, Alex and Knut were probably playing the transistor radio Inez had lent them. From the *salon* came the resonant tones of the first movement of the symphony.

He smiled as he realised that he was unlikely to be disturbed were he to pay a visit to Rory's 'studio'.

Slowly he climbed the remainder of the stairs and went along the landing to the back staircase leading to the attics. The studio door was open. As he switched on the light he saw the easel, the canvas on it covered with a light cloth.

Closing the door behind him lest someone should notice the light, he went forward and lifted the cloth.

For a moment he stood staring, lost in an admiration which was purely academic. There before him were Inez's eyes, her expression, the tilt of her head, the very texture of her white skin; there, the burning flame of her red hair, the delicate blue shadows at the base of her throat. Rory had captured her likeness to perfection.

Then his eyes moved down to the body and he gasped. It was the body of a seductress, offering herself with the proud knowledge of her power to fulfil the promise that lay in every soft curve. This was not Inez, his wife, the Baroness Leyresse. This was the body of a wanton.

He closed his eyes. Then he opened them for a second look. Memories were flooding his mind—memories of the young girl he had married and the humiliation he had suffered on their wedding night. As in the painting, so had his young bride, Inez, offered herself to him, promising him her abandonment to the delights of the flesh. He had failed in his response and shown himself to be an inadequate lover. In the years that had passed since then, he had come to terms with his impotence. Inez had soon ceased to be the eager, hot-blooded woman he had married. Or so he believed until now. Now he saw that nothing had changed. The seductress was still there, offering herself once more, renewing all the agony of the past, trebling it since she was not offering herself to him.

In this moment of painful truth, the Baron's self-control snapped. The jealousy that had been gnawing at him took complete possession. He picked up a palette knife lying by the easel and was about to slash at the canvas in a frenzy of impotent rage when his eye was caught by the sketches that had been lying beneath the knife.

He snatched at them, his green eyes no longer icy but fiery. The nude sketches of

Inez's body lay grasped in his hands as he looked feverishly from one to the next. Here, open to the gaze of the world, was the body of his wife, known only too well, he now realised, to the artist who had drawn her. The sketches had no facial detail but there could be no doubt they were of Inez—the voluptuous curve of the hip, the suggestion of strength even in the most supine of the poses, the slimness of the waist, the invitation of her breasts, her softly rounded arms, her long slender legs.

The first rage of anger left him. In its wake followed an ice-cold fury. The hands holding the sheets of drawing paper trembled. Slowly the habit of years reasserted itself. He had only once permitted emotion to overrule his reason, he reminded himself, and he had come near to killing a man. If he were ever to do the same again, he wished at least to be in command of his actions rather than a slave to his passions.

The sketches, after all, proved nothing—unless it were that his wife had no modesty, no pride. He had given Inez a title but it seemed he had failed to turn the peasant girl into an aristocrat. Her pretensions to good breeding were superficial. Beneath the surface lay the truth . . .

But what was the truth?

The Baron was once more in control of himself. He reflected reasonably that the young Englishman had an exceptional talent.

He was an artist and a very, very promising one. To an artist, a nude was merely a figure to be used as a model. He viewed it as dispassionately as a doctor might study a nude patient. Rory needed such anatomical details to enable him to reproduce the figure on canvas, the floating green chiffon of the dress barely concealing the outlines of the body beneath.

But behind the artist was a man, the Baron argued with his own logic, and he knew little enough about Rory Howes! Could he or any man fail to be susceptible to such a woman as Inez? He might dislike her, despise her, hate her even, but he could not fail to want her. If such was Rory's feeling, he could not be blamed for the inevitable. No, the blame lay at Inez's door. She was the one offering herself shamelessly, cleverly, wantonly, her whole body vibrant with sexuality.

The Baron put down the sketches and replaced the knife on top of them. His eyes went back to the portrait and despite himself, he knew he could never destroy it. At the same time, he could not hang it in view of others, for they would know what kind of woman Inez was beneath her aristocratic façade. If he hung it in his bedroom where none but the servants would see it, he himself would know no peace. Each time he looked at it he would feel again the agonies of his impotency; see himself not as the rich, powerful baron who cleverly kept a devoted young wife by his side, but as a pathetic, ageing man on his knees at the side of his wife's bed, begging forgiveness for his failure to be a man.

The memory of his torment rose again to taunt him. If Inez had shown sympathy, understanding, patience . . . but she had laughed at him, ridiculed him and so completed his castration. He had continued to love her, to desire her. On a number of occasions, his courage heightened by wine, he had demanded his rights as a husband. But the cost to his pride made those occasions more and more rare as the years went by until he ceased going to his wife's bedroom.

As once he had stood outside his wife's door, hesitant and trembling with uncertainty, torn between pride and desire, so now he stood looking at the portrait, wanting to possess it yet knowing it could bring him no lasting happiness. Then, as now, he could not destroy the object of his desire.

He turned away, his face grey with spent emotion and fatigue. The violence had gone out of him and only the bitter aftermath remained. The years had taught him patience, if nothing else. He could wait. For the moment, portrait, artist, model could remain unharmed. But when the right time came, he could and would extract his full quota of revenge.

CHAPTER TEN

Rory was tired. For the last two days he had painted with a fierce concentration that absorbed all his energy. The portrait was almost finished and he had no doubt now that it was far better than anything he had dared hope to produce. At last there was a true likeness to Inez, but it had cost him a great deal in nervous energy to achieve it. The most taxing effort of all had been to keep Inez at arm's length without actually antagonising her.

He now knew that Knut had been right in suspecting that Inez was in love with him, or at any rate, wanted him for a lover. At first he was flattered and excited, but these emotions quickly vanished and with them any temptation to enjoy what she was offering him. Now he had no feelings of affection or desire for Inez, Baroness Leyresse, but he was in love with his painting of Phryne, the Greek courtesan whose crimes were forgiven because of her unrivalled beauty.

Like the judges of ancient times, Rory could not bring himself entirely to condemn Inez for being as she was, nor ignore the fact that she was the model for the best piece of work he had ever done. She had inspired him to produce even better than his best. If he felt anything at all for Inez, the woman, it was pity.

He disliked himself for not being more honest with her. But he dared not offend her. He knew that such was Inez's capacity for anger when she was aroused, she would be capable of destroying his work; perhaps turning him out of her home before he had completed the portrait. He feared that Inez, believing herself scorned, might well revenge herself by ruining the one thing dearest to him—his painting of her.

Rory refused to allow himself to think beyond the final completion of his work. He knew he must then hand the portrait over to the Baron. Deliberately he refrained from imagining what view the Baron would take of it. He, too, might destroy it and Rory could not tolerate the idea. It was easier to forget such a possibility and concentrate upon the finishing touches.

Unfortunately the weekend party was about to disrupt his efforts to do so. Tired though he was, he would have preferred to continue every day of the week until it was completed. But Inez had informed him that work must stop now until the guests had gone. For the next three days she expected Rory to behave as a normal guest in her house.

Rory now sat in the armchair in his room watching Alex and Knut unpacking the costumes from the wardrobe where they had been put away in readiness for the party. They were laughing and joking and he felt very much apart from them. It was not that they were deliberately excluding him from the fun. It was he, himself, who was unwilling to relinquish the creative urge uppermost in his mind. He knew he was being surly and unfriendly but, partly due to exhaustion, he was unable to overcome his disinterest.

Alex helped Knut don one of the monk's robes. She pulled the cowl over his head as he fastened the rope around his waist and stood back to survey the effect.

'It's wonderful!' she said, her voice that of an excited child. 'Look, Rory, Knut could really be that poor young man who was forced into a monastery.'

Knut's blue eyes twinkled.

'If I am the lay brother, then you shall be my novice, lady love. Come over here, my pretty darling, that I may kiss those lovely lips!'

He pounced on Alex and with mock romanticism, began to kiss her hands, her arms and then her face.

'For heaven's sake, stop behaving like an idiot!'

Rory's voice caused Alex and Knut to break apart and stare at him in amazement. Neither could find anything suitable to say and it fell to Rory to add on a more level note:

'You've no idea how ridiculous you look in that get-up, Knut, especially with Alex in jeans. The pair of you look . . . well, indecent!'

It was not what he really felt. The truth was

he had objected to the sight of Knut kissing Alex, albeit in fun. He was now as embarrassed as they by the boorishness of his remarks.

With an effort he forced himself to smile as he stood up.

'If you are both intent upon making yourselves look ridiculous, I suppose I'd better enter into the spirit of the thing and try on my robe. You put on yours, too, Alex. Maybe Knut will look better when all three of us are dressed up.'

Knut, with his usual sensitivity, had a very good idea what was wrong with Rory but kept his thoughts to himself.

'Go on, Alex! Go next door and change. You'll spoil the effect if you try to put that nun's habit over your jeans! And turn down that transistor, Rory. Pop music is hardly the right background for the *trois religieux*!'

Rory put on his habit. Despite his earlier mood, he grinned at his reflection.

'It's surprisingly effective!' he admitted. 'I don't think I'd recognise either of us easily. We'll get hot dancing in these.'

They were busy exchanging remarks about each other when the door opened and Alex came back into the room.

Rory's gasp was audible. He had been quite unprepared for the effect Alex created dressed as a nun. Her long fair hair was hidden by a wimple. Her young face, pale, perfectly

220

shaped, was extraordinarily virginal. Against the creamy white of the soft veil that framed her cheeks, her blue eyes looked even larger, innocently wide; her mouth a delicate curve. Instantly, he wanted to transmit her image to paper. From the folds of the cream-coloured habit, her two small hands appeared grasping a jet black rosary. She looked dedicated, untouchable—and immensely desirable.

His heart jolted. This was the girl he had already held in his arms on two occasions. He had kissed that mouth, seen in those eyes his own reflection. He knew the feel of that young body hidden now by the long folds of white cloth. She was both familiar to his senses and yet totally new. It was as if he were seeing her for the first time.

'Alex, you look quite lovely!' he said, moving towards her as if he could not help himself. 'I must paint you just the way you are at this moment. You are really beautiful!'

The colour raced into Alex's cheeks and she glanced nervously at Knut. He came to her rescue at once.

'And so say all of us!' he endorsed Rory's praise. 'You'll be the sensation of the evening in that garb, Alex. It's so very simple and yet quite bewitching. No wonder nuns usually wear black!'

The tension was eased and they all relaxed into laughter.

'I wasn't quite sure whether to carry the

rosary or not,' Alex said, still very conscious of Rory's eyes fastened upon her. 'I don't want to seem sacrilegious. At the same time, the black is a small relief from so much white.'

'You mustn't change a thing,' Rory said quickly. He was quite unable to take his eyes off her. He had forgotten his portrait of Phryne. His mind was filled with visions of his next painting. He would call it 'The Bride'. Indeed, no secular bride could be more virginal, more beautiful than Alex.

Ideas were pouring through his mind in a swift, creative urge. He remembered that he had once wanted to paint Alex as a Madonna in the blue dress she so often wore. He would do so later on. In complete contrast he would also enjoy painting her in her scruffy old jeans, hair blowing across her face, eyes laughing, the two Great Danes leaping at her side.

'You will model for me, won't you?' he asked anxiously.

Knut raised his eyebrows.

'I somehow doubt if your beautiful Baroness will give up her place to Alex without a fight,' he said dourly. 'If you intend to paint Alex, you'd do better to wait until we get home to England, Rory.' He suddenly saw his opportunity and added quickly, 'Alex and I were only saying this morning that we'd both like to leave here as soon as your portrait of Inez is completed. We'll take Alex back to England with us, Rory. What do you say?'

Rory nodded. A few more days would put the finishing touches to Phryne. He had suddenly lost all interest in his present creation. His mind was full of ideas for his next work. If he could not paint Alex here at the abbey he would be only too willing to return home if she was willing to go with him.

'Do you really mean you want to give up your job here?' he asked Alex. 'I thought you intended to stay for a year.'

'I'm free to go whenever I wish,' Alex told him. 'In one way I don't want to leave but I think Knut is right—there's an atmosphere here I can't explain which frightens me. Knut feels it too. There's really only one reason I can't bear the thought of going away . . . and that's Tristan. I expect you think it's silly of me to feel so sentimental about a dog, especially one that doesn't even belong to me.'

'Perhaps Inez could be persuaded to sell Tristan to you,' Rory suggested but without any real hope. 'I don't think she really cares much about him—only as an adornment, if you know what I mean . . . the fabulous Baroness flanked by her aristocratic beasts.'

Knut shot him a look of surprise. Usually it was he who made any derogatory or sarcastic remarks about Inez and Rory who defended her. Moreover, it was barely twenty-four hours since he had last suggested to Rory that they go back to England and Rory had flatly refused. Someone had changed his mind and

Knut did not doubt that it was Alex.

He felt a moment of regret. If Rory and Alex fell in love, so would end his last glimmer of hope that Alex might eventually turn to him. Realising from the first that Alex did not return his growing affection for her, he had kept a tight rein on his feelings. But now, as Alex and Rory looked at one another across the room, he knew he had been foolish ever to imagine that Rory might remain indifferent to Alex's charm.

For Alex's sake he was happy; happy for Rory, too, if this meant he had finally escaped from Inez's domination. He intended to do everything he could to smooth their way, for he had no doubt that when Inez reached the same conclusion about Rory as he had, she would leave no stone unturned to disrupt this newly discovered love.

Alex, meanwhile, was far from certain as to the meaning of the look she had glimpsed in Rory's eyes. She could not forget the memory of those sketches of Inez, nor quell the ugly suspicions that they had aroused. She did not question Rory's desire to paint her, but this could mean no more than an artist's appreciation of a new model for his next creation.

His unexpected willingness to leave Inez and return to England might have no significance beyond the fact that Inez certainly would not want Rory to paint her, Alex, at the abbey. Her confusion was heightened by her uncertainty of her feelings for Rory. She could not ignore the belief that he had been and perhaps still was Inez's lover. Alex wanted to believe the relationship was entirely a working one, but even if Rory was blind to the look in Inez's eyes when they rested on him, Alex could interpret their meaning, and Knut, too, had seen it, far sooner than she had.

She found herself considering now with a cold uneasiness that Knut might well be justified in his other criticism of Inez. He had called her 'evil', 'cruel' and 'ruthless'—adjectives she had thought wildly exaggerated and prejudiced. Spoilt and selfish were descriptions she had thought more fitting. Now she was not sure. Even Knut's crazy notion that Inez herself had poisoned poor Tristan no longer seemed ridiculous, although Alex had continued to argue fiercely with Knut that no one in their right mind would go to such shocking lengths to satisfy the vindictive side of their nature.

'You cannot judge Inez as you would a normal woman,' Knut had insisted. 'No one could thwart her and expect to get off lightly. And Tristan has continually shown a marked preference for you.'

'Not even Inez could want to kill her own dog!' Alex had insisted.

'She didn't kill him. She gave him just enough poison to make him ill. I think she knew just what she was doing. Let's face it, Alex, Tristan had a few rotten days of pain and misery and you were distraught. I believe she achieved exactly what she set out to do.'

Alex shivered despite the warmth of the heavy nun's habit. She was beginning to catch a little of Knut's anxiety; his fear that if they all stayed on at the abbey much longer, something awful would happen. If Knut were right about Tristan being deliberately poisoned because he showed too much affection for her, Tristan might be safer if she were far away from him. The dog followed her everywhere and, no matter how hard she tried to ignore him and thus force him to give his attention to his mistress once again, he steadfastly refused to go near Inez, even displaying a nervous inclination to sit as far away from her as possible.

Since Alex knew nothing of the brutal kick Inez had so recently given the dog, Tristan's fear of Inez puzzled her. Obviously, he could not have known who poisoned him so there was no clear reason why he should behave as he did. Alex could only guess that in the uncanny way dogs had of divining a human's thoughts, Tristan sensed Inez's mood, and was nervous because of it.

Alex had no real hope that when she left the abbey Inez would consider selling Tristan to her. Even if by some miracle Inez did agree to do so, it would mean separating the dog from his mate, Isolde. She would have to steel herself to say good-bye to him when the time came and try to forget him. No doubt he would forget her, too, and settle back into the life he had known before she arrived at the abbey.

Her happiness gave way to a feeling of depression.

'I'm going to change out of these clothes,' she announced. 'I'm afraid of getting this white fabric dirtied before the ball.'

Rory watched regretfully as Alex left the room. If he could have had his way, he would have taken her to the studio this very moment and begun his painting of her.

He saw Knut's eyes on him and laughed sheepishly.

'Okay, you win! Alex is a hundred times more attractive than Inez. I give you credit for noticing it before I did. But with Inez in the room, one tends not to see any other woman.'

For once Knut forbore to argue with his friend. As they removed their fancy dress costumes, he said quietly:

'Don't let anything hurt Alex, Rory. It has taken her a long while to get over the death of her David. She is very vulnerable, you know.'

Rory nodded.

'Don't worry, Knut. We'll get her safely away from this place as soon as I've finished Inez's portrait. I have to finish it. You do understand that, don't you?'

'Yes,' Knut agreed. 'But I'm holding you to

227

that promise of "as soon as possible". I think these next few days could be very unpleasant if you aren't careful, Rory. Don't do anything to antagonise Inez. I just don't trust her. Nor, come to that, do I care very much for the look in the Baron's eyes. I think he knows his wife is crazy about you and doesn't like it. Take care!'

The warning, dramatic though it was, did not sound in the least unreasonable. There was an atmosphere in the abbey, intangible, yet real enough. Everyone's nerves were strung just a little too tight. It was as if there were an electric current in the air and a wrong word or gesture might spark off an explosion.

Rory resolved to take Knut's advice and be as attentive to Inez as he could bring himself to be. He must not give the slightest indication of the way he felt about Alex. For everyone's sake, this was not the right time for him to admit, even to himself, that he believed he had fallen in love. That admission must wait until they were all back in England, safely out of harm's way.

*　　　*　　　*

It was seven o'clock. Downstairs in the brilliantly lit *grand salon*, the five-piece Italian orchestra had tuned their instruments and were awaiting the entrance of the first costumed guests. Already seated in the huge room were several of the elderly friends of the

Baron who had been detailed by Inez to form the panel of judges. Prizes were to be given for the best female and best male costumes. The thirty competitors were to descend the stairs, pass through the hall and into the *grand salon* in prearranged order. The musicians, meanwhile, would play music appropriate to the costume of the wearer.

These arrangements had been enthusiastically agreed by Inez's guests who now clustered on the landing at the top of the staircase, laughing and chattering in several languages.

Alex, Rory and Knut were to make their entrance last of all. This had been Rory's idea and he had managed to talk Inez into agreeing to it, despite the fact that she herself had wanted to create the grand finale.

The three of them, attired in their religious robes, were hidden behind the silk draperies in one of the alcoved window recesses in the front hall. From there they could watch the parade without themselves being seen.

The orchestra struck the first notes of music and the haunting melody of 'Greensleeves' spread outwards from the *salon* to the hall.

There was a murmur of voices from the top of the great staircase, a rustling of silken dresses and an audible gasp as people made way for the Baroness Inez Leyresse, dressed as Anne Boleyn. Slowly, regally, enjoying the sensation she was creating, Inez descended the stairs.

Her dress was of deep, emerald green velvet, the wide skirt encrusted with tiny brilliants. The low-cut neckline of the close-fitting bodice was edged with mink and wide bands of the same fur cuffed the sleeves. A tiny crown of brilliants topped her elaborately styled, red-gold hair. Real diamond and emerald rings flashed and sparkled on her white hands as she held up the heavy folds of her dress to aid her descent.

She looked fabulously beautiful—proud, stately, aristocratic. Such was the success of her posture and her costume that it would not have seemed ridiculous if someone knelt before her and kissed her hand.

'She is certain to win first prize in that get-up!' Knut said matter-of-factly. 'It's fantastic!'

Behind Inez came her husband, the Baron. He was less spectacularly but nonetheless flamboyantly dressed as the first Duke of Buckingham. His costume had obviously been copied from the painting in the National Gallery—white taffeta breeches looped high above the thighs, long white silk stockings and yellow shoes with jewelled buckles. There was a jewelled garter just below his left knee. His flame-coloured velvet cape was edged with white taffeta and there was a royal order around his neck in addition to the great loop of gold cord attached to his sword, from which hung two golden buckles.

His thin, gaunt face and hooked nose were outlined by a stiff lace collar; and on top of his head was a black velvet cap with three tiers of white plumes.

'It suits him very well!' Alex said as he passed by them in Inez's wake. 'It is almost as if he belonged to that era.'

The music changed to a 'gallop'. The Count and Countess Wienborg came slowly down the stairs. The plump Countess was disguised as a sixteenth-century horsewoman in a violet velvet habit, the long skirt looped. A violet beaver-trimmed hat perched on her head had a flowing veil. She carried a silver-handled whip and wore silver embroidered gauntlets. Over her long black riding boots were jewelled spurs.

Beside her, the Count was dressed as an eighteenth-century chevalier of the French court. He repeatedly took pinches of snuff and amused the onlookers with elaborate sneezes. He was only just recognisable beneath his white-powdered wig tied back with a black velvet bow. His pale blue satin knee breeches and coat did little to improve his robust figure and bandy legs.

Rory and Knut exchanged grins. They had met the Count on his last visit to the abbey and found him as amusing as his wife was dull.

But Alex was trying to establish the identity of the next contestant. The music had changed once more and was playing a slow march.

Down the stairs came a tall, thin man garbed in black from head to foot, a black cap covering his head, a black mask covering his face. In his hand he carried an executioner's axe which he raised theatrically as he passed one of the women. Her scream delighted the onlookers who gave the executioner a slow handclap as he walked in time to the death march across the hall into the *salon*.

'This is a fancy dress dance *par excellence*!' Knut remarked approvingly. 'I never thought the costumes would be so elaborate. We're going to look very drab and dull by comparison!'

A Chinese Mandarin in glittering orange brocade coat and trousers was followed by a grotesquely masked Hunchback of Notre Dame. The French film star made her entrance as Lucretia Borgia in a white satin dress cut so low that it revealed most of her ample bosom. Gustave, her Swedish companion, accompanied her as an Italian courtier.

One after another the guests made their way down the stairs to join the ever growing numbers in the *salon*. Soon, only a few remained on the landing and Alex, Rory and Knut slipped out of their hiding place. Using the back staircase, they took their place on the landing. When the music changed to a religious theme they moved forward in single file, heads lifted as if in exhaltation at a heavenly vision.

As they entered the *grand salon* there were audible gasps from the onlookers. The men gaped in undisguised admiration of Alex. The women shifted uneasily in their elaborate costumes, aware that none of their finery, the jewellery, the glitter could compare with the simple beauty of this young girl.

As Alex passed by them there was a moment when every woman present felt a passing breath of sadness for their lost youth, their lost innocence, for that ethereal side of their nature lost with childhood. The men, too, were sad. Wealth, success, power, background—none of these could help them realise that half-remembered dream of boyhood—to love and be loved by a girl like this. The ugliness of life itself had tainted each and every one of them, so that each knew, deep within himself, he could not touch Alex without passing on the taint of greed, of intrigue, of selfishness, of power. She was beauty beyond their reach.

The moment passed and the crowd began to applaud. The applause grew in volume as the three young people bent to kneel at the foot of the great high-backed chair where Inez was enthroned as Queen of the Ball. There could be little doubt now as to whom the judges would award first prize.

Inez's hand, as she held it out to be kissed in a parody of the era they were theatrically emulating, trembled with fury. Not even the warm look of admiration in Rory's eyes could soften her heart.

'How dare you wear those robes!' she said, her voice too low for anyone but the three of them to hear her. 'It is sacrilege!'

But no one else in the room seemed to think so. The three young people were instantly surrounded by congratulatory competitors and there was a surge of men demanding that Alex dance with them after dinner.

'I'm afraid Alex has inadvertently stolen Inez's thunder!' Knut whispered to Rory. 'I knew Alex would look fabulous but I never imagined she'd create quite such an effect. Inez is really angry, Rory. Can't you go and make your peace with her?'

Reluctantly, Rory moved away from the circle around Alex and went to Inez's side.

'You look fantastic in that costume,' he complimented her. 'If I had not painted you as Phryne, I would have wanted to paint you as Anne Boleyn just as you are tonight.'

A little of the tension eased from Inez's body when Rory spoke so admiringly. But she was not yet ready to forgive him.

'You have made me very angry!' she said. 'I understand now why you refused to tell me earlier about your fancy dress costumes. You knew very well I would refuse you permission to wear those clothes!'

Rory looked genuinely surprised.

'Honestly, that thought never crossed our minds,' he said. 'We wanted to surprise everyone, nothing more. How do you think I look as a monk?'

Inez's mouth curved into an ironic smile.

'Not your most seductive,' she said in a low voice. 'Somehow I do not think of you as a celibate.'

By the tone of her voice as much as by her choice of words, Rory knew that Inez had recovered from her anger. Relieved, he laughed.

'I'm a wolf in sheep's clothing,' he jested. 'But I mustn't monopolise you, Inez. I'm sure everyone else is wishing to congratulate you. Perhaps there'll be a chance for me to dance with you later?'

Inez felt her heart jolt with heady anticipation. Despite the bad beginning to this evening, it seemed now as if everything would yet turn out as she had planned.

'I will make sure that I am free to dance with you, Rory,' she said. 'Not just once, but many times.'

'That will be marvellous!' Rory said with false enthusiasm. Still further encouraged by this reply, Inez put her hand over his and squeezed it gently.

'Later, tonight, I may dance *for* you!' she whispered. 'You have never seen the flamenco danced, have you? I have a Spanish costume and I will perform just for you, Rory.'

He nodded, trying not to show the embarrassment he was feeling. He would have had to be both deaf and blind not to understand the message transmitted by Inez's eyes and her tone of voice. The evening now threatened to be a thoroughly difficult one. He wanted to be with Alex; to dance with her as often as he could. The very last person he wished to be with was his hostess. He was going to require all his concentration and tact to avoid Inez's advances without appearing rude or indifferent.

'I think your husband is objecting to the way I am monopolising you,' he said by way of excuse. It was true enough that the Baron was staring at them. 'I'll go and make polite noises to your guests, Inez.'

Inez frowned.

'If I don't care what Bernard thinks, why should you, Rory? It is my party and I shall behave as I choose!'

Nevertheless, she did not try to detain him. The evening had only just begun and she and Rory could be together far less obviously later when the lights were turned down low and the dancing started. Bernard was indeed staring at her and, despite the defiance she expressed to Rory, she was aware of the danger of provoking her husband too far or too publicly.

The champagne flowed freely as the servants circulated the room with trays of glasses. Rory found himself cornered by the French film star. Alex was being monopolised by the young Swede, Gustav. Watching Alex smiling up at the tall blond boy, Rory felt his mood take an even deeper plunge downwards. He would be lucky to have even a few dances with her. She looked so enchanting, he knew every man in the room would be eager for her company. He did not blame them but blamed himself for having been blind to Alex's attractions for so long and wasting all his chances to interest her in himself. Knut had hinted on several occasions that Alex liked him; might even be falling in love with him. And he, wrapped up in his painting, had foolishly ignored her.

When dinner was finally announced, he made his way quickly to Alex's side. Ignoring the Count who was about to escort her into the dining room and the Swede still hovering on her other side, Rory took her arm determinedly and said:

'You're sitting with me, Alex!'

She looked up at him and smiled.

'Well, don't look so angry about it!' she teased him gently. 'I'd be delighted!'

He relaxed at once and smiled back at her.

'Good girl!' he said softly. He began to walk with her through the hall to the dining room. 'I'm sorry if I barked at you. Truth is I had a difficult session earlier on with Inez and then I saw you being charming to our dear Gustav and . . . well, I suppose I was jealous. Forgive me?'

Alex felt a rush of happiness engulf her. This was a new Rory, possessive, attentive, caring. He wanted to be with her as much as she wanted to be with him.

Because of the large number of people, the meal was laid out as a buffet, from which guests could help themselves to whatever delicacy took their fancy. There were huge lobsters, vast Mediterranean prawns decoratively and colourfully arranged around cut-glass bowls of rich yellow mayonnaise. There were oysters, fresh salmon in aspic, whole crabs. Two chefs stood carving turkeys and joints of English sirloin, venison, veal and pork. In the centre of the table lay a whole roast suckling pig.

'There is enough food here to feed Inez's guests three times over!' Alex whispered to Rory. 'I suppose the staff will eat the leftovers.'

Waiters moved among the diners with trays of red and white wines. The South American group had taken over from the Italian one and played quietly in the background. The noise of conversation rose in volume. At one end of the room Inez stood toying with her food as her eyes strayed continually to Rory and Alex. She refused the wines but continued to drink champagne, her white skin flushed with alcohol, her eyes brilliant. The automatic smiles which she gave to those who addressed her held no hint of the dangerous mood she was now in.

With ill-concealed impatience, she waited while the table was cleared and the gâteaux, fruits and other desserts were brought in by the servants. She was complimented again and again on the magnificence of this banquet, but for the first time in her life, she was totally uncaring of her reputation as a hostess. Only one thing mattered now—Rory. She had waited for him long enough.

Her head seemed to be on fire, her mind split into two compartments. Whilst murmuring polite replies to those around her, the voice in her head carried on its own conversation. 'Why don't you turn your head and look at me, Rory?' the voice insisted. 'I am here, waiting for your glance! You must know how much I want you. I need you. *Look at me!*'

But he had no eyes for anyone but Alex at his side.

Coffee, brandy and liqueurs were served in the hall. The guests began to filter through to the *grand salon* where the orchestra was already playing dance music. It was ten o'clock and the evening was about to begin.

Inez felt as if her whole body were charged with electricity. It had been her custom at other parties she had given in the past, to start the dancing with Bernard. But tonight she wanted that first dance with Rory, no matter how Bernard resented it; no matter what the other women thought. None would dare to speak their thoughts to Bernard or to her and Inez did not care one jot how they gossiped among themselves. Let them say Inez Leyresse had taken this young boy as her lover! Their suspicions would, she hoped, soon be well-founded.

As if a sixth sense had made him aware of his wife's intention, the Baron approached her. He put his hand on her arm. His fingers were cold despite the heat of the room.

'Shall we take the floor, my dear?' he asked.

Inez's mind spun. She looked at her husband blankly.

'Shall we begin the dancing?' he said again, quietly but firmly.

'I have not finished my coffee, Bernard.'

There were only the dregs left in the bottom of her coffee cup. Inez saw his eyes go down and quickly turned her head away as that steely green glance came back to her face.

'I think we should commence the dancing,' he said, his voice implacable.

'In a minute!' she said irritably. 'Don't fuss, Bernard. I do not wish to dance yet.'

'But I think we should.' The Baron's voice was ice-cold. 'Our guests are becoming restless.'

Inez hesitated. Instinct warned her that this was no battle of wills over a dance. Bernard had somehow guessed her desire. He was laying down a direct order. To deny him was to admit her disregard for him.

She glanced quickly around the room. Rory was standing talking to Knut. Alex was not with him. In another five minutes she might not have so good an opportunity. If she danced with her husband now, when she returned, Rory might have found himself a partner.

'I'm sorry, Bernard, but I really don't wish to dance just yet. Why don't you invite the Countess to partner you? She would be delighted by the compliment.'

The Baron made no reply. He walked away from her as if her rebuff was of little consequence to him. If he felt insulted, he gave no visible sign of it. Somewhat to Inez's surprise, he approached the Countess Weinborg and bowed over her hand. A moment later, they moved off together towards the dance floor.

Inez let out her breath in a sigh of relief to be rid of him. But she could not in all decency follow him too quickly onto the floor. Nor could she afford to wait too long lest Rory invite someone else to dance. Throwing caution to the winds, she made her way over to him. With a curt nod to Knut, she said to Rory:

'The first dance is nearly over, but I am holding the next one free for you.'

Rory had no alternative but to appear delighted. In fact he was only waiting for Alex to return from feeding the dogs—something she had not had time to do before dinner because of the fancy dress parade—in order to take her onto the dance floor.

Knut, grinning secretly, tactfully removed himself. The stiffness of his leg might prohibit him from dancing with Alex but at least it had the advantage of excusing him from dancing with Inez!

'I wish you would change those clothes!' Inez said to Rory. 'I prefer your own. I find those monk's robes disagreeable to my mood.'

'But you look perfect in your dress!' Rory parried skilfully. 'I am sure your gypsy costume cannot do you the same justice!'

Inez smiled, her good humour restored.

'Ah, but you shall see, Rory. For all those hours you have studied me so closely, you still do not know all about me. I can be many women, Rory. You will discover this is so.'

Rory's growing embarrassment at this kind of verbal badinage with Inez made him feel that even the dance floor would be preferable. He suggested they go through to the other room and courteously took her arm. Beneath his fingers her flesh was burning hot and he could feel the trembling of a muscle in her forearm. Her state of high tension communicated itself to him and he felt even more uneasy.

The first dance ended and the notes of a soft Italian love song heralded a tango. Rory and Inez moved onto the floor just as the Baron and the Countess came off it. The two

242

couples passed each other within inches. The expression on the Baron's face imprinted itself on Rory's mind and remained there as Inez melted into his arms. The man's eyes had been a steely grey-green; his mouth had been twisted in a grimace that was a parody of a smile. It was a cruel, ugly face, divested of its customary hauteur, its delicate aristocracy, its intellect. It was full of unmistakable malignance.

Inez saw it, too. Unlike Rory, she knew very well the reason for it. But she did not care. For the first time since Rory had kissed her in the studio, she was back in his arms, his body close to hers, his cheek only a breath away from her lips. She felt sick with desire. Her legs were trembling so violently she was unsure if she would be able to follow his steps.

As she stumbled, Rory instinctively held her more tightly. Sighing, she relaxed against him and he felt her cheek pressing against his.

He tried to ease away but Inez murmured:

'Don't be afraid, Rory. What does it matter who sees us.'

Rory's heart plunged. Knut was being proved right in all his predictions. Inez was in love with him. Hers was not the behaviour of an idle flirt. Nor was she merely amusing herself. She was deadly serious.

'Inez, please!' He managed to draw his face away from hers. 'You don't understand. I'm not afraid of people seeing us. It's just that . . .

I don't share your feelings. You are a very attractive woman but . . .'

'But you are not in love with me!' Rory only just caught the words, spoken in a low husky voice. 'But that doesn't matter. I love you, Rory, and that is enough. Once I have shown you how I can love, you will never want another woman. Trust me, Rory. I will make you love me!'

'You're out of your mind,' Rory found himself whispering back. 'You have a husband, Inez. Besides, I . . .'

She gave him no time to explain. She broke in:

'You have never thought about us the way I have, Rory. It is a new idea to you and you are a little shocked.' She gave an excited laugh. 'You need time to become used to the thought. When you do, you will know as I do that Bernard does not matter. Nothing matters but you and me together. No, don't say anything now. I will give you time. Like the Fairy Godmother, I will give you until midnight. Look at me, Rory. Now and all evening long, look at me and imagine what our loving would be like. Think of those drawings you made of me. Watch me when I am dancing for you. Then decide!'

Her voice was bordering on the hysterical and Rory began to wonder if she had had too much to drink, if this could be making Inez so hopelessly indiscreet; and blind, too, to the way he felt about her. Or to the way he did not feel about her. If there had ever been a time when he had felt desire for her, it had long since gone. He wanted nothing to do with her. She not only frightened him by her revelations, but she repelled him, too. His embarrassment rendered him speechless.

Mercifully, the dance came to an end. Inez tried to persuade him to remain on the floor but Rory insisted it would be carrying indiscretion too far.

Reluctantly, Inez agreed to return to her guests. She refused to consider that Rory really did not want to dance with her. Emotion held her in its grip and because she so desperately wished it, she succeeded in convincing herself that Rory had actually promised an assignation at midnight.

Rory escaped into the crowd. Catching sight of Alex, he grabbed hold of her and took her onto the dance floor. He was so unnerved by Inez's behaviour he was about to tell Alex of his ordeal. But then she smiled up at him, a sweet, radiant smile, and he found it impossible to speak of Inez. He did not want to wipe that look of innocence from Alex's eyes; nor let the sordid image of Inez cloud his own thoughts. He preferred to forget Inez, to bury his face in the fragrant silkiness of Alex's hair and to feel her slim young body melting in his arms. It was as if he had come out of a nightmare into a beautiful dream.

245

'Are you happy?' he asked, urgently wanting her to be so.

'Of course I am!' Alex replied. 'I am having the most wonderful time.'

She wished she could tell Rory that he was the reason for her happiness; that it was only because of his presence that the fancy dress parade had been so exciting; only because he had wanted her beside him at dinner that the meal had become a fairy banquet; only because he was dancing with her that her cup of happiness was full to the brim.

'I'm happy, too,' Rory told her. He had believed the evening ruined, after that unnerving dance with Inez. But now it did not seem in the least important. He was holding Alex in his arms and wanting nothing more than to go on dancing with her all night long.

It was Alex who broke the spell after three successive dances. They must, she said, make sure that poor Knut was not all alone. However, when they finally located him, it was to find him talking animatedly to a Swiss lady who had spent a few holidays in Norway not far from Knut's home.

'We need not have worried about him,' Rory said, as the look of concern left Alex's face. But he loved her the more for her thoughtfulness.

They went to sit on the stairs where they could see the whole panorama of guests but where they had an illusion of privacy. Rory held tightly to Alex's hand. She leant back against him and he put an arm around her shoulders.

'We sat this way the night Tristan was so ill,' Rory reminded her. 'It seems ages ago now although it's scarcely any time since it happened. You know, Alex, I've been an awful fool.'

'In what way?' Alex asked. She wondered if Rory could hear the rapid beating of her heart.

He gave a sheepish grin.

'Well, wasting so much time,' he said. 'I mean, I was so wrapped up in my painting, I never stopped to think about the more important things in my life.'

Alex drew in her breath.

'Isn't your career the most important thing, then?' she asked. 'It's right that it should be.'

'No, it isn't!' Rory said. 'I don't want success at the price of personal happiness. People are more important than paintings and you are more important to me than my portrait of Inez. But I've only just realised it, Alex. I've been an idiot.'

Alex gave a deep sigh. Rory could not have said anything to make her happier.

'Knut and I did wonder once or twice if it was your painting or your model which was keeping you so enthralled,' she said mischievously. 'I'm glad it wasn't Inez!'

Suddenly Rory found himself able to talk about Inez—to tell Alex what had happened

247

and how appalled he had been to find himself caught up in the situation.

'I know it's probably silly of me,' he said, 'but I'm honestly a bit scared, Alex. Inez doesn't seem to want to take any hint I throw out that I'm not interested. It isn't easy, rejecting a woman like Inez. Apparently the fact that she is married doesn't seem to bother her in the least.'

'Poor Inez!' Alex murmured. 'It must be horrible for her, being married to a man she doesn't love and loving another man who doesn't care about her.'

Rory tightened his arm around her.

'I imagine you're the only girl in the world who could pity Inez,' he said. 'You've every right to dislike her. Maybe you are right, Alex, and I ought to feel sorry for her. But at the moment, I can only feel resentful that I allowed her to monopolise me and keep me from you.'

'Not all the time,' Alex reminded him. 'We had those marvellous days, you and Knut and I, when Inez was in Paris.'

'And our brief moment in that horrible cellar!' Rory agreed laughing. 'I wonder what the old monks and abbots would say if they saw the revelry going on this evening!'

'Don't!' Alex said. 'I don't want to think of ghosts and curses and evil. I'm too happy.'

Gently, Rory turned her face towards him and kissed her.

'Me, too!' he said. 'And this is only the start! We're going to have some marvellous times together from now on.'

The next few hours passed in a haze of contentment for Alex. Rory was either dancing with her, holding her close against him, or sitting with her on the stairs as they sipped champagne, his arm around her shoulders. She was blissfully ignorant of the effect their behaviour was having on Inez. Rory noticed but deliberately blinded himself to the consequences. When Inez danced near them, he purposefully buried his face in Alex's hair, avoiding Inez's eyes. When he and Alex needed a rest from their exertions on the dance floor, he waited until Inez was looking elsewhere before slipping away to their secluded seat in the semi-darkness of the staircase.

He was determined that nothing and no one should spoil the evening. He wanted to keep the starry-eyed radiance in Alex's eyes untarnished. Her happiness overflowed and enlivened his own growing excitement. He did not try to analyse his feelings. If this was falling in love, he thought, then he was content to fall. He had never been so happy or so convinced that the girl beside him was utterly right for him, the perfect companion, the most beautiful and charming woman in the world. Her response to him was without artifice— total, warm, giving. Rory sensed that she too

249

had abandoned herself to the evening.

At midnight, a roll of drums heralded the serving of refreshments. This was to be followed by an announcement by the Baron of the winners of the fancy dress competition and the distribution of the prizes. There was a brief lull in the general noise of conversation whilst a search was made for the Baron.

When eventually he was located, he looked strangely flushed and dishevelled.

'Wonder what he's been up to!' Rory said to Alex. 'He looks as if he's been drinking and that's not like our Baron—the most abstemious of men as a rule!'

The Baron's speech did indeed sound a little slurred as he took his place in front of the microphone. Beside him, one of the servants had placed a table on which lay a dozen or so beautifully wrapped packages.

With suitable accompaniment from the orchestra, the names of the prize winners were announced. There was enthusiastic applause from the onlookers as the first prize was awarded to the nun and the two monks.

Rory held Alex's hand as they went forward to receive their gifts. Knut grinned delightedly.

'I told you we'd be a sensation!' he muttered as they walked away with their prizes. 'But did you see Inez's face, Rory?' he added as they went to the stairs to unwrap their packages. 'She was shooting murderous glances at you. Have you been neglecting her?'

Rory's reply was inaudible as a fresh round of applause broke out for the second prize winner—the Hunchback of Notre Dame. A third and fourth prize were awarded followed by a consolation prize for the most humorous costume. And finally, the Baron announced there was an award for the most beautiful dress. This, he told the assembly, he knew everyone would agree should go to Inez.

There was a gasp of admiration as the Baron presented his wife with a tiny unwrapped leather jewel case. The lid was open to reveal a huge ruby and diamond ring.

'For those of you ladies who might be interested,' the Baron's voice rose above the envious cries of the women, 'the ring is of unusual antiquity. It is said to be an exact copy of one owned by Lucrezia Borgia and has a hidden cavity for poison!'

There was another gasp from the guests at Inez's elbow and they drew back instinctively. Inez's face was pale and inscrutable.

'However,' the Baron continued in an amused tone of voice, 'the poison has been suitably replaced with my wife's favourite perfume so there is no need for anyone to feel apprehensive!'

Knut's blue eyes were no longer smiling.

'I believe this is the Baron's way of letting Inez know he knows she poisoned Tristan,' he said quietly. 'Very subtle! Very devious!'

'Surely not,' Alex said nervously. 'I still can't

believe she did so. You don't believe it either, do you, Rory?'

'I don't know,' Rory answered truthfully. 'And what's more, I don't want to think about it. Let's open our prizes.'

For Alex, there was a magnificent bottle of Chanel scent; for the two boys, boxes of expensive Havana cigars which, as neither of them smoked, they said they would give away as Christmas presents.

The Baron announced that the dancing would now continue. Inez edged away from the circle of admirers around her and with her head held high, walked to the stairs. Her eyes flashing brilliantly, her cheeks flushed, she stood at the foot of the staircase and looked up at the trio above her.

'Rory,' she said imperiously. 'I think this is our dance.'

It was not a request but an order. Rory, prodded surreptitiously by Knut, had no chance to refuse. He rose to his feet and reluctantly went down the stairs.

*　　　*　　　*

Inez, like her husband, had been drinking steadily throughout the evening. Though only her heightened colour betrayed the fact, inwardly the alcohol had robbed her of the last vestiges of caution.

As Rory took her onto the dance floor, she

said accusingly:

'You have been avoiding me all evening, Rory. No, don't speak. I know you only wished to be tactful. But Bernard has gone to bed. He left after his little prize-giving ceremony. There is nothing to fear now. No one is watching us.'

She pressed closer against him and felt his resistance.

'Don't be afraid, *chéri!*' she said in a low passionate tone. 'I will take care of you. I will love you as no other woman could. You know I'm in love with you, don't you, Rory?'

'Inez, please . . .' he began, but she would not allow him to speak.

'I have waited so long for this night,' she interrupted him as if his replies were unnecessary. 'In a few minutes I shall dance for you—*just for you*, Rory. Then we will escape. We will go to the studio—no one will see us there. Then, at last, we can be together. We will become lovers.'

'Inez, you know that isn't possible. Besides, I . . .'

'You are afraid of love, Rory. Do not be. We were destined for each other. I know that now. All my life I have waited for you. I have never truly loved another man. Fate knew that one day you would come to me. We cannot fight against our destiny.'

'You're crazy, Inez!' Rory said, but she merely laughed.

'It is true I am a little mad—mad with love

253

for you. That is as it should be, Rory. Nothing matters but love. You will see. Trust me.'

She broke away from his arms, still laughing.

'I will go and change now into my other costume. I will dance for you. Then you will see that I am not Queen Anne Boleyn whom you must treat with respect, but a gypsy woman waiting for your love.'

Rory stood in the centre of the dance floor watching in horror as Inez ran across to the musicians and spoke to the leader. He saw the guitarist nod and then Inez hurried away up the staircase. She did not seem to notice Alex or Knut still sitting there.

Rory began to walk towards them but stopped halfway. If Inez really was a little insane, and she sounded crazy enough to him, he did not want Alex involved in any embarrassing scene that might ensue. He decided to wait by the dance floor and see what would happen. At least, with so many of her guests present, there must be a limit to any indiscretion Inez might commit.

High above Rory's head in the picture gallery hidden by shadows, the Baron also waited. He had seen the look on his wife's face as she danced with Rory; and he knew her too well to believe that she would relinquish her young admirer to Alex without a fight. He had noticed Rory dancing and sitting out with the girl and seen Inez's eyes continually searching the room for the young couple.

Inez had been unwise to fling down the gauntlet by refusing the opening dance with him. Her second indiscretion was her selection of Rory for her first partner. Now, when she thought he was no longer observing her, he would watch from his place of concealment just how far his wife intended to go in her attempts to seduce her reluctant Englishman.

CHAPTER ELEVEN

At the first click of the castanets, the dancers drifted off the floor, aware that something was about to happen. When Inez made her appearance, few realised that the woman in the scarlet and black Spanish costume was their hostess. They assumed a member of the South American band was providing a cabaret interlude.

The beat of the guitar joined with the castanets which Inez held above her head and clicked in a slow steady rhythm. Her body, swathed in the tight scarlet dress with its deep border of tiered black frills, undulated gracefully in time to the throbbing of the guitar. Her high-heeled, black-strapped shoes, revealing tiny slender ankles, began to tap the floor.

Head held high, her dark eyes blazing with

excitement, she made her way towards Rory. The beat of the music remained slow but with a steady, near imperceptible, increase of tempo. The guitarist followed Inez, a few feet away. Some of the guests began to clap in time to the music but they stopped as the speed of Inez's castanets and the tapping of her feet quickened.

Even for those who did not know the meaning of the dance, there was no mistaking its expression of passion, of love. There could be no mistaking either, that Inez was dancing for Rory. Several of the men were amused, believing that Inez was merely teasing the young man who stood watching with more embarrassment than pleasure. One or two were envious, wishing Inez had chosen to honour them. But there were others who glanced nervously over their shoulders looking for the absent Baron, wondering how their host would take this exhibition of sensuous provocation directed towards a young and handsome man.

Inez neither knew nor cared what they thought. She was completely caught up in the wild stirring music to which her body responded with all the pent-up feelings of the past weeks. She knew that she had never danced better, and was inspired by the sight of Rory's eyes watching her and the excitement she was evoking. The atmosphere of the room was electric with tension.

Up in the gallery, the Baron's face paled. Hands and legs trembling, eyes narrowed to thin slits of green glass, he stumbled away, no longer able to endure the scene of his defeat. Certain of his wife's intent, he now took for granted Rory's susceptibility, believing that no man could resist such a woman. He felt no anger towards Rory. His every emotion was concentrated on the determination to extract revenge upon the woman he loved. He had no other thought, no other wish, but this.

Had he waited a few minutes longer, he would have seen that he was totally mistaken in his judgement. Just before the flamenco reached its fiery climax, Rory succeeded in breaking free from the near hypnotic trance in which he had been gripped since Inez's dance began. He knew that he must get away quickly, even if leaving before the music stopped would be insulting to Inez. She was only a yard or two away from him now, her body swaying, eyes flashing, every movement a deliberate provocation, a challenge, an invitation. To go before the finale was cruel but the only way he could think of to tell her that her behaviour, far from being welcome, was an embarrassment to him. The time for prevarication and politeness was gone.

Taking a deep breath, he moved surreptitiously backwards into the crowd behind him. Deliberately, he refrained from looking at Inez's shocked face. He walked quickly past the standing couples and made his way to the stairs.

Knut and Alex stared down at him. They, too, had been watching the dance and were fully aware of Rory's dilemma.

'Tell Inez I've had to go to bed!' he said to Knut. 'Say I've got food poisoning—anything you like. Forgive me, Alex, I'll explain tomorrow.'

He hurried upstairs and into his bedroom, locking the door behind him. Sitting down on the bed, he tried to calm himself. One thing only was certain—that he could no longer remain at the abbey. Knut was right and the sooner they all left the better. His painting did not matter. Quite possibly after tonight, Inez would have lost all interest in it. He had publicly insulted her and it would be surprising if she did not turn him out tomorrow. That might make it easier than having to explain to the Baron their sudden decision to leave.

The dance had now ended. Inez paused only briefly to acknowledge the thunderous applause that followed before she hurried after Rory. Still in her world of make-believe, she found an explanation for his sudden departure. She told herself that Rory had intended no insult but had rushed away towards the end of her performance only in order to be at the studio to await her. She convinced herself that her dancing had had the desired effect and that he was as wildly

258

impatient to possess her as she was to possess him.

When Knut barred her way up the staircase, she tried to push him aside. He said firmly:

'Rory asked me to tell you he is not at all well, *Madame*. He thinks it may have been the crab—food poisoning. I'm afraid he has been very sick and has gone to bed.'

Inez stared at the Norwegian uncertainly. For a moment her confidence flagged. Then her face cleared. She smiled. Naturally Rory would have felt it necessary to give his friends an excuse for his absence. Rory would be in the studio waiting for her.

'I'm so sorry he is unwell!' she said. 'Please give him my sympathy. Now if you will excuse me, I must go and change.'

Knut sat down heavily beside Alex, his face comic with astonishment.

'I don't understand it! Inez didn't seem in the least upset by Rory's defection,' he said to Alex. 'I just don't believe it. Nobody could mistake the way she was dancing for Rory. It was an open invitation. I'm ready to swear she wasn't teasing him. She was in deadly earnest. And I'll swear he was running away . . .'

He broke off, seeing the expression on Alex's face.

'Now, Alex, forget whatever is going through your mind. Inez may be beautiful and I'll grant her flamenco was the most seductive dance I've ever seen, but Rory isn't interested.

259

There's no assignation, I'm sure of it. What's more, I'll go up to his room and prove it, if you want.'

'No!' Alex's voice was sharp with dismay. 'I don't really believe it myself, Knut. It's just that, well, I wouldn't altogether blame him if . . .'

'Yes you would and so would I. Rory knows as well as we do that Inez is evil. She is, Alex— a dangerous, evil woman. Anyway, judging by the way you and Rory were dancing tonight, I'd say it is you Rory wants, not her. And I don't blame him for that!'

With an effort, Alex smiled. She could not forget the radiant confidence she had seen in Inez's eyes as she had turned away from Knut to continue up the stairs.

'I hope you're right,' she said.

But despite the warmth of the atmosphere she shivered and allowed herself the comfort of holding tightly to Knut's hand.

*   *   *

It was Alex who first gave the alarm that the dogs were missing. They had been shut up during the party and Alex and Knut had let them out for a last run before going to bed soon after Rory. But the following morning, when Alex went down to let them out, the gun room was empty.

She made a quick search of the *salons*. Old Gilbert was directing the servants who were cleaning up the rooms before the guests came down for breakfast. No one had seen Tristan or Isolde.

Alex widened her search. It was possible one of the servants, brought up to the abbey for the weekend and unused to the household routine, had let the dogs out into the grounds. She hurried outside. The skies were a heavy leaden grey and the air unusually quiet. Glancing up at the sky, Alex shivered. A storm was brewing. Even now the first few flakes of snow were drifting down onto her uncovered head and settling in her hair.

She stood in the courtyard calling the dogs. There was no answering bark from Tristan. She called several times more before returning to the abbey to begin another search of the ground floor rooms. Two of the guests, Gustav and the Count, had come downstairs for breakfast. Half-heartedly, they joined in the hunt.

Alex began to feel seriously worried for the first time. The dogs were too large to escape notice for long.

With great unwillingness, but feeling it her duty to do so, she sent word to Inez via her personal maid, Denise.

Within a few minutes Denise returned with the message that Alex 'was not to be so stupid—the dogs must be somewhere!'

'She was very angry with me for disturbing her,' Denise said, shrugging. 'My lady is in one of her very bad moods. I shall have trouble today. You also, *Mademoiselle*, if you do not find the dogs. She will pick on anyone when she is in this kind of temper.'

Alex ran upstairs and knocked on Rory's door. He was still fast asleep but opened his eyes at the opening of the door and was fully awake by the time Alex had explained what was wrong. He dressed and joined her downstairs as quickly as possible.

'Don't get in a flap,' he said reasonably. 'Two great beasts like Tristan and Isolde cannot remain hidden for long. We'll soon find them, darling.'

The endearment was a momentary comfort to Alex. But as the minutes and then the hours went by and Tristan and Isolde gave no sign of their whereabouts, Alex was near to tears. Rory, too, looked worried.

'Suppose Knut was right and Inez did try to poison Tristan the other night! Suppose this time she has succeeded!' she said miserably.

The same thought had crossed Rory's mind but he made light of it.

'Even if Inez had been crazy enough to do that, we would have found the bodies by now,' he said reassuringly. 'The dogs must be somewhere. We'll search again.'

He felt tired and nervy. Late last night Knut had come to his room and reiterated his opinion that they should all leave the abbey at once. They had agreed finally that they must approach Inez as soon as she appeared the following morning and announce that all three of them would be leaving as soon as possible. Unfortunately, the absence of the dogs had prevented them furthering their plan to spend the morning helping Alex to pack.

A search of the cellars proved fruitless.

'Where *can* they be?' Alex asked helplessly. 'With more than seventy people in the abbey, I don't see how the dogs can stay lost for so long. None of the guests or the servants have seen them since yesterday. They must be outdoors somewhere.'

'Perhaps there's an outhouse of some sort where we haven't yet searched,' Knut suggested. 'Let's go and talk to Gilbert. He has lived here for years. He may know some place we haven't thought of looking.'

The old man listened to their account of all the places they had tried. He shook his head.

'There is nowhere else,' he told them. 'Only the old ice-house and in any case the doors would be shut and barred. The dogs could not get in even if they tried.'

'All the same, we'll look there,' Rory said at once. 'What is an ice-house, anyway?'

As they put on their outdoor clothes once more, Alex explained that the ice-house had been built centuries ago by the monks. It was an ancient method of refrigerating food. The method was simple but effective. A hole was excavated in the mountainside to form a store house. Blocks of ice were placed around the walls and covered in sawdust.

'The Baron explained how it worked one day last summer,' Alex told the boys. 'He said it was a very efficient way of keeping food fresh in the summer months. In the old days, there might be whole carcasses of deer, for instance, which would need preserving and the ice-house was the perfect place. The monks had to walk to the valley to buy fish and other perishables so they stored as much as they could in the same way we use a deep-freeze nowadays.'

None of them expected to find the dogs in such a place, although it was just possible if the doors had been left open they could have gone inside for shelter. It was snowing heavily and any paw marks in the grounds would long since have been covered by the thick white flakes.

The double wooden doors of the ice-house were secured from the outside by a heavy iron bar.

'There is really no point in trying to open up the place,' Knut said. But at that moment, his eye caught a sliver of white on one of the doors. The outside bark of the wooden support had been peeled off—recently, too, judging by the freshness of the scarring.

Rory had noticed it, too. He and Knut looked at one another in dismay. The same thought lay in both their minds. If the dogs had been poisoned and hidden inside, Alex

264

must not be allowed to see the corpses.

'We're wasting time just standing here,' Alex said. She began to lift the heavy iron bar. 'Come on, help me!' she cried. 'We've got to make sure they aren't in here!'

Rory took a deep breath, inwardly praying, as was Knut, that he'd been letting his imagination run away with him. Of course the ice-house would be empty.

But the iron bar lifted easily and the two doors swung open, impeded only by the soft snow piling up outside. Alex pushed past the boys into the dark interior before either of them could stop her. Then she tripped and fell.

'Oh, my God!' Rory whispered as he and Knut hurriedly pulled Alex to her feet. He pushed her aside and knelt down. In the darkness it was impossible to see much, but enough light filtered through the doors for him to identify the two inert bodies as they lay, one upon the other.

'Help me, Knut!' he said and began to half-lift, half-drag the uppermost dog towards the doorway.

It was Isolde. There was no sign of injury to her lifeless body—only raw, red patches on each paw where she had obviously tried to scratch down the door. There was no froth at her mouth, nothing to indicate poisoning. The body was stiff. Aghast, Knut whispered:

'I think she froze to death!'

After one horrified glance at Isolde's body, Alex rushed back inside. Frantically, she lifted and tugged at Tristan's body. Her eyes were filled with tears and she closed them, unable to bear what she knew must face her.

Rory's voice caused her to open them again.

'I think his heart is still beating!' he was shouting. 'He's still alive, I'm sure of it. Quickly, Knut, help me!'

He tore off his anorak and laid it on the snow. Then with Knut's assistance, they rolled Tristan on to the improvised stretcher.

'You go on and find a warm place to put him,' Rory ordered Alex. 'Get some brandy, and some hot water bottles. And phone the vet. Hurry!'

As Alex ran off, he and Knut struggled to lift the dog. Tristan weighed about a hundred and twenty pounds and for a moment Rory was unsure if the cloth of his anorak would support its burden. But the material held firm. Slowly, laboriously, they struggled back through the thick snow towards the abbey, the body of the unconscious dog swaying between them.

Alex had raised the alarm. As they approached the drive several men came out to assist them. Four more went to collect Isolde. But rescue for her had obviously come too late. There was no spark of life visible and the brandy Rory tried to force down her throat had no effect.

Tristan, however, was still breathing, though so slowly that for long minutes it seemed as if he, too, were dead. But Alex insisted his heart was still beating and eventually they all saw him draw a slow, shallow breath. His body was ice cold. They were afraid of putting him too close to the fire in case the rate of returning circulation was harmful or painful for him. But they covered him with blankets and put hot water bottles around him.

When Inez appeared, the three of them were grouped around Tristan as he lay near the stove in the boiler room. Her face was ashen. She looked ill. Knut thought inconsequently that she also looked quite old. She was clearly shocked.

'Someone told me Isolde was dead.' She broke off and knelt on the dusty floor beside the dog, disregarding the delicate fabric of her dress.

'Tristan!'

Although she only spoke the one word, her tone was so distressed that Knut seriously doubted that this terrible deed had been perpetrated by Inez. But someone had locked the dogs in the ice-house, and if not Inez, who else was crazy enough to do such a horrifying thing?

'Alex has telephoned the vet,' Rory said. 'He'll be here soon.'

Inez opened her mouth as if about to speak, but then her lips closed to a thin, tight line.

She stood and without one glance at Rory, said to Alex:

'Tell Monsieur Govin he is to do everything he can to save Tristan.'

Then she turned on her heel and left them, her dress dusty, a smudge of dirt across one cheek, her face paler than ever.

'I don't understand it!' Knut said. 'I am certain she was responsible for Tristan's last illness, but this time . . . he broke off, shrugging his shoulders in perplexity.

Alex looked at him uncomprehendingly.

'You can't honestly believe someone deliberately locked the dogs in that ice-house intending them to die?' Her voice faltered. 'No one would leave two harmless animals to freeze to death! You must be out of your mind, Knut.'

'Someone is!' Rory interposed quietly. 'Someone put that bar across the door. The dogs couldn't have shut themselves in.'

The three of them fell silent. It was too much for any sane person to accept.

The old butler came to the door with a fresh supply of hot water bottles. There were tears in his eyes as he looked at the dog.

'Pray to God, *Messieurs, Mademoiselle,*' he said simply. 'Then perhaps Tristan will survive.'

He, too, looked older and frailer this morning.

'Inez ought to retire the old boy,' Rory said

when he went out. 'He looks as if last night's party was too much for him.'

'Gilbert will never retire,' Alex replied. 'He served the Baron's father and he'll go on working until he dies. The Baron told me he had attempted to pension him off on several occasions, but he won't go. He's devoted to his master.'

Gilbert returned a few minutes later, accompanied by Monsieur Govin. The vet at once gave Tristan an injection and the huge dog's heart began to beat more strongly. A short while later he opened his eyes.

'He should recover,' the vet said tersely. 'What we have now to guard against is pneumonia. You said both animals spent last night in the ice-house? If that is so, it is a miracle Tristan survived the ordeal. But for the protection afforded him by the other dog's body, he, too, would have succumbed to the cold. *Quel désastre! Quel accident!'*

None of them felt it necessary to inform him that this had been no accident. It was for Inez to enlighten whomever she thought fit.

Tristan was given another injection and Monsieur Govin left, promising to return later in the day.

In the salon Inez's guests crowded around her, excited and curious to know what was happening. They knew the dogs had been discovered in the ice-house and all were repeating the vet's remark that it was a terrible

269

accident. Inez did not contradict them and seemed content to allow her visitors to draw their own conclusions. She accepted their condolences with apparent indifference and looked almost unconcerned when Gilbert informed her that one of the gardeners had buried Isolde.

Knut, who had left Rory and Alex together to minister to Tristan, studied the Baroness's reactions closely. He could not understand her. He still doubted that she had done this dreadful thing. At the sound of the lunch gong, the Baron finally appeared.

At the sight of her husband approaching her, Inez's white face became suffused with colour. Her eyes narrowed and her walk, as she went forward to meet the Baron, had the slow stealth of a cat stalking its prey.

'Well, Bernard, you have missed most of the excitement,' she said in an icy voice that nevertheless trembled. 'Have you heard that poor Isolde is dead? If so, you may also have heard that Tristan is alive; yes, alive! And with every chance of getting better. Does that surprise you? Is it not a miracle?'

The Baron coughed nervously. Inez showed signs of age this morning, Knut thought, but her husband looked almost as old and frail as Gilbert. But he held his head high as he met his wife's gaze, his green eyes as brilliant as ever, but unsmiling.

'That must be a great relief to you, my

dear,' the Baron said calmly. 'Who would have supposed that any living thing could survive a night in that dreadful place! One would imagine that death would be an inevitable consequence to dog . . . or human.'

At this moment Knut felt certain it was the Baron Leyresse who had been responsible for the dogs' incarceration. He must, indeed, be mad, Knut decided. Inez's behaviour at the party must have been the last straw. She had provoked her husband beyond endurance and driven him out of his mind.

Knut felt a fierce renewal of his anxiety to leave the abbey. But he knew he could not go unless Rory and Alex went with him, and Alex would never agree to leave whilst Tristan's life hung in the balance. And Rory would not leave Alex. So they must all remain, and let events take their course.

It was with the greatest uneasiness that Knut watched the Baron take his wife's unresisting arm and lead the way to the dining room as if nothing had happened. The guests followed behind their host and hostess, talking amongst themselves. They were like figures on a stage, unreal, walking as if they were playing their parts, the villain and the villainess leading the way.

Knut turned on his heel and hurried away from them. He had to exert the greatest self-control so as not to run through the big front door, out into the snow; not to run and run

271

until he had left the abbey far behind him.

His fear was irrational but very real. When he had lain on the mountainside in the snowstorm, he had expected death; but not even then, when it cannot have been far away, did he feel its approach as surely as he did right now.

CHAPTER TWELVE

The storm was worsening. All the lights in the abbey were switched on despite the daylight hour. The sky was so heavy with ominous dark clouds that even at lunchtime it appeared to be dusk.

Many of Inez's guests were contemplating a premature departure. Although due to stay the whole weekend, they knew that the road to the abbey could become impassable after a particularly heavy snowfall and some of the visitors had appointments the following Monday morning in Paris.

Beyond a polite request that no one need leave before the scheduled time, Inez made no serious attempt to keep the house-party intact. By nightfall, all but a stalwart few had gone.

Inez dismissed all the servants hired for the occasion. There now remained only her own staff, numerous enough to cope with the few remaining guests.

With so much of her day taken up with these various departures, Inez had no time to consider how best she could re-establish a relationship with Rory. Throughout a sleepless night, she had lost her ability for self-delusion and been forced to accept that her plans had so far failed miserably. Humiliated, thwarted, angry and despairing by turns, she had paced her room hour upon hour trying to determine where her approach to Rory had been at fault; why he had ultimately chosen Alex in obvious preference to herself.

Staring at her face in the mirror, devoid of make-up and drawn with fatigue and tension, she pondered bitterly her lost youth and questioned whether this had been the sole cause of her rejection. If it were true, there was no hope for her, she told herself, close now to despair. But as the hours wore on, she succeeded in convincing herself that it was not her beauty that had failed her, nor her power to attract, but that Rory, from the very beginning conventional in his manner towards her, had scorned her because she was another man's wife.

Exhausted, as the dawn tried to break through the snow-laden sky, Inez reproached herself for not making it more obvious to Rory that she would give up anything in the world for him, even if it meant asking Bernard to divorce her. She should have told Rory sooner in their relationship that her marriage was only a façade. She convinced herself that had Rory realised she loved him enough to run away with him, he would not have formed the impression that she wanted no more than a casual affair. For Rory to risk arousing Bernard's wrath for a mere flirtation was clearly stupid and she, herself, had been stupid not to realise his real reason for avoiding any involvement.

Continuing this hopeless self-delusion, Inez found a measure of relief. On the edge of physical and mental collapse, she had fallen into a fitful sleep from which she woke a few hours later in an intensely frenetic state. Outwardly she gave no sign of it, her willpower enabling her to appear calm and normal. She had greeted her guests at breakfast with smiles and small talk and might have succeeded in a return to a normal frame of mind but for the shock of hearing what had happened to the dogs.

Inez had no doubt that Bernard was responsible. Her guests naturally assumed that the dogs had wandered into the ice-house and the doors had been blown shut, incarcerating them accidentally, but the instant Knut had pointed out that he and Rory had had to remove the iron bar in order to open the doors, she had realised that this was Bernard's retaliation for her last night's provocation; that he had planned their death.

She had half-expected repercussions, but

none so terrible as this. He must have known how deeply she was obsessed with Rory and chosen this frightening and horrible way of warning her that if she pursued her desire further, he might kill her, too, rather than lose her.

Knowing her husband as she did, these suspicions did not seem extraordinary. Bernard had always been violently jealous and vindictive. She knew also, that to drive him too far was to turn the introverted, controlled restrained aristocrat into a madman. For him to have chosen such a form of revenge was quite in keeping with his nature. There was small comfort for her in the knowledge that he had failed to destroy the favourite of her two dogs.

But understanding his reasons did not alter her desire for retribution. He may have thought he could play his trump card and frighten her into submission, but he had merely shown her how, at long last, Rory could be hers.

Not until dinner on Sunday evening did Inez see Rory. He had spent most of the day with Knut and Alex nursing Tristan. The three of them had jointly decided that it was necessary for them to appear for the meal, but resolved to have as little to do with their host and hostess as possible. Inez ignored Rory. The way she deliberately refrained from either speaking to him or looking at him was markedly obvious, the more so since she questioned both Alex and Knut as to Tristan's progress. Apart from this, she devoted her attention entirely to her husband. If not exactly loving towards him, she was as near to showing him affection as any of them had ever seen.

'I just don't understand it,' Knut whispered to Rory as the meal ended and they walked back to the *salon* for coffee. 'If the Baron were the one responsible for last night's horror, how can Inez bring herself even to look at him, let alone smile at him?'

Rory shuddered.

'I don't know and I don't want to think about it any more,' he said. 'We've talked of nothing else all day. Though I must say I find it strange that Inez has said nothing to correct the impression the dogs met with an accident.'

Knut sighed.

'All one can imagine is that she knows the Baron had an excellent motive for wanting retribution and is now trying to make amends for the way she humiliated him last night. Perhaps she's afraid he'll find some way to finish off poor Tristan.'

'In that case, one of us must stay up with Tristan at all times until he's better,' Rory said flatly. He attempted a grin. 'Well, at least I seem to be off the hook. Inez isn't speaking to me! That's one slightly more cheerful aspect of this nasty business.'

During the next hour, conversation centred mainly on the weather. The radio was emitting regular storm warnings. It was fortunate, the Baron said, that so many of their guests had cut short their stay for it looked as if the road might well become impassable during the night, if it were not already so.

'We will not be short of food if we are cut off from the valley,' Inez announced brightly. Her eyes looked feverish in her pale, exhausted face. Even the placid Countess, who had decided to stay on for the remainder of the weekend, noticed Inez's fatigue. She remarked that it might be a good thing for all of them to have an early night.

'You must be tired, my dear. You look all in,' she told her hostess tactlessly.

'I had no idea I looked so frightful,' Inez replied in a cold, brittle voice.

The Countess murmured that she had not intended to sound uncomplimentary, but the Baron, putting an arm around Inez's shoulders, said:

'To me you look far more beautiful tonight than at the party last night. But perhaps that is because I prefer to see you dressed as my wife rather than as Anne Boleyn . . . or a gypsy!' His smile was twisted.

Only Knut saw the twitch of Inez's shoulder as she tautened beneath her husband's embrace, and guessed that the Baron's barb had found its mark.

277

He caught Rory's eye and they both rose to their feet.

'We're taking turns to sit up with Tristan,' Knut said. 'So if you will excuse us, we're going to get some sleep now as Alex is taking the first watch.'

The Baron seemed uninterested in this announcement but Inez nodded as if in agreement.

The Count and Countess also rose to leave and it looked as if everyone would retire. But as the Baron stood up, Inez put a restraining hand on his arm.

'There are one or two things I wish to discuss with you before we go to bed,' she said, her voice soft and persuasive.

As Knut walked with Rory through to the gun-room where Alex was sitting by the fire with Tristan, he said caustically:

'Perhaps Inez is going to have it out with him now. I don't believe any of that show of affection she put on tonight. I think she hates him. I wonder if he knows it and was just playing the part of the devoted husband this evening.'

But Rory refused to discuss Inez. He didn't want to think about her, but about Alex. He wanted to regain the wonderful carefree happiness he had shared with Alex on the stairs the previous night; wanted to see that look of love for him come back into her eyes; wanted to be able to tell her how much he loved her. Neither Inez, the Baron, Knut, nor even the dog, could hold his concentration for long. His mind and heart were full of Alex.

He was grateful when Knut decided tactfully to make himself scarce and went up to bed. At long last he could sit down beside Alex.

Her head was bent over the dog and the fall of her hair hid her face from him.

'Alex, please look at me. I haven't had a chance to talk to you alone all day and there are several things I must say to you. Please, Alex?'

She turned to face him, her eyes serious but not condemning.

'It's about last night,' Rory said. 'I don't know what thoughts went on in your mind when I rushed upstairs so suddenly and left you with Knut. I want to explain why I did so.'

'You don't have to,' Alex said quickly.

'I think I do,' Rory persisted. 'I don't want to go into any of the details but stupid though it sounds, I was running away from Inez. She had some crazy idea that she and I . . .'

'Don't go on, Rory!' Alex broke in, her eyes gentle with understanding. 'I do understand now. When Inez hurried upstairs after you, I was silly enough to wonder what you really felt about her; if you had made a secret assignation. But I realised I had no right to feel jealous. And anyway, I didn't really believe that you . . . you and she . . . were

279

lovers.'

'Never!' Rory said violently. This time he succeeded in drawing her close against him. 'I never loved her, Alex. I was fascinated by her but I never loved her. I think I've loved you all along—right from the first night when you appeared like a guardian angel in that blue dress of yours. I do love you, Alex. Very, very much! Tell me you believe it, despite the way things must have looked to you on occasions.'

The last vestiges of doubt left her. Alex drew a deep sigh of relief. Then she smiled.

'I believe you. And now you've got to believe me when I say I love you, Rory. I think I began to love you the first time I saw you, too. I didn't realise it at first because I was so sure I could never love anyone after David. But I do.'

'Then that makes me the happiest man in the world,' Rory said. When he finally stopped kissing her, Alex broke away from him, smiling breathlessly.

'I'm so happy, Rory—or I would be if only we could leave this place. I'm beginning to hate it more and more.'

Rory stayed silent. He could think of nothing that might reassure her. He, too, felt as if they were living on the edge of a nightmare.

'Even if we wanted to "escape",' he said with an attempt at humour, 'we couldn't do so right now. The last radio report said the storm was worsening and the Baron said the road to Valory was almost certainly blocked.'

Alex shivered. Not even the comforting feeling of Rory's arm around her shoulders could lessen her mood of apprehension.

'I wonder what the penalty is for stealing dogs in France,' Rory went on. 'It's at the back of my mind that when we do go, we should take Tristan with us. The trouble with stealing him is that he's a bit too big to hide in our luggage!'

Alex gave a tremulous smile.

'Anyway, he won't be fit enough to travel for several days at the minimum. I can't leave him, Rory—not even if we really are in danger. Does that sound very selfish of me?'

'Far from it!' Rory said, hugging her. 'I myself wouldn't leave Tristan even if you were willing to. He seems to have become part of our lives somehow—yours and mine. Perhaps that is because he's twice been near to death and we've nursed him back to life together. It's as if he belongs to us now. I wonder if we could persuade the Baron to sell him to us. Maybe he'd be glad to do so if he knew it meant me leaving here sooner.'

'But Tristan is Inez's dog, not his,' Alex reminded him.

They sat silent for a few moments, watching the dog's slow but steady breathing.

'Thank God, at least, for modern drugs,' Rory murmured. 'The vet said there was little likelihood of Tristan developing pneumonia now. He's going to pull through, Alex, and that's all we should be worrying about for the moment.'

Neither realised that it was not Tristan's life that hung in the balance at this moment. Death stood not an hour or two away from them, unavoidable and inevitable, awaiting only a brief lull in the tumultuous storm before calling to collect its victims.

CHAPTER THIRTEEN

When the Baron did not appear at breakfast, Inez dispatched Gilbert to her husband's room to see if he was unwell.

The old servant returned gaunt-faced and trembling.

'*Madame*, he is not there,' he told his mistress. 'And his bed has not been slept in!'

Inez sighed. 'Don't be stupid, Gilbert!' she said sharply. 'Of course he slept in his bed last night. Where else?'

The Count looked up from his coffee.

'Go and see if the Baron is in the library, Gilbert,' he suggested. 'He may have fallen asleep there reading a book.'

'That is possible,' Inez agreed as Gilbert shuffled away. 'When I went up to bed last night Bernard said he had one or two papers

282

he wished to look at before retiring.'

Rory looked across the table at Alex. In her eyes there was a reflection of his own misgivings.

Knut, seated beside him, said in a low tone: 'Now what's up!'

They continued their breakfast in silence until Gilbert returned. He looked even more shaken and worried.

'The Baron is not there, *Madame*. I questioned all the servants but none of them has seen him this morning.'

'Pull yourself together!' Inez said sharply. The old man's voice was bordering on tears. 'Of course your master is somewhere about. Tell the servants they are to make a methodical search of every room—the attics, the cellars, everywhere.'

The Countess put down her knife and actually stopped eating long enough to say tactlessly:

'It was only yesterday we were searching the abbey for your poor dogs, Inez. I suppose it is inevitable that in a place this size things do get lost occasionally. Don't you sometimes feel the abbey is a little *too* large, Inez, my dear?'

'No, I do not!' Inez said coldly. 'And Bernard is hardly an object that gets lost. He has probably fallen asleep in a chair where the servants have not noticed him. Finish your *petit déjeuner*. Your coffee will be getting cold.'

'Would you like us to help search for the

283

Baron?' Knut asked. But Inez curtly refused his offer. She seemed unwilling to accept any suggestion that her husband was absent other than by his own choice.

Twenty minutes later one of the footmen reported that there was no trace of the Baron despite a thorough search of the abbey, and that Gilbert had collapsed from nervous exhaustion. Did the Baroness wish them to search the grounds, the man enquired.

'You must be on the point of collapse yourself to suggest such a thing, Louis,' Inez said, sighing impatiently. 'As if anyone in their right mind would go out of doors in this weather. Your master is not an idiot, Louis.'

'But, *ma chère*!' the Count broke in with a frown. 'If Bernard cannot be found indoors, then surely . . .'

'Oh very well, if you think it best!' Inez snapped. 'I'm certain it is a waste of time. The servants cannot have searched the building properly. But by all means they can look outside if you think for one moment Bernard can have been crazy enough to go outdoors.'

She stood up and turned to look at the five people sitting at the breakfast table. She was wearing the black slacks and tunic top in which Rory had first seen her. This morning she looked younger again, autocratic, graceful. Her slender figure was framed by the great window, her red hair a flame against the dark grey sky. She looked strangely beautiful.

284

Suddenly she smiled.

'You've no idea how worried you all look!' she said in a low, mocking voice. 'You cannot seriously believe anything terrible has happened to Bernard?' For the first time in twenty-four hours, she looked directly into Rory's eyes. 'You, Rory, are a young man of great common sense and perception. Does not the idea of my husband going for a walk in last night's storm strike you as absurd?'

Rory caught his breath. There was something in Inez's manner that he found unnerving. He was reminded of a cat playing with a mouse. Clumsy with nervous reaction, he moved his arm and sent his plate crashing to the floor.

'*Mais qu'est que c'est?*' Inez said in a smiling reproach. 'Everyone seems so *enervé*! In a minute, you will all be making me nervous, too!'

Rory stood up, his face white.

'I'm going to help look for the Baron,' he announced. He was now seriously frightened that some further outrage had been committed.

Knut rose with him.

'I'll come with you,' he said quietly.

As they left the dining room, Knut said:

'I hope you are not thinking what I am thinking, Rory. It's really too crazy to contemplate but I think we ought to search the . . .'

'To search for the Baron!' Rory broke in quickly, unwilling to hear Knut voice his own growing fears. 'Let's try to keep sane even if everyone else in this establishment is round the bend.'

Knut nodded. He had always disliked and mistrusted Inez, but never until now had it crossed his mind that she might be capable of murder. He was relieved that Rory appeared not to share his horrible suspicion that she had poisoned her husband with the same cold-blooded ruthlessness that she had poisoned her much-loved dog.

He reminded himself that they had no proof she had administered poison to Tristan. It had never been established where the poison had come from. It was obvious that if a careless servant had been responsible he would deny his guilt. Rory, Alex and he had all assumed Inez to be the culprit with no evidence to back their suspicions.

Nevertheless, Knut's instinct was too strong to be ignored. Something was very wrong somewhere and the Baron's disappearance only added to the uncertainty.

He caught Rory's arm.

'Suppose Inez knew the Baron had shut the dogs in? Suppose she wanted retribution for Isolde's death?'

'Oh, for heaven's sake, Knut!' Rory broke in angrily. 'You're letting your imagination run away with you. We all are. Now put your ski-boots on and let's get going!'

But by the time they were dressed to go out in the storm, one of the footmen came stumbling through the thick snow to the garden door. The man looked like a ghost, his face, hair, clothes covered with snow, his eyes burning with shock.

'What is it?' Rory asked in French. 'Speak up, man!'

The servant gasped out his terrible news.

'The Baron is dead, *Monsieur*!'

Stammering with nervous excitement, he went on to relate how he and another servant had discovered the Baron frozen to death in the same ice-house which had claimed Isolde's life.

'I don't believe it!' Rory said stupidly, although he could see instantly by the horrified expression on the man's face that it was true.

'I do!' Knut said sharply. 'And what's more, we're going out there to look, Rory. I want to know if someone put that bar across the ice-house doors. If they did, then this was no accident. It's murder!'

He grabbed the servant's arm and asked if it was he who had found the Baron's body.

'No *Monsieur*! It was Gilbert. After a glass of cognac he revived and insisted upon continuing his search. It was he who thought to look in the ice-house, poor fellow.'

'Where is he now?' Knut asked.

'Guarding the body of the Baron. Gilbert is

very distressed, *Monsieur*. He loved his master deeply. I'm afraid the shock might kill him.'

Knut and Rory hurried out into the snow. It was falling thickly enough to blind them and it was some minutes before they found their way to the ice-house. The sobbing of the old butler reached them even before they pushed open the heavy doors. Gilbert was kneeling by the stiffened corpse of his master, keening and weeping, the tears coursing down the grooves of his wrinkled face.

Gently, Rory raised him to his feet. The old man was on the point of collapse and Knut took his other arm to help support him.

'I don't like having to question you just now, Gilbert,' he said gently, 'but I must ask you this. It is important. Do you understand? For your master's sake, I must ask you. When you came here, were the doors barred? Gilbert, answer me truthfully. *Were the doors barred*?'

The words seemed to penetrate the old man's grieving mind. He shook his head in denial.

'You are sure? Absolutely sure?' Knut persisted.

Gilbert raised his head, staring up at Knut from his blurred, watery eyes. His voice, though barely above a whisper, was suddenly firm, strong.

'I am quite sure, *Monsieur*. I understand very well why you ask. You are thinking of the dogs. I, too, held the same suspicion as you hold. But it was not so. My master cannot have been murdered. The doors were unbarred. It must have been an accident!'

The effort required to make this declaration proved too much for him. His frail body collapsed into unconsciousness. Together Knut and Rory carried him back to the abbey.

Half an hour later they went to find Alex. She was sitting with Tristan in front of the gun-room fire, her face white with shock. Rory put his arms around her.

'I still can't believe it!' Knut said. 'Poor old Gilbert swears it was an accident but I'm sure Inez did it. *I'm sure of it*!'

Rory frowned.

'I know how you feel, Knut, but I'm equally sure the old man wasn't lying. He made it clear enough he, too, had suspected Inez, but had been obliged to change his mind when he found the doors unbarred. Poor old fellow. He's in a bad way!'

'If only we could get a doctor to him,' Alex said. 'It could be days before the road is cleared. They won't even attempt to bulldoze a way through until it stops snowing.'

'At least the telephone is working,' Rory said in a vain attempt to bring a little comfort to their situation.

'The Count has telephoned the *gendarmerie* and the Mayor to report the death. They're coming up here as soon as the road to the abbey is clear. It's odd that the Mayor has to be notified, but this seems to be a French custom.'

Alex held tightly to Rory's hand.

'I hate to think of the poor Baron still out there in the cold,' she whispered. 'It seems so . . . so inhuman just to leave him there.'

'The Count said the police have ordered that nothing is to be moved,' Rory told her.

'I suppose the police have to make sure it was an accident,' Knut said thoughtfully. 'I don't see how they can reach any other conclusion. Even if someone had persuaded the Baron to go to the ice-house, with the door unbarred he could as easily have got out as in. And Inez couldn't have forced him out there. He must have gone of his own accord.'

'I suppose we should feel sorry for Inez,' Alex said. 'It must be a terrible shock to her, even if she didn't love him. The Countess has given her some kind of sedative and sent her to bed.'

'I'm more concerned about poor old Gilbert,' Rory said. 'He really did love the Baron. I think I'll go and see how he is. I've never seen anyone break up so quickly.'

Gilbert had been laid on the sofa in the servants' sitting room. There were pillows beneath his head and several rugs covered him.

Inez's maid, Denise, was kneeling beside him, crying softly. Seeing Rory, she lifted a tear-stained face and said:

'I think his heart is giving out, *Monsieur*. If only the doctor could come! And the Curé. *Monsieur* Gilbert would not wish to die unconfessed.'

Gilbert was unconscious but when Rory asked Denise if anyone had a stimulant which might help to revive him, he opened his eyes and stared at Rory with a strange intentness. He seemed anxious to speak but Rory could not make out the meaning of his words. He pushed Denise gently aside and knelt in her place.

Slowly, trembling, Gilbert's frail white hand came out from beneath the covers and gripped Rory's arm with surprising strength.

'Life is leaving me!' The words were quite audible. 'It is my heart, *Monsieur* . . .' He paused as if drawing on the last vestiges of his strength. Then he said, 'I do not wish to die with a secret on my mind. I had thought it best to remain silent, but my conscience will not permit me. Not even for my beloved master can I die with a lie on my lips. May God rest my soul and may the Baron forgive me, but I must tell the truth.'

Rory felt his heart jolt.

'What is it, Gilbert? What is it you want to tell me?'

It was not hard to believe the old man was dying. He looked unbelievably frail, his lips pinched and blue, his eyes sunk in his face.

'My master killed himself!' The words were

clear. 'God forgive him!'

'You must not imagine such a thing. I'm sure it was an accident, Gilbert,' Rory said with as much conviction as he could muster to relieve the old butler's distress.

Gilbert tried to speak but pain gripped him. When the spasm passed, he moved his right hand slowly across his body. The clenched fist fell open and a scrap of paper fell onto Rory's palm. It was crumpled and tattered but when Rory unfolded it, the writing was quite clear, if unevenly scrawled. It bore the words:

'Inez. My love. My life. My death.'

'It was beside his body,' Gilbert gasped. He drew a long, shuddering breath and then his face became suddenly peaceful.

Behind him, Denise whispered:

'I think he is dead, *Monsieur*!'

She pushed past Rory and bent forward, feeling for a pulse in the pathetically thin, bony wrist. Crossing herself, she turned away, her eyes full of tears.

'The shock was too much for him, too much!' she said.

Rory stood up with a feeling of despair. Here was yet another death which he had been powerless to prevent.

He walked out of the room, holding the crumpled slip of paper Gilbert had given him. He felt a sense of loss at the death of this loyal, honest, devoted servant.

'He really cared about the Baron,' he said to

Knut and Alex when he had passed on the sad news. 'I know he was very old but I wish he had not died in such circumstances. He was torn between honesty and loyalty. The thought of the Baron committing suicide deeply upset him and there would seem to be little doubt that it was suicide.'

'But his fear could be quite unfounded,' Knut said thoughtfully. 'This note proves nothing, Rory. It's a matter of how you interpret it. "*My life. My love. My death.*" Suppose you preface those words with "*the reason for*". It gives them a very different meaning, doesn't it?'

Rory and Alex looked at him aghast.

'You really think Inez killed him. *But how*?' Rory asked.

Knut's face was stern.

'I think it's possible, though I'm not sure how. I just don't believe any man would choose to commit suicide in such a macabre way. If the Baron had wanted to end his life, he could have shot himself. He had all those pistols in that cupboard over there. He could easily have staged an "accident" with one of them. Why choose such a slow death? It doesn't make sense.'

'Perhaps if he had been the one to kill Isolde, he was trying to make some kind of retribution by killing himself the same way,' Alex suggested, biting her lip. 'He might have felt guilty—tried to make amends by forcing on himself the same suffering.'

'I doubt it,' Knut said bluntly. 'I think he fully intended to kill both dogs in order to hurt Inez. Having made up his mind to do so I don't think he would have been in the least sorry afterwards. I think he deliberately chose such a revolting way for the dogs to die to torture Inez. If he were sorry at all, then I think it was only a regret that he didn't succeed in finishing off poor Tristan, too.'

'And if Inez knew it, she could have decided to give her husband a dose of his own medicine,' Rory murmured thoughtfully.

'Exactly!' Knut agreed. 'Except for one fact—*the doors were not barred*. As we agreed earlier, even if she'd got him inside the ice-house, he could easily have come out again.'

'Suppose Inez had somehow persuaded the Baron to go to the ice-house last night,' Rory said slowly, 'and she did bar him in. Then later, in the early hours of this morning, she went out and removed the bar to make it seem like an accident?'

Knut nodded, his eyes filled with excitement.

'No one would have missed the Baron during the night,' he said. 'Inez would have known she had eight or more hours to do as she wished without fear of interruption. She *could* have done it!'

Alex interrupted them.

'I don't believe it. I think you are both

letting your imaginations run away with you. No one in their right senses would have gone out in the storm last night. Not even Inez could tempt the Baron to go out in the middle of the night, and she certainly couldn't have forced him there against his will.'

'Inez could have persuaded him out there if she'd made up her mind to do so. He always did what she wanted. But if she did go out, she'd have got very wet doing so. If we could find the shoes she wore, we'd have our proof, Knut.'

'But do we want proof?' Alex asked, her voice almost a whisper. 'Even if all you suspect is true, Rory, do we want to be the ones to prove it?'

'Alex is right,' Rory said thoughtfully. 'It isn't for us to play detective, Knut. We're guests in her house.'

'Nor is it right that Inez should get away with it if she is guilty!' Knut argued. 'She might harm someone else! No one should be allowed to get away with murder.'

'Let's leave it to the police to sort it all out,' Rory suggested. 'We'll tell them we have the note; tell them what happened to the dogs. We'll tell them everything we know and suspect. Then it's up to them. Agreed?'

'Would it not be fairer to speak to Inez first?' Alex asked. 'She has never done us any harm. On the contrary, she has been very kind in many ways to all of us. I don't like the idea of accusing her behind her back.'

Knut's face hardened.

'If Inez did kill her husband, then she must be insane, Alex, and therefore not responsible for her actions. The fact that she has not yet harmed us does not guarantee she wouldn't try if she is guilty and knows we've guessed how she did it.'

'*If* she killed him!' Alex said doubtfully. 'We are only guessing and it's a pretty wild guess. We're suspecting her of murder, Knut. That's an awful thing to contemplate.'

'But if she did do it, it was an awful thing to have done,' Knut reasoned. 'I understand your reluctance, Alex, and your doubts, Rory, but remember this—if Inez is innocent, our phone call to the police can't harm her. The police will merely think we are the insane ones. They probably will anyway!'

Rory nodded. If Inez was a murderess, then no one at the abbey was safe and that meant Alex's life was at risk as well as everyone else's. Alex might easily be Inez's next victim if Inez suspected he was in love with her. He alone had considered the fact that Inez had a double motive for killing her husband. The way she had spoken on the night of the dance had clearly indicated that she would allow no one to stand between him, Rory, and herself.

He took Alex's hand and led her to the alcove in the hall from where they could sit and watch the library door. Alex's hand was very cold, her face pale.

'I don't want to believe it!' she said in a small, scared voice. 'I've been telling myself that Inez couldn't have done such a terrible thing, yet deep down . . .'

'I know,' Rory said quietly. 'And in a way, it's even harder for me to face up to the possibility. I can't help feeling I'm in some way responsible. I ought to have realised far sooner than I did how Inez felt about me. But I was so wrapped up in my work, I didn't want to know.'

'You can't possibly blame yourself, Rory,' Alex said quickly. 'You never encouraged her, did you?'

Rory shook his head.

'No, but I suppose I didn't discourage her either. There was one day in particular, in the studio—Inez removed all her clothes and I made a number of sketches of her. I should have realised then—I suppose I did—what she wanted. But all I could think about was the chance to draw her, paint her the way I wanted. I deliberately closed my mind to the obvious.'

Alex drew a deep breath of relief. She had so often wondered about those sketches. Now she need never think about them again.

'Poor Inez!' she said. 'I hope it isn't true, Rory. I hope it was an accident!'

Upstairs in her bedroom, lying on the bed, Inez cradled the telephone receiver to her ear, trying to stifle her quick nervous breathing. She had heard the bell tinkle when Knut had taken the downstairs phone from its cradle. She had lifted the receiver on the extension by her bed, just to reassure herself that the call had no importance.

Until that moment, it had not seriously crossed her mind that she would be suspected. Her plan had seemed faultless. With the heavy snowfall covering her footprints, there was no evidence to prove she had returned to the ice-house to remove the bar from the door. And with no bars across the door, there was no reason whatever why Bernard should not have got out if he wished. The police could reach only one of two possible conclusions—that it was suicide, or an accident.

When Knut first started speaking, she nearly laughed. The gendarme obviously thought the Norwegian was a lunatic. But as Knut continued to insist that he knew what he was talking about, and elaborated his theory, the man had begun to wonder, then to consider and finally to accept the possibility that the Baroness Leyresse might have murdered her husband. He would, he told Knut, inform the Mayor at once and consider what action to take. For the time being, nothing could be done since the road to the abbey was impassable. He impressed upon Knut that he must make sure that nobody left the abbey before he arrived.

As soon as Knut replaced the receiver, Inez did likewise. Her face was ashen as she slipped off the bed and hurried over to the wardrobe to search for the fur boots she had worn during the night.

It seemed impossible that she had overlooked such a small but serious piece of evidence—small but important enough to indict her. Fortunately Knut's phone call had warned her in good time of her careless oversight. She smiled as she considered how fate had played into her hands, or was it, she wondered, her instinct safeguarding her. But for her eavesdropping, she might not have had time to hide the boots.

But the smile faded as her fruitless search became more and more frantic. Her whirling mind would not focus on where she had put the boots when finally she had returned to her bedroom. She could not recall into which of her many cupboards she had thrown them.

Suddenly she remembered. She had simply taken them off and fallen exhausted into bed. Denise, the maid, must have removed them when she brought in the morning coffee. They were probably now in the airing room, drying.

Her first frantic instinct was to rush downstairs and find them. But at the door her last remaining vestige of caution stopped her. Knut might already have seen the boots. For her now to remove them, hide them, destroy them, was to lend credence to his accusation of

299

her guilt.

Inez paced the floor, her hands twisting together as she tried to calm herself. If she were to leave the boots where they were, no one could disprove her if she said she had been out after breakfast, joining in the search for Bernard.

She halted, considering the matter. Her mind quietened and her thoughts became clearer. Knut had spoken to the police of a note left by Bernard, found by Gilbert. He had not said what was written on that note. She had been so frightened by the reference to her footwear that she had forgotten this far more damning piece of evidence.

Weakly, Inez collapsed onto the bed.

What was in the note? She must make Gilbert tell her. If she knew what Bernard had written, she could think up some reasonable explanation that made his accusation less damaging, less incriminating. But even as the thought struck her, she realised that the old servant would want her brought to justice if he suspected she had murdered the master to whom he was so totally devoted. Gilbert had never liked her; would be glad to see her brought down.

The first paralysing attack of fear struck her. Last night and in the early hours of this morning, she had given no thought to the possible consequences if her plan misfired. It had seemed one hundred per cent fool-proof.

The only difficulty she had envisaged was in devising a way to persuade Bernard to go out in the dark to the ice-house.

It had not proved as difficult as she had feared to get him there. When everyone else had retired to bed, she had taken her husband completely by surprise. She had gone to stand behind his chair and had placed her hands on his shoulders as if in affection.

'I want to tell you how sorry I am,' she had said, feeling the muscles of his neck tauten at her touch and at the soft conciliatory tone of her voice. 'I have behaved very badly, Bernard, and I owe you an apology. Can you ever forgive me?'

At first he had been reluctant to speak. But his silence was an indication that at least his mind was not totally closed against her. Whatever jealous thoughts he entertained about her and Rory, he had not yet entirely hardened his heart towards her.

'I must have caused you great distress, my dear,' she continued. Behind his back she had smiled at the convincing warmth in her voice. 'I want you to know that whatever you may think about my behaviour, nothing has lessened my deep regard and affection for you. I was obsessed for a little while. Like some silly servant girl, I imagined myself just a little in love with my portrait painter. Oh, I know it was absurd of me, ridiculous. But you and I . . . we have not been very close these past years,

301

Bernard, and I was lonely; and very susceptible to the admiration and adoration Rory gave me. I was flattered that such a young man could find me attractive. I know now that it was all meaningless. No one could ever love me as you have done, Bernard. Fortunately, you brought me to my senses before any harm was done.'

He had spoken then for the first time.

'I admit I thought you were beyond reason, Inez.'

Inez had moved quickly to the front of his chair and knelt at his feet, laying her head on his knees. She was certain now that he still loved her, was still powerless against her charms.

'You are not a man who shows his feelings with sentimental words,' she said. 'But you found a way to tell me you love me, Bernard. You showed me, when you so nearly killed both my dogs, that you would stop at nothing to prevent me continuing to make such a silly little fool of myself; to bring me to my senses. And you succeeded, *mon cher*. I needed just such a jolt to force me out of my stupid romantic dreams. Now I am back to reality; to the realisation that you love me very deeply; that you are my husband and the only man I want.'

For one long minute he made no sound, no movement. Then his hand came out to rest on her head and he began to stroke her hair. She

302

had won.

'I took a big chance, Inez,' he had said. 'You might never have forgiven me. Perhaps if Tristan had died as I intended, you would have hated me for what I did. But you hurt me beyond measure; tormented me; insulted me. I could think of no other way to show you that I could take no more of it. Ah, Inez, my wife, my love, my life. If I lost you, life would be meaningless. I think you know that. We understand each other, do we not?'

From then on it had been easy for her to lull him into believing what he longed so much to believe—that she loved and admired him. Soon she was able to raise the subject of the dogs again; to profess a curiosity as to exactly how he had managed to persuade the animals to go into their pre-ordained tombs.

'That was not difficult,' he had assured her. He had taken a large quantity of turkey and venison from the kitchen and the dogs had followed him willingly enough to the ice-house.

Although Bernard, himself, had had no qualms in carrying out his intentions, he had expected that a woman would be squeamish, sickened at the gruesome manner he had chosen deliberately to shock and horrify her. But now he realised that far from frightening Inez, she saw his behaviour as a kind of tribute to herself; was even enjoying and sharing with him the sadistic flavour of it.

Inez had not shown him such warmth and affection since the early days of their marriage. A new hope had been created at the back of his mind—that perhaps at this late stage of their life together, he might yet win her completely. It occurred to him that he had been too soft, too indulgent with her. A woman of fire and passion might respond better to harshness, even to cruelty if worship left her cold. He, himself, felt no revulsion for this apparent streak of masochism in his wife. He found it strangely erotic and she left him in little doubt that she was excited too. Gripping his arms with surprising strength, her eyes glittering, she had said urgently:

'Bernard, do you remember that night not long after we were married . . . we were marooned in that mountain hut in the storm . . . you made love to me . . . it was magnificent . . . you were so commanding . . .'

She had jumped to her feet and pulled urgently at his hand.

'We can be lovers again, *chéri*—don't you see? It can be as it was that night . . . we will go to the ice-house . . . take this rug . . . make believe we are back on that mountain with the storm raging. It will be all right, you will see . . . trust me Bernard! You do want me, don't you?'

Inez, alone in her bedroom, recalled her feeling of triumph as she stumbled behind Bernard through the deep snow towards the ice-house. There was no fear that they might be seen. Before they had gone more than a few yards, the thickly falling snow had covered their footsteps from the abbey like a white blanket. She had laughed in exultation, actually enjoying the wild fury of the snow flurries and the wind against her face. The old man in front of her had guided her towards the scene of his own destruction and she enjoyed the irony of it. By morning he would be dead— and she would be free. The last barrier between her and her love, Rory, would be gone.

Free! The thought now danced through her mind with quite another meaning as she recalled the note Bernard had written before he had succumbed to the cold. The freedom of life itself was at stake. Did they still have the death sentence in France? Could she actually be guillotined?

The thought brought a fresh wave of panic. As it grew within her mind, she lost the ability to think calmly; to play out her part to the end. Bernard's note assumed a terrifying importance. She should have known that Bernard would not give up life without one last effort to revenge himself upon her. In her imagination, she saw his spidery blind writing, scrawled in the blackness of his icy tomb. As her fear increased she saw how slender were her chances of denying her guilt. There were too many people like the Norwegian who might testify that she had fallen madly in love with Rory. The girl, Alex, might add her testimony. Even Rory himself . . .

Inez covered her face with her hands. In this moment of fear for her very existence, the cold, hard facts about Rory superseded the crazy dreams and hopes. He did not love her. He had never loved her. If he knew she had murdered her husband, even suspected it, he would turn against her. He, too, might testify; say in court how she had attempted to seduce him that day in the studio. All her guests at the fancy dress ball would testify how she had danced for him. Even her maid, Denise, would not remain loyal.

Inez knew then that she stood little chance of survival. To stay at the abbey in an attempt to brazen out her innocence was to risk life itself. Rory was lost to her. She had nothing now to keep her here. She must save herself. If she could only get down to Valory she could escape to Paris, fly to South America where her father would protect her; buy her safety if need be.

At that moment the telephone rang. She gasped and reached for the receiver. Someone downstairs lifted the phone in the library. The call was from the gendarme, informing Knut that the severity of the storm was slackening and the snow ploughs were going to attempt to make their way up to the Abbaye St. Christophe. He, the Mayor, the doctor and the

Curé would follow as close behind as was feasible. With good fortune, they would arrive within the next few hours.

Inez replaced the receiver quietly. Her drawn white face screwed into a facsimile of a smile. Once again she had been forewarned. Luck had not entirely deserted her. Her mind raced. There were snow tyres on the car as well as chains. The road leading down to Valory was not too steep at the higher level. At the lower level, where the hairpin bends became more precipitous, the snow ploughs would be in action. She could force a way past them. Even if she were seen by the gendarme, it would take time for him to turn his car. She could be well on her way before they could catch up with her. Her car was a powerful one. She had money and her jewellery which was worth a fortune in any country.

Inez went to her dressing table drawer and took out the key to the safe. Seconds later, the safe door swung open and she pulled out the first velvet-covered tray of jewellery. She gave a cry of horror. On top of the black velvet, surrounded by emeralds, diamonds, rubies, lay the knight's ring.

She dropped the tray and stood paralysed, watching as the ring rolled away from her, then turned and came towards her in slow motion. She stood perfectly still, holding her breath until it stopped finally in the space between her bare, cold feet.

To her guilt-ridden, fearful mind, it lay there like a symbol of evil and a warning of disaster and death.

*   *   *

'I think the storm is nearly over!' Rory said, standing at the window and staring down into the courtyard below. 'The sky is much lighter and . . .'

He broke off, peering more closely through the latticed glass.

'There's a car outside!' he said. 'That's strange.'

Knut came to stand beside him. 'It's Inez's car and Inez is in it,' he shouted. 'No one else has hair that colour. My God, Rory, she must be out of her mind. She won't be able to drive far in that snow.'

Alex came to join them. All three watched silently as the car skidded, recovered and began to move out of the courtyard and through the abbey gates.

'Someone ought to stop her,' Knut said. But he made no move. Rory's face was grim.

'You can't even see the road,' he muttered. 'She must be guessing where it is from the markers.'

The car's progress was very slow. To the three observers it was as if they were watching a film in slow motion. They could not believe Inez could get much farther. Every yard brought a wave of snow thrown up by the tyre chains. Smoke poured from the exhaust.

But although on two occasions the car came to a standstill, each time Inez managed to reverse and go forward again until finally, the big Peugeot disappeared round the first bend.

The three of them continued to stand by the window as if mesmerised.

'She must have listened to those phone calls!' Knut said more to himself than to the others. 'She's trying to make a run for it before the police arrive.'

'So she did do it!' Rory commented. He felt sick.

'She'll never make it—there won't be room to pass the snow ploughs and the police car.'

Knut looked up at the sky, frowning.

'I really thought it was clearing up,' he said. 'But the storm isn't over yet. Did you hear that thunder?'

The rumbling noise to which he referred seemed to grow louder. Alex gave a sudden sharp cry and pointed up the mountain.

'It isn't thunder!' she whispered as she stared horrified by what she saw. 'It's an avalanche. It's gathering momentum . . .'

Her voice broke and she pressed her knuckles against her mouth to stifle her cry of horror. The slow-moving mass of snow was several hundred feet away, yet they could hear as well as see the snapping pine trees as it pursued its relentless path downwards. It gathered even more snow as it swept on with a noise like the rumbling of an express train.

Rory put his arm round Alex. His face was as white as hers. The sight was awesome.

'It's all right,' he said. 'It's not coming this way!'

'No!' Knut agreed. 'But look, Rory, it's going to hit the road. God! How terrible!'

It was level with them now, gathering speed, sweeping down anything in its path. Nothing could stop it as it raced downwards towards the valley.

In its wake came a strange silence. The same thought lay in each of their minds as their eyes followed the scene of barren desolation the avalanche left in its wake. Had the mass of snow suffocated the snow ploughs and the cars on its downward journey?

The air in the room suddenly seemed stifling. Rory opened the window. From the valley rose the faint sound of a warning siren, too late to herald the disaster that must have already reached the town.

Alex covered her eyes.

'It's horrible!' she whispered.

Their voices sounded tremulous. All three of them were shaking. Downstairs one of the maids began to scream hysterically.

Rory looked at Knut, his eyes uneasy with fear.

'I know it's probably not the best time to say it,' he remarked in a small thin voice, 'but with

Gilbert and the Baron both dead, and perhaps Inez, too, I can't help thinking about the Valbanon curse. Reason tells me all these disasters are just coincidental, but at the same time . . .'

'Don't let's think about it,' Knut said wisely. 'I prefer to think it was just Fate. Fate brought you and me here in the first place; in a way, Fate brought Alex here too. None of us could have foreseen what would happen, far less prevent it. It happened because it had to happen. If you are going to start questioning the whys and wherefores, then why did Tristan survive when poor Isolde died? One just has to accept these things.'

It came as no surprise to any of them when eventually the first of the snow ploughs fought its way through to the abbey and reported that a Peugeot had been swept past them down the mountainside. The men had no idea that there had been someone in it, unable to believe that anyone would voluntarily have driven a car down a road that even their snow plough had had difficulty in traversing.

The second snow plough arrived, quickly followed by the car bringing the gendarme, the Mayor, the Curé and the doctor.

As soon as the body of the Baron had been brought to the abbey and the cause of death from hypothermia ascertained, inquiries were begun. The Count and Countess, the servants, Rory, Knut and Alex were questioned individually and together by all four men. Written statements were drawn up and signed. Rory was interviewed again and yet again, the Mayor as well as the gendarme becoming more blunt as the hours went by in the wording of their questions. They were trying to elicit the exact relationship between Rory and Inez.

The portrait was brought down from the studio. Seeing it for the first time through the eyes of others, Rory could understand their suspicions. In a strange way, he understood through his painting how infatuated he had actually been with his model. But equally, he realised how dead all feeling had become for the subject of his painting. It was a part of his life that was over; an experience which had matured him both as a painter and as a man. Later, when he could see these last weeks in retrospect, he hoped he would have learned something from them. For the time being, he was incapable of any emotion other than a desire to be finished with the questions; to be as far away from the abbey as he could get.

A phone call from Valory confirmed what everyone knew must have happened—Inez Leyresse was dead. The old Curé voiced all their thoughts when he said simply:

'Perhaps it is for the best.'

The Mayor certainly thought so. The Baron and Baroness Leyresse had been important and influential people in his community. It would be very disagreeable to have a scandal attached to their family name. From the evidence so far, it did look like murder—and of a most unsavoury kind, too.

The gendarme agreed. There was no proof that the Baroness had killed her husband. Neither the note in the Baron's handwriting, if it were his, nor the wet boots of the Baroness were actual proof of guilt. The Baron's horrible death could have been an accident; could have been suicide. None could be certain. His superiors would have to be informed; would ponder, as he had done, the possibility of murder. He, himself, preferred not to believe it. And with the Baroness dead, there was no murderer to be brought to justice.

The doctor could throw no light on the situation other than to confirm that the Baron had frozen to death. There was no sign of violence done to his body, no question of his having been doped or poisoned. Privately, he believed that the old man had probably decided to end his life. But there was nothing other than the questionable suicide note to substantiate his suspicion.

As for the Curé, he kept his thoughts strictly to himself. Of all people, he reminded himself, he must be the last to talk of the power of evil. It was his duty to refute the very idea of witchcraft, of spirits able to survive death and wreak their vengeance on the living. Besides, the Baron and his wife had made many generous donations to the Church and he would much prefer them to be buried in Holy ground where only their Maker would know their guilt and pass judgment on them.

The Count was called in for a private consultation with the Mayor. A simple old man, neither perceptive, nor curious, the Count ridiculed any idea that the Baron could have killed himself; he was equally emphatic in his refusal to accept that the Baroness could have killed him.

'I have known both of them for fifteen years or more,' he said indignantly. 'They were a devoted couple, ideally suited. The situation is perfectly plain to me, *Monsieur le Maire*. The Baron must have been worrying about that unfortunate episode with the dogs and gone out to the ice-house to try to establish what had happened. It was late at night, he was tired—perhaps that last brandy he had as a nightcap was a little too much for him—and he fell asleep. The doors blew shut in the storm, and, poor fellow, he froze to death while he slept. As to the three young guests—they are of good character—I'll stake my reputation on it. My wife will confirm what I have told you. To entertain any other idea is absolutely absurd and I am surprised that you, the Mayor of Valory, should hold these very damaging ideas.'

'Can you also account for the Baroness's

inexplicable departure in her car?' the Mayor asked, feeling obliged to pursue the matter further.

'My dear fellow!' the Count replied scathingly. 'You do not seem to understand the situation very well. The poor Baroness was utterly distraught when she heard what had happened to her husband. What devoted wife would not be? Even my own dear wife was hysterical. It is my opinion that the Baroness, bravely attempting to stifle her grief, put too great a strain upon herself, and her mind became unhinged. Regardless of the conditions outside, she made up her mind to drive to Valory for assistance for her husband. Quite probably she did not grasp that it was all too late. I think she was trying to come to you or perhaps to *Monsieur le Docteur* for help. A brave woman. We should not sully her memory with such unworthy suspicions.'

Rory, Knut and Alex were called in once more and invited to read the Count's statement.

'On reflection, after reading what the Count has stated, do you wish to withdraw the various allegations you have separately and jointly made?' the Mayor inquired. Frowning slightly, he added, 'It does indeed seem strange to me that having received such lengthy and considerable hospitality here at the abbey, you would wish to repay your host and hostess in such manner.'

'That isn't the point . . .' Rory began, but Knut gave him a quick kick beneath the table.

'It is possible we have been mistaken,' he said. 'And I assure you it was not with any ill-will that we voiced our suspicions. We did so because we felt it our duty to tell you what we knew and what we thought. If you do not see fit to pursue the possibilities we mentioned, then it is your prerogative to disregard them. As far as my friends and I are concerned, we want only to be permitted to go back to England as soon as possible, to forget the whole thing.'

'Aaah,' said the Mayor, leaning back in his chair and nodding at the gendarme beside him. 'It is as I thought. These young people have been letting their imaginations run away with them. If we are all agreed, then I think we will consider our inquiries at an end. It is clearly a case of accidental death. *Monsieur le Docteur* has already issued a death certificate. *Monsieur le Curé* has said he will arrange the burial. Our friend, the gendarme, will make out the necessary report for his superiors and the formalities can be concluded.'

'So that's that,' Knut said as they left the room and went upstairs.

'It's an odd sort of justice,' Rory protested.

'I know what a stickler you are for facts, Rory,' Knut sighed. 'But don't you see, no one wants to believe us. Our version is too gruesome, too fantastic.'

Alex agreed.

'I don't want to believe it myself,' she said.

'Come to that, nor do I,' Rory said with a grimace.

'Then remember, both of you, that even *we* don't know the truth. Maybe Inez didn't do it. Maybe it really was an accident. Those doors could have blown shut.'

'Yes, but . . .' Rory broke off, grinning sheepishly. 'You're right, of course, Knut. We don't know. We can't help the Baron now. Nor can the wretched Inez harm anyone else.'

'The person we would hurt if we could prove what we suspect is Eloise,' Alex said, surprising the two boys. They had both forgotten the existence of Inez's child. 'It would be a terrible thing for her to live with. Knut is right. We must put it out of our minds.'

'I suppose the daughter will inherit everything, even the abbey,' Rory said reflectively. 'The last surviving Leyresse.'

'Eloise won't live here—she hates the place,' Alex told him.

'I don't blame her, so do I,' said Knut. 'There is an evil atmosphere here despite all the luxury, all the beauty. I can't get away quickly enough.'

'Nor I,' Rory agreed. He looked at Alex and, as if sharing the thought, together they said: 'Tristan!'

Rory grinned.

'I don't see why we shouldn't take him with

317

us!' he said. 'He'll have to go into quarantine, of course, as soon as we reach England. I'll talk to the Count, Alex. We'll buy Tristan if that will make it legal for us to have him, though I don't suppose the Count will care. It's fortunate for us he's here to see to everything.'

'I suppose I'd better telephone my family and tell them to expect me back in a few days' time,' Alex said.

Rory caught her hand.

'Don't do that,' he said impulsively. 'I want you to come home with me, Alex, meet my parents and . . . hey, Knut, where are you off to?'

Knut grinned at him from the doorway.

'Nowhere in particular,' he said, 'but I know when I'm not wanted. What is that English saying of yours? Two's company, three's a crowd!'

'But of course we want you . . .' Alex began but Knut had slipped out of the room closing the door behind him.

'Do we want him?' Rory asked as he put his arms around Alex and drew her against him. 'I think Knut is a lot wiser than we are, Alex. He knew long before I did that you were the right girl for me.'

'He knew before I did that I was in love with you,' Alex agreed smiling.

Rory looked into her eyes with an answering smile.

'So I suppose he knew, when he left us alone, that I wanted to ask you to marry me. Not yet, of course. Not for a year or two, when we're both a bit older and my career is established; but some day, Alex, will you marry me?'

She closed her eyes and her head found its now familiar resting place against his shoulder.

'Better ask Knut,' she said. 'I'm sure he'll tell you I am certain to say "yes".'

We hope you have enjoyed this Large Print book. Other Chivers Press or Thorndike Press Large Print books are available at your library or directly from the publishers.

For more information about current and forthcoming titles, please call or write, without obligation, to:

Chivers Press Limited
Windsor Bridge Road
Bath BA2 3AX
England
Tel. (01225) 335336

OR

Thorndike Press
P.O. Box 159
Thorndike, Maine 04986
USA
Tel. (800) 223-2336

All our Large Print titles are designed for easy reading, and all our books are made to last.

M